"I am launching my first packs now."

The first group of four packs hurtled out of their bays, drives flaring as they emerged beneath the carrier's nose.

At the same time the carrier *Valthyrra* held herself on a course to intercept a sistership, ready to do whatever she could to distract the *Dreadnought*. Yet another carrier was there first, turning the full power of her main battery against the *Dreadnought*, heedless of the discharge beams ripping along her shields. The alien weapon continued to focus the greatest part of its attention on the stricken *Kaeridayen*, blasting away sections of her unprotected hull. *Kaeridayen*'s nose and wings were gone already, torn apart by internal explosions and burning furiously.

"*Valthyrra*, be careful!" The commander warned. "If you lose impulse scanners, we'll be blind and helpless. The *Kaeridayen* has to have lost hers—"

"*Trendaessa Kaeridayen* is dead," *Valthyrra* said softly. "Her main computer grid is destroyed. What remains of her crew is trying to abandon ship, and we have to buy them time."

She locked her conversion cannon on target and discharged a stellar reserve of energy, fearful of how the *Dreadnought* would respond . . .

D0324582

Also by Thorarinn Gunnarsson

STARWOLVES

STARWOLVES:
BATTLE OF THE RING

STARWOLVES:
TACTICAL ERROR

Published by
WARNER BOOKS

STARWOLVES DREADNOUGHT

THORARINN GUNNARSSON

WARNER BOOKS

A Time Warner Company

WARNER BOOKS EDITION

Questar® is a registered trademark of Warner Books, Inc.

Cover design by Don Puckey
Cover illustration by John Harris

Warner Books, Inc.
1271 Avenue of the Americas
New York, NY 10020

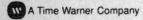 A Time Warner Company

Printed in the United States of America

First Printing: January, 1993

10 9 8 7 6 5 4 3 2 1

PROLOGUE

They were the Starwolves. Hunters of the Stars. Warriors of the Endless Night.

They were bred for war, designed to function at ease under the deadly conditions of high speeds and sharp, crushing turns demanded in spaceflight. No living being could compete with them in battle. Not even the most complex computer guidance system could out-fly them. Created to serve as simple machines of war, they would in time evolve into the greatest and most noble of races, most deadly of enemies but truest of friends, champions of justice but cold and merciless warriors.

But eighteen centuries before Velmeran, Commander of the legendary carrier Methryn, insisted that he and his people were not machines and brought the ancient war of the Starwolves to an end, matters were very different indeed. The Starwolves were smaller, weaker and less clever than they would become, never thinking to question the single purpose of existence which they had been designed to fulfill. They fought their battles in blind faith, failing to consider the greater strategies that would have ended that unending war.

Then a greater menace came from beyond unknown stars, destroying all things for the sake of destruction alone, giving battle without any greater purpose than to seek out and ravage all civilized life. And so it was that the Starwolves were called upon to defend the very enemy they had been created to destroy. But how they would respond, and just how much their own will could influence the instincts that had been programmed into their very nature, were matters impossible to predict. . . .

1

—1—

The convoy began dropping out of starflight, each ship a minute behind the one before it. Mostly they were medium bulk freighters, small enough to be quick and agile but large enough to be useful, although every fifth ship was a powerful Union battleship or heavy carrier. Each ship coasted for a few minutes after emerging to carry itself clear of the area of emergence, before braking with forward engines just in time to join up with the main convoy, drifting deeper into the system that was its destination. Twenty-seven had already gone sub-light and eight more would join up with the group in the next few minutes. If all went well, they would all settle into orbit within six hours, making a less tempting target for the Starwolves.

Union Fleet Command had some odd and rather ineffectual notions about the true definition of subtlety. The transport of millions of tons of chemical explosive ordinance could have been done more quietly by moving a ship or two at a time; a convoy under military protection only called attention to itself, no matter how quietly and quickly it tried to move. And if the Starwolves discovered the convoy, three battleships and two carriers could hardly offer even the slightest protection.

A curious state of war had existed between the Starwolves and the Union for over thirty thousand years, sometimes in active and merciless hostility, and sometimes in a tense truce that might exist for centuries. The Starwolves were self-appointed protectors. As long as the Sectors and their vast trade monopolies dealt fairly and peacefully with the lesser colonies, the independents and the few aliens within the space they controlled, then the

3

Starwolves were willing enough to keep the truce. But the Sector families and their monopolies existed for the sake of greed; they preferred to take what they did not own, destroy the competition offered by the independents, and the Starwolves were always swift to punish tyranny. No one knew what motivated the Starwolves, except perhaps some instinct for altruism that had been programmed into them.

Perhaps that was the whole point; the Starwolves were an artificial race, created for the purpose of fighting the Union. Although vaguely human in appearance, they had been bred by complex genetic engineering methods, for quickness, endurance and tremendous strength, to make them perfectly suited for the crushing accelerations of space-flight. The Union could not begin to match the technology of their immense carriers and nimble black fighters. Or even if they had, the Union still possessed no pilot capable of flying against a Starwolf nor even of surviving the deadly conditions aboard such a ship. Indeed the Starwolves would have won their war long ago, except that the Union was able to resist them by size and numbers alone. The Starwolves were thought to have only eighteen ships, with perhaps ten packs of fighters aboard each. With its limitless resources, the Union could afford to lose a small fleet more easily than the Starwolves could lose a single fighter.

But that was never to suggest that the Union accepted such losses, not when its ultimate goal was to defeat the Starwolves either by slow, steady attrition or an overwhelming cascade of resources. There seemed to be some small hope in that scheme, for the Starwolves were inexplicably unwilling to be ruthless. They might prey upon shipping, or make occasional strikes at important military targets, but they would not take the war into the Union itself, and destroy its ability to make war by removing its means to renew its lost resources.

Therefore the loss of several million tons of explosives, or even the ships that carried it, was hardly a matter of great concern in the larger scheme of things . . . except, of course, to the crews of those ships. If the Starwolves did find them, the escort of three battleships and two carriers would have been futile, even laughable. Starwolves seemed to have an uncanny way of knowing in advance things that the Union tried to keep secret. They were too clever to fool, too swift to evade and too powerful to fight.

Such thoughts had been very much on the mind of Captain Janus Tarrel every moment of the journey. Hers was the ultimate responsibility, not just as captain of her own battleship, the Carthaginian, but as executive commander of the entire convoy. The official position at that moment was that a state of moderate tension existed between the Union and the Starwolves, which was to say that certain greedy Sectors had been trying to expand at the expense of the colonies and the Starwolves had responded predictably. That response had so far taken the form of a general, unpredictable attack on military and company shipping, a tactic designed to defeat the Union's ability to take a hostile stance. The Starwolves would not hesitate to utterly destroy this convoy with its cargo of explosives destined to subdue unruly colonies.

"All ships are down from starflight," the surveillance officer reported. "The convoy will be firming up within five minutes."

"What surveillance contacts do you have?" Captain Tarrel asked, knowing that she would have been told of anything new or unusual as a matter of normal procedure.

"Three contacts running in system, all identified commercial ships on the established shipping lanes. No contacts at all within two point seven light hours."

Captain Tarrel found that less reassuring than she had wished. She would have felt better if she could rely upon having any warning, but the Starwolves had a habit of dropping out of starflight right on top of their prey. They possessed accurate achronic scanners that could see across whole light years without a time delay. Her own scanners had an increasing lag that made them worthless past a few light hours, and were almost blind to a ship still in starflight.

"Time to destination?" she asked.

"Five hours, forty-seven minutes," the helm officer responded, channeling the navigational grid to the main viewscreen.

Chagin, the first officer, walked quietly over to join her at the central station where they could see the viewscreen clearly. "Do you wish to increase our speed and arrive sooner?"

Tarrel shook her head impatiently. "This many large engines flaring in such tight formation would shout our presence to Starwolf scanners three sectors over. It would be better for us to just coast in."

"Is there any reason to be nervous?"

"Nothing beyond the obvious," she said. "For all the good that we can do, they might just as well not include a military escort. I suppose that it gives the freighters some time to scatter while the Starwolves take us apart."

A flash of light flickered across the viewscreen, and several seconds later a concussion like distant thunder rolled along the length of the ship like a wave. The members of the bridge crew paused for a moment at their stations, waiting until they were certain that it was not themselves that had been hit. Captain Tarrel just waited, knowing that the surveillance officer was already consulting his scanners, although one thing was immediately clear. One of the freighters, and her cargo of perhaps a million tons of deadly ordnance, had exploded.

"That was Velvet Queen by process of elimination," surveillance reported after a moment. "She had been running six kilometers left and slightly down from our position. Scanners record very little debris of any size, so she must have been largely vaporized by the blast."

"What contacts?" Tarrel demanded.

"No contacts before, after or during the explosion. No drive emissions. No weapons paths. I see no indication yet that Velvet Queen was destroyed by external forces."

"Then you rule out the possibility of attack?"

"By no means. I simply have no evidence of attack at this time."

Tarrel nodded. "Try to obtain confirmation of that from the other ships in the fleet. And get visual identification of as many ships as possible on the various viewscreens."

These were tense moments, hardly less frightening than being under open attack. Tarrel had to make some very quick decisions about the safety of her convoy, and she did not yet know for certain that they had indeed come under fire. Accidents did happen. Velvet Queen had been carrying nearly two hundred thousand orbit-to-surface guided bombs of five tons each, all in unpressurized cargo bays open to various forms of radiation and extremes of temperature. At the same time, that was hardly a fragile cargo. Those bombs had been designed to penetrate planetary atmospheres without projected shielding, just their own tough ceramic shells. With no other supporting information, the only way that Captain Tarrel had of judging whether or not they were under attack was to wait and see. She stood in the center of the bridge, glancing about at the viewscreens of various sizes that now showed different sections of the fleet.

This time, she happened to be looking right at one of the bulk freighters as electrical discharges rippled over its hull hardly a second before the vast ship disappeared in a brilliant flash.

"Disperse the convoy!" she ordered without hesitation. Starwolves could chase down only so many targets at a time. "Group the military vessels with carriers in the center. Stand by at red alert."

"Same as before," the surveillance officer reported. "No contacts. No evidence of physical or energy-based weapons being fired. No drive emissions. This time I did record a sudden flare of energy from the ship itself, as if it was being destroyed from within."

"Do the Starwolves have any weapons like that?" Tarrel asked.

"Not that I know of."

"Is there any way you know of that Starwolves could attack a ship without showing themselves?"

"They would have to be firing from very low starflight speeds, but still fast enough to evade our scanners. Even at that, they would have to deliver one shot from extremely close range, less than two hundred meters. Not even Starwolves are that precise."

Tarrel had to agree. The situation seemed completely hopeless. They could not fight an enemy they could not even see, and grouping the fighting ships had not diverted the attack to themselves. She weighed her options very quickly and decided upon the only scheme that might save at least a portion of the convoy. Bulk freighters continued to explode all about them, at widely separate locations about the dispersing fleet as if the enemy was all about them . . . or perhaps standing off at a great distance and taking shots. Perhaps the Starwolves had invented a weapon which was undetectable in its deployment, and useful from such a distance that the attacking ship was not required to reveal itself.

"Order the convoy into starflight as quickly as they can get there," she directed. "Any destination that lies in their path. Signal our sister ships to stand by to run at any moment. We'll be going as soon as the convoy looks safe."

"What are we doing?" her first officer asked. "Can't we fight?"

"If you have any constructive ideas on how to fight this, you tell me," she said. "About all we can do for those freighters is to sit close and try to draw the fire."

Fortunately they had kept their speed to eighty percent that of light to decrease the time needed for their final run to their destination. They needed only a final sharp acceleration to carry themselves up to starflight threshold, a matter of only a couple of minutes even for bulk freighters. As soon as those ships began disappearing without exploding, Captain Tarrel knew that the survivors were safe. By that time, only four seemed likely to make it clear. But the unseen enemy had left the military ships completely alone, either saving them for sport or simply picking off the freighters before they could escape. She found that a disquieting observation in itself.

"Order the other ships to break and flee into starflight," she ordered. "Let's get the hell out of here as fast as we can. Relay to the battleships to circle around once they are clear. We have to make some determination about the status of the station and remaining system traffic."

"All ships acknowledging."

"Then let's scatter."

Tarrel had already predicted two events. The escape of the fighting ships would be noted, especially now that the freighters were gone, and the larger, slower carriers would lag behind and find themselves selected as the most inviting targets. The five military ships suddenly darted away, each one in a different direction, and it turned out that she was wrong in her second estimate. The intelligence of their enemy was cold, calculating and merciless. The battleships were most likely to escape, generators normally reserved for heavy cannons and shields pouring vast amounts of power into their over-sized engines, and so they were targeted first. The first went in a matter of seconds, overloaded generators exploding with enough force to put a sizeable dent in a planet. The second battleship lost power and was left adrift for a long moment while lightning rippled over its hull. Observing this final attack visually, Captain Tarrel wondered if she could protect her ship.

"Standing to threshold?" she asked.

"Ninety-seven percent at this moment, Captain."

"Full power to the hull shields, even if the diversion of power slows our transfer into starflight."

"Captain?" Chagin asked, surprised.

"Do it now," she snapped.

That order was obeyed only just in time. In the next moment, a tremendous rush of energy washed over Carthaginian's hull. The shields took the initial assault, and forces that would have ripped the giant ship apart erupted over her hull. The shields held only a matter of seconds before they failed, power couplings burned out from the overload. But the ship escaped in that same instant into starflight, her transitional shock wave shaking off the devastating effects of the weapon discharge.

Carthaginian had barely survived. Devastated by the attack, she was still spaceworthy but in no condition to fight. Too many of her high-power systems had been destroyed trying to shed an overload of energy, even though she had caught only the edge of that devastating weapon's force. After circling in starflight for a full hour, Captain Tarrel had her brought back into system as close to the inhabited planet and its meager station as safely possible. A parabolic loop around the system's star and then around the planet itself helped to cut the immense ship's speed with a minimum use of the drives and their betraying energy signatures.

Tarrel had already relayed her warning ahead to the station, sending the local traffic to cover and dampening all major energy emissions. But closing the system to traffic did not solve the problem of ships already in flight, not when most commercial vessels needed a couple of hours either to get themselves to transition velocity or make they way back to the station. The matter was largely irrelevant under any circumstances. There was no indication that making a ship emission-silent decreased its visibility even to known Starwolf technology, only that unobtrusiveness made it a less inviting target when more tempting ones were at hand. Captain Tarrel had always felt helpless enough in dealing with Starwolves, but that was nothing compared with the helplessness of this situation.

Ignoring normal approach protocol, Carthaginian made a rapid advance to the station, matching velocities during a final, crushing loop about the planet, and nosed in to a docking sleeve. Captain Tarrel had been required to trust a great deal to the abilities of her bridge crew in that maneuver, and almost as much to luck. The echoes of that hard docking were still ringing through the ship as she left the bridge for the nose lock. Only a couple of minutes later she reached the military command post and the offices of the Sector Commander. Dan Varnloy was a man she had known well in the past, the captain of the first ship on which she had served as a senior officer, the same ship that was her present command. She knew that she could talk to him easily, and that he would believe her assessment of the seriousness of the situation. He had agreed quickly enough with her recommendation to close the system.

"Jan, what have you been doing out there?" he asked the moment she entered the main office. "We saw ships exploding in rapid succession, but there seemed to be something strange about the whole affair. We never recorded any weapon flashes."

"Neither did we," Tarrel said. "Nor did we see any attacking ships, as if we were being picked off by something still in starflight. No ships, and no weapons traces. It was as if we were being hit with a weapon that poured a tremendous amount of destructive power into a ship's hull without the need for either the attacking ship or the download beam making itself known. But I am only guessing. There are certainly other possible weapons that might have had the same effect."

"Could it have been mines made to escape scanner detection?" Varnoy asked.

"There seemed to be no detonation of any mine, unless it could have been drawn to a ship and discharged. But the nature of the energy discharge did not suggest that."

"Did any of the ships survive the attack?"

"As far as I know, only the Carthaginian," she explained. "We were hit just as we were on the edge of transition, and we shook off the discharge by escaping into starflight. I've had the data from the event shunted over to your main computers."

They retired to a terminal for a couple of minutes while Commander Varnoy looked over the report. The data was completely raw, not yet organized in any fashion, but the message was plain enough. "That was a clever move on your part, but you were still lucky."

"I know that," Tarrel agreed. "I still don't see what we can do to defend ourselves against this attack, or even detect it. There's just not enough data to suggest how it is being done."

"You're actually being fairly generous in your estimation of just how much hard data we actually have."

She nodded. "If I can stick out my neck a little farther, I have to admit some doubt that this is even a Starwolf attack."

Varnoy glanced at her. "Just a suspicion, or can you be specific?"

"Suspicions on specific observations at this time," she said. "This seems to be a sudden and very big jump in Starwolf technology. At the same time, I have to admit that fairly simple adaptations of existing techniques might be giving very dramatic results."

"Granted, on both counts."

"The attack also seemed pointlessly cruel," she added. "Starwolves can be very cruel, when they have the need. But they make very certain that you get the message of whatever lesson they want to make. And they can be very compassionate as well. This was very casual and undirected, almost like an automated weapon picking off our ships at random."

"An interesting point," Commander Varnoy admitted. "I still believe that we will find Starwolves behind this, and that the cold, brutal manner of the attack was to satisfy the requirements of a field test of some new weapon. But if we can't pin it to them any time soon, we have to consider the possibility of a new enemy. Any more ideas of what to do about it?"

Tarrel shook her head. "We recorded no data that could have been used as an indicator of attack or the location of the attacking ship, and no way to trace or even estimate direction of fire. They might be right on top of us, and they might be sitting light-years away. I just don't see any way to fight back."

"We need more data, and I don't see any way of getting it except the hard way."

The station alarm lit up at that moment, red alert proximity three. Something out in the system was happening, probably dangerous. Captain Tarrel looked up, knowing already what it must be. One of the commercial vessels still out in the system had just come under attack. Commander Varnoy looked up at her, his steady gaze unreadable, before he turned to the communications monitor.

"What have we got?" he asked briskly.

"A pocket freighter coming into system just exploded," the response came immediately. "No indication of attacking ship or weapons, but we treated it as an attack under the circumstances. Should we send out the system fleet?"

"Negative," he answered without hesitation. "Have the entire fleet move off from the station and stand by, cargo ships and tenders as well. Order all private and commercial ships out of the system in the opposite direction from the last attack."

"Your orders understood and relayed." There was a momentary pause. "Sir, we just lost another ship, this one much closer than the first. We have moved up the alert status to proximity two."

"Give me a system map indicating the sites of the two attacks."

They glanced briefly at the system schematic that came up on the monitor, enough to see that the line of attack was moving directly toward the inhabited planet and the station.

"Commander, evacuate the station," Tarrel urged him. "Send everyone down in any life boat and small shuttle with minimal energy emissions that can take them as quickly as possible to the planet."

"We have over four thousand people up here," Varnoy protested, then nodded with great reluctance and turned back to the communication monitor. "Order all major power systems on the station shut down. Order all civilian personnel to evacuate the station immediately. They are to proceed to planet surface. No ships will be standing by to evacuate personnel; use emergency pods and shuttles only. Order all private ships at station and unable to disembark immediately to be abandoned."

"Your orders understood and relayed."

"Commander, I have to get to my ship immediately," Tarrel insisted. "We might be able to buy some time. . . ."

"The hell you will!" Varnoy declared, turning on her. "You have to get your ship the hell out of here as fast as you can move. You have the only direct records and observations on this enemy, so your only concern is to get yourself intact to Sector HQ by any means possible. I haven't yet decided whether to use our own ships to buy time. For as little effect as it would likely have, I think that I would rather send all ships to safety now. Can you protect yourselves in any way?"

"No, all we have on line are drives and partial navigational shields. No scanners except some passive, and no battle shielding."

"Then time is the one defense you have," Varnoy told her.

"I'll call ahead and have Carthaginian standing by to move the moment you come aboard. Now go."

Captain Tarrel left without a word of farewell or a glance back, and she did not even think to ask until it was too late whether he meant to join the evacuation or stay at his post. So much probably depended upon whether or not there was time to clear the entire station of inhabitants. The halls of the station were filled with people hurrying to find shuttle bays and life boats, many of them struggling to carry small children or valuable records. All in all, this was a relatively small station serving a limited colony. They might just all get away, especially if the unseen enemy was having to maneuver or decelerate to attack. And if the major power systems were shut down, there was some reason to hope that the station would be spared destruction. She still held to her pet theory that high-level emissions drew attention from the automated attack systems of their adversary.

She made it to Carthaginian's nose lock quickly enough, in spite of the confusion in the station. She sealed the lock herself and released the docking grapples manually, and the battleship began sliding backward out of her berth only a few seconds later, drawing back somewhat faster than her usual habit. Tarrel approved completely, although she was given to wonder just who had the helm at that moment.

By the time she reached the bridge, they were already pulling clear of the station and turning about to maneuver clear. The area was full of ships; even the Sector Fleet was running, so there was no doubt that Commander Varnoy had considered them ineffective in covering the evacuation. The ships were moving up from the station, away from the planet below, while the shuttles and pods were dropping away quickly toward atmosphere. Anything else would have made navigation completely impossible.

"What does it look like outside?" she demanded, hurrying to her seat before accelerations put her against the walls.

"We have nothing absolutely certain since the station stopped relaying active scanner data," the surveillance officer reported. "I have recorded the destruction of two more ships, one within two light-minutes of the planet and one just outside of orbit."

"What the hell do they want?" Tarrel asked quietly. The Starwolves would never wantonly take out a tactically unimportant station, just for the sake of destruction. "Take us out of this system as fast as this ship will move. Our destination is Sector Headquarters.''

"Still maneuvering for room to run, Captain," the helm responded. "The local traffic is rather heavy."

"Make it quick. And give me the station centered on the main viewscreen.''

There was no indication of attack at first, until a small freighter pulling away from the far side of the station suddenly flashed like ball lightning for a prolonged moment before it exploded. At least the little ship's destruction was relatively feeble, since her generators had not yet been brought up to power to feed her drives. A second freighter exploded, then one of the ships of the system fleet and a freighter still at dock. The explosions continued to intensify, until Tarrel was certain that they had come under multiple simultaneous attack. That had not happened during the earlier attack. The ships had been taken out one by one. Beneath her awareness of this change in tactics and demonstration of new abilities, she realized that it meant they had probably just lost their only chance of escape.

"Get us under way if you have to go through something," she snapped.

Carthaginian began to move forward rapidly, still swinging around her nose in the process. But the viewscreen remained fixed on the station, and Tarrel could see clearly the moment the assault was turned upon the station itself. Great arcs and branches of lightning began to leap over the far end of the station, as small portions of its components began to explode in a series of sustained blasts. Tarrel thought the effect was much the same as if the beams of some powerful weapon were being played across the surface of the immense structure, pouring in raw energy until metal exploded, white-hot, nibbling away at the five mile long station. In spite of that concentrated barrage, ships still fleeing the station were still being taken out at regular intervals. If this attack came from a single ship, then it could divide its attention and firepower among many targets.

Moments later, the members of the bridge crew were pressed into their seats as the Carthaginian began to accelerate rapidly toward her transition into starflight.

The Carthaginian arrived at the military complex of Vinthra five days later, the best speed that the rather abused battleship could manage. At least the time allowed her crew to make what repairs they could, so that she did not limp into port nearly a derelict. Captain Tarrel did not know until later, but her proud ship was in fact severely scorched from the discharge of energy that had nearly destroyed her. At least the active scanners were mostly back into the grid by the time they arrived, and the hull shields were fully operational after extensive rewiring. Carthaginian was an old ship, her frame and most of her hull over two hundred years old, although she had seen no less than five complete refittings in her life. After switching out some damaged components, the old battlewagon could easily go out for another two hundred years, assuming that Starwolves and other mysterious things bumping about the stars did not make short work of her.

Carthaginian was a lucky ship. She had fought Starwolves, minor encounters to be true, twenty-one times in her long career, five of those encounters resulting in her unscheduled refittings. Once she had even been captured and sold back, that being one method Starwolves had for earning their living. Now she had survived two brushes with this new, devastating weapon. Captain Tarrel considered that to be nothing short of a miracle, failing to credit that this matter was largely due to her own cleverness and her uncanny ability to know when it was time to run.

A meeting of the Sector's senior coordinating officers was scheduled as soon as Carthaginian came into the system, the data she carried and the personal observations of her captain very much in demand. Although Janus Tarrel was young, she did possess a gift of listening to, understanding and remembering everything she heard, and that gave her a wealth of experience to call upon that was not necessarily her own. She knew what to expect from this meeting, so she was not taken by surprise. The minds of armchair admirals with policies cast in stone followed predictable paths. They accused her first of fabricating the whole affair to excuse her incompetence in losing the entire convoy. They questioned her resourcefulness in failing to find a way to protect her convoy against this new weapon, although they could think of none themselves. Finally, having failed to discredit her, they politely asked her advice. Which they largely ignored.

Her one, curious ally through all of this was Victor Lake, the young Sector Commander. They had served together in their earliest days as junior officers, including that first assignment aboard the Carthaginian, and at one time they had been quite close. Lake had come from what was now a rather obscure branch of the ruling Sector Family, unimportant enough to think that the only favors his connections would gain him had already been granted in his commission in the Sector Fleet. But he was clever, earning for himself first a ship, then the post of System Commander, and finally the unexpected title of Sector Commander.

He was not loved by his senior commanders. Coming from the Sector Family, he did not believe the propaganda and hollow beliefs that his seniors worshiped, but he was more capable for his more realistic views, and so respected for his abilities. He was very well-liked by his commanders and captains in the field, largely because he was no more cruel to the colonies than policies he could not control forced him to be, and also because he did not expect heroic, futile gestures in facing the Starwolves.

Captain Tarrel had actually not seen him in the two years since his sudden and unforeseen promotion to Sector Commander. His new duties had brought him to Vinthra, and she had immediately been given command of the Carthaginian by his order. She often wondered if that had been compensation for a relationship that was no longer expedient, both excuse and reward for making herself scarce.

Commander Lake had remained largely silent during those times when the mood of the council had turned hostile toward her. They had both recognized the importance of allowing the matter to blow over by itself, although that did not help to sweeten her opinion of him. When all was said and done, he had decided upon the course of action, although his decisions were in certain respects surprising. The council had recommended attempting contact with the unknown attackers, using a small fleet of drone cruisers as bait. Tarrel did not expect to be given command of that mission herself.

She hurried out into the corridor the moment the meeting adjourned, hoping to demand some word from Commander Lake on several subjects. She was almost surprised to find that he had waited for her; in her own philosophies, she had believed that he had been trying to shun her company since his promotion.

"You wanted to talk?" he asked casually, almost daring her to be angry.

"I want to talk business at least," she responded. "If nothing else, I would like a better idea of what you expect of me."

"That is not unreasonable," he agreed. "We can speak privately in my station office. Will you accompany me?"

"Is that an order?"

"If this is business, then it is an order."

They walked together, for his offices were only a short distance down the corridor on that same level. Tarrel refuse to be intimidated by any man she had taught to be half-way good in bed; she had never kept his company for the sake of his sexual abilities, but because they were like minds. While his response so far seemed to argue otherwise, she was satisfied that he was not going to pull rank on her simply as a ploy to keep her silent. They could still talk. Once she felt certain of that, she found that she was no longer so anxious or annoyed over the matter.

Despite his words, Lake took her not into his office, but into his private quarters. The Carthaginian's shuttle bays were no larger than this suite of apartments, its decor rich but understated. He watched her as she looked about. When she saw him staring, he smiled wryly as if sharing some subtle jest.

"Would you like something to drink?" he asked.

She shook her head. "Not while I'm working. You know me better than that."

"Are you working?"

"I'm thinking about business. You pay me to think, remember?"

"I suppose I do," he agreed. "So, what are you thinking?"

"First of all, I'm thinking that you might be using me as bait."

Lake considered that briefly, and decided that he should pour himself a drink. "Do you know, the trouble with my new job is that I often have to think like a mercenary. I wish that there was no need of mercenary thinking in the military, but there it is."

"You propose to send me out to face that thing again, and you expect me to be understanding?"

"No," he agreed simply. "It might not be fair to ask you to stand up to that thing one more time. If cannon fodder would get the job done, I would send those fossils I have to keep around as resident experts. *You* seem to have some idea of how to handle this situation."

"I keep running away?" Tarrel asked.

"You do have to survive long enough to learn something.

And that is very much the point. I'm going to give you a small convoy of old ships, anything we can find in a hurry that is nothing but scrap. We can have those slaved to your navigational system so that they will fly in formation around your own battleship, and then we'll send you to locate the area where that thing was last known to be. When it starts nibbling away at your convoy, you'll know that you've made contact and you have a few moments to attempt communications. If they don't answer, then you get the hell out.''

"You seem to believe that this is not Starwolves.''

Lake shook his head. "Starwolves don't behave like that. They can be damned dangerous, especially if they catch you doing something they don't like. But they do live by certain rules of their own making. I can't say that I really give you much hope of success, but we might learn something more by provoking another attack. If they don't talk, and if you don't find some way to fight them, then find yourself some Starwolves and discover what they have to say on the subject.''

"If the Starwolves really are behind this, that would be looking for more trouble than I could handle,'' Tarrel reminded him.

"Yes, I know that,'' Lake agreed. "Those are the chances we have to take. If this situation is as desperate as I suspect—as you seem to suspect—I would even be willing to make an alliance with the Starwolves against this new threat.''

"The Sector Families are not going to like that.''

"Perhaps not,'' he agreed. "And they will have to accept certain restrictions upon their ambitions, to appease the Starwolves. But, if they want to stay in business, they will just have to accept it. I know how to sell the idea to them, so no trouble there. I'm speaking to you this candidly now, so that you will understand my own plans enough to act as my agent when you leave here. You might well find yourself in the role of diplomat, either with these new attackers or the Starwolves, and the alliances you make could save or destroy the Union. I want you to feel free to do whatever it takes.''

"You could go with me,'' Tarrel pointed out.

"I wish I could. The fact is, I'm about to do the Union itself a dirty trick, and you have to help me. If I try to go, Councilor Debray will want to know why, and end up replacing me with a professional diplomat. That person will be under direct orders to guard the Union's dignity and commercial interests at any cost, not realizing that the cost would be those very things they want to protect. There's more going on here than you know. Things are a lot more serious.''

"What do you mean?" Tarrel asked plainly.

"No mention was made of this during the council—most of those idiots don't even know yet—but there have been five known attacks just like the one you saw, most of them worse," Lake explained. "You just happen to be the first witness to survive. That's why I can say with great certainty that the Starwolves probably are not behind this. Someone is systematically destroying all traffic, all the stations, even the satellites, every piece of hardware we have in space, system by system. If Starwolves were resorting to such dire tactics, they would be trying to force us to surrender before they destroy our spaceflight capabilities completely. And under those circumstances, they would want us to know that they were the ones doing this to us."

Tarrel frowned. "I don't believe that you were going to tell me all this at first."

"I'm not supposed to. I just don't see how you can do what I need for you to accomplish without knowing it. So, will you take the job?"

Captain Tarrel looked profoundly surprised. "Oh, I suppose I just didn't understand. I didn't know that I had any options. I thought that this was an order. You know, the things that you senior officers tell underlings to do and you expect done no matter what."

"I know about orders. I just want to know that you are devoted to this mission."

"And what if I say that I don't want to volunteer?" she asked, but Lake was not inclined to humor her. She hurried on, "I'll do it, of course. And you can trust me to do my best. That's the only way to bring myself and my crew out of this alive."

"I'll have your drones standing by within the next twelve hours. I've already sent crews aboard your ship to repair her damage and make some necessary modifications. Is there anything special you expect to need?"

"Can I get Carthaginian painted before we go out?"

"You're likely to need it more when you get back."

"Then paint it again," Tarrel insisted. "I don't want to present my ship to Starwolves looking like a tramp."

Lake considered that briefly. "All right, you get your paint.

Who knows what might impress Starwolves? They eat prodigiously, and they seem to like furry little animals and other cute things. People who have talked to them say that they are never what you would expect, that they can be intelligent, gentle and in many ways rather innocent. Other than that, I really don't know what I can tell you."

"I'm really not worried about the Starwolves, as long as I can get their attention before they scorch my ship. It's the things I can't see that worry me more."

Captain Tarrel returned to her ship a couple of hours later, having argued with the refitting crew about the installation of external missile racks on Carthaginian's hull. Getting that had taken some persuasion on her part, since the battleship already carried four dozen missiles in internal bays, and also because the crew chief had been reluctant to give additional ordnance to a ship on a diplomatic mission, and possibly also from reluctance to give weapons to a ship that was likely doomed anyway. But Tarrel wanted weapons that she could use without betraying her intentions by opening bays or powering up a system. Any trick that she might have up her sleeve would be a great help, considering the disadvantage she was at already.

She found that her crew had shrunk considerably in one respect, and grown somewhat in others. She found herself with only three complete bridge crews, a basic maintenance crew and a handful of other necessary specialists. Lake, forever frugal, had left her with just enough to keep her ship running while risking the fewest lives possible. Her crew had expanded by one, a rather clever but harmless-looking young man, wearing the insignias of an executive officer, whom she found sitting in her chair. Since she already had a second-in-command, the rank of executive officer could mean just about anything from mission commander to special advisor or observer. She decided that he was going to be an observer, and he had better not observe anything from her chair ever again.

"And just who are you?" she asked sharply as she checked the progress reports on the ship's refitting.

"Lieutenant Commander Walter Pesca, reporting as ordered," he responded briskly, affording her a very snappy salute.

Oh, the bright and eager type. "Why are you on board my ship, Mister?"

"I was recommended as an advisor. I'm an alien contact specialist with extensive training in linguistics. If you find new aliens, I'm supposed to learn how to talk to them and try to guess whether they are telling the truth. If we end up talking to Starwolves, I'm supposed to try to figure out their language so that we can eavesdrop on them. Sector Commander Lake thought that you might find me useful."

"You might be useful," she agreed guardedly, "but you are not a command officer. And only command officers can sit in my chair."

"I won't forget, Captain."

"Since you were sitting in my chair, do you know what happened to my first officer?" Tarrel asked.

"Right behind you, Captain," Chagin said, coming up behind her at that moment. "I was just down checking the installation of the missile racks you wanted."

"You know, those missile racks are not really a very good idea," Pesca remarked brightly, pleased to be helpful.

Tarrel glanced at him. "I found this person in my chair."

Pesca looked very nervous. "There didn't seem to be a senior officer on the bridge."

"There doesn't have to be a senior officer on the bridge when the ship is secure at station," she told him. "And like I said, you're not a command officer anyway. Have you ever been on board a ship before?"

"Yes, of course!" he insisted in injured tones. "I've traveled on the couriers many times."

"Couriers? That's like tourist class," Tarrel exclaimed. "Did Commander Lake choose you for this mission personally?"

"Yes, I believe so."

Tarrel shook her head slowly. "You know, I've just become aware of a plot to assassinate the Sector Commander. Assuming that I survive to come back for him. Chagin, has anyone sent down word about where they expect us to find this monstrosity?"

"Captain, that information was given to me to relay to you," Pesca offered hopefully, seeming more sure of himself once he was discussing business. "The Dreadnought has been following a predictable path along projected patterns that have been shunted down to your computers. Given the anticipated travel time for the convoy, we should be able to intercept the Dreadnought in the Standon System in eight days. Orders have already been relayed ahead to have the local traffic cleared and the station abandoned.''

"Dreadnought?" Tarrel asked.

"It's a very old word for the largest class of battleship."

"Yes, I know that. It just seems to suggest a very great certainty that the Starwolves are not behind this."

"That does seem to be the suspicion, although I suppose that you know more about that than I do," Pesca said. "The term Dreadnought is one that is not used for any of our ships and it also differentiates this ship from the known Starwolf carriers. Assuming, of course, that it isn't a modified carrier."

"That's what they're paying us to find out," Tarrel commented. "Find yourself a cabin near the bridge where I can find you in a hurry."

"Thank you, Captain," Pesca said, and withdrew.

"Well, what do you think of Wally?" she asked.

"He seems competent enough, once his brain comes on-line," Chagin remarked dubiously. "They have to paint portions of the hull before they can hang all the missile racks, but everything should be done in time."

"Good. I want those missiles rigged to fire without going through the main weapons computer or targeting scanners. We should be able to do that ourselves without upsetting the station crews."

"They find us strange enough already over the missile racks," he agreed.

"Good. Then tell them that I want every drone in the convoy rigged to explode from full generator overload on a signal from here."

Chagin looked vaguely impressed. "Would that really destroy this thing?"

"No, I doubt that," Tarrel said. "I was just thinking about something. When I was very young, I believed that little monsters danced in my room at night. I thought that if I could turn on the light quickly enough, then I might catch them by surprise before they could hide. I was thinking about doing something like that with our Dreadnought."

Chagin had to think about that for a moment before he realized what she had in mind.

—2—

Carthaginian led the convoy into the system, dropping abruptly out of starflight well out on the fringes and maintaining near-light speed as they hurtled directly in. This was, as far as anyone could know, the best guess of where they could expect to find the Dreadnought. The Standon system, their original destination, had already been attacked while the convoy was in flight. The small commercial station and base for the System Fleet was gone, although every ship that could move or be moved had fled. They found this system in much the same condition, indicating that the mysterious enemy ship had been here, too. They could not know yet whether it had gone on again, seeking other prey.

In spite of the best efforts of the computer grid to maintain the convoy in perfect formation, the ships running in that widely spaced configuration were of various sizes, types and stages of disrepair. Some were so decrepit that their engines and generators surged and faded, some constantly and others at unpredictable intervals. As far as Captain Tarrel was concerned, that was just as well. The Dreadnought appeared to respond to high-energy emissions, and this sad lot was making all manner of tempting noise.

"Disperse the convoy to wide formation," she ordered as soon as the group of ships had settled in from their transition from starflight. "Arm all self-destructs except our own. Wally, stand by with your communication."

Lt. Commander Pesca had learned to bear his nickname with good grace, assuming it to be a compliment or term of affection.

He remained blissfully unaware that the Captain simply found it difficult to afford him the dignity of a military title.

"Communication standing by," he responded. "Do you still wish to send on the light-speed bands as well?"

"Let's not leave any stones unturned," Tarrel answered. "Broadcast your communication now."

Pesca had put together a rather competent first-contact communication, repeated in every major language he knew, including some that were entirely mathematical in nature and transmitted on both achronic and standard radio bands, as many as the ship could handle. They did not expect an actual dialogue with the Dreadnought, but any response might give them a fix on its location and possibly reveal something about its nature. At least they would know where to look.

"We already have a response," Pesca announced only a few seconds after the transition began. "One brief message on a single achronic band. Less powerful than a Starwolf achronic carrier, but more distinct."

"What about the message?" Tarrel asked impatiently.

"The computer can't identify anything familiar about it."

"Any guesses?"

Pesca considered that briefly. "It is a machine code and very brief. I suspect that we have just been hailed with a recognition code. If we respond properly, we get to talk. If not, we get blown away. That suggests to me that the Dreadnought is entirely machine-driven."

"Clever boy," Tarrel remarked to herself, thinking that Wally might just win back his rank at this rate. "Do you have a direction on that signal?"

"I'm putting it up on the navigational grid now, Captain."

Tarrel glanced at the navigational monitor, a large screen between the helm and navigator's stations just before her. To her alarm, the source of that signal was nearly directly behind and slightly above their own flight path. It was probably moving in to intercept. Carthaginian was following the convoy. At this point, they were the most tempting target.

"Move us quickly up through the convoy until we are leading," she ordered frantically. "I want a safe lead on those ships as quickly as we can get it. Stand by the self-destructs."

"We can't detonate those ships while we're anywhere within the convoy," Chagin reminded her.

"Yes, I know that. I just hope that we can get through before that thing takes out too many of our ships."

She did not add that, with the Carthaginian accelerating quickly through the convoy, her powerful main drives would be giving out some very appealing emissions. She considered the risk to be worthwhile. Indeed, they were almost through the convoy before the first of the ships suddenly exploded.

"Are we clear?" she asked.

"Give me thirty seconds more and we should be able to ride out the shock wave without damage," Chagin reported.

"Make that forty seconds more," the surveillance officer added. "We might not get a reading if we're too close, and we need the lead time to make a good identification."

"I'll give you every second I can. Just stand ready."

A second ship was taken out before the minimum time to safely detonate the convoy. Captain Tarrel counted the seconds to herself, but the loss of a third ship just short of the surveillance officer's mark convinced her that it was time to go. The delay in executing the order would take care of the rest, with some to spare. If she lost too many ships, the plan would not work.

Every ship in the convoy exploded its generators from a forced overload at the same moment, the combined blast enough to destroy a planet but spread over a fairly large area of space. And the leading edge of that blast was coming right up Carthaginian's tail. Fortunately the battleship was already traveling nearly fast enough to outrun even the flash, and she had begun moving to the very edge of transition threshold since the order to detonate. She needed every second she could get to stay ahead of the shock wave, which would be just as deadly to her systems as the Dreadnought's high-energy weapon unless it had some time to dissipate.

"I have it!" the surveillance officer announced. "Positive contact!"

"Blessed be!" Tarrel declared. "Take us on into transition. We might be lucky enough to avoid the shock wave completely."

As soon as Carthaginian was safely into starflight, she joined Chagin and Pesca at the surveillance station for a look at what the scanner had been able to detect. Even Carthaginian's most accurate and powerful active scanners had been unable to identify any trace of the Dreadnought. But the explosion of the convoy and the tremendous energy involved had acted like a powerful flash or strobe, briefly illuminating the mysterious ship, and the passive scanners had been aimed past the flash to capture the reflection from the Dreadnought. The information collected had not amounted to much, the most intriguing item being the visual representation of achronic scattering of tachyons emitted by the blast. To their frustration, all it showed was a featureless gray cylinder with rounded ends.

"Is that the ship?" Pesca asked.

Chagin shook his head. "That's just the reflection from her hull shields, if I had to guess. I don't like guessing anything about the monster, but I have seen that often enough to be certain."

"That's it," the surveillance officer agreed.

"Do we have a size on that?" Tarrel asked.

"I can give accuracy to within ten percent. We have a length of twelve kilometers by just under three across. No indication of just how large the ship inside that shield might be, unfortunately. The Dreadnought's visual and electronic invisibility is probably some function of the shield, which must be extremely powerful. Otherwise we should have had some reflection from the ship itself."

"Perhaps five times the length of a Starwolf carrier, but wider and much thicker," Chagin mused. "Probably several times the mass."

"I really don't believe that it could be Starwolves," Tarrel said. "Well, we know a lot more than we did, but not enough."

"What do you think, Captain?" Pesca asked.

"We obviously can't handle this ourselves. Let's get our information to a courier, and then we'll go find ourselves a Starwolf."

The first problem in finding a Starwolf was knowing just where to look. The Union knew only that there was at least one carrier to every sector, and that each carrier ran a regular patrol through that sector. The actual course of that patrol varied according to need, and the patrol changed regularly so that the presence or absence of a carrier could not be anticipated. There had always been some suspicion that the Starwolves employed drones or reconnaissance flights of smaller ships, and that they kept surveillance devices in some of the more important systems, but that had never been proven. All that could be said for certain was that the Starwolves were well aware of just about everything that went on in Union space, while their own habits remained very obscure and their comings and goings were largely unpredictable.

Captain Tarrel's response to this problem was as clever and effective as circumstances allowed. She made the best determination she could about just where in the Sector Starwolves were most likely to be found. Carthaginian was taken into that region at the battleship's best speed, and they began issuing an achronic message that Lt. Commander Pesca had assembled, the best he could manage for the purpose of attracting Starwolf attention in a constructive as opposed to a destructive manner. This matter required many hasty explanations on Tarrel's own part, since System and Fleet Commanders they encountered along the way were not sympathetic to a Union battleship advertising for the chance to talk with Starwolves. It had even gotten them fired upon in one rather remote and provincial system, but the diplomatic pass issued by Sector Commander Lake himself settled all other arguments. Especially since refusal to recognize that pass could be considered an act of treason.

A full week of searching brought them their first positive lead. Not only had a Starwolf carrier passed through one independent system only three days earlier, it had stopped for planet leave and had left only a few short hours before. Independents were not as a rule willing to help the Union, but a single battleship trying to attract the attention of Starwolves was such a novelty that they were willing to help. As they obviously saw it, if a Union battleship wanted to find trouble, who were they to interfere? Unfortunately, they did not know where the Starwolves had gone next.

Tarrel retreated with Chagin to the reference terminal on one corner of the bridge, for a hasty consultation with the local star charts. Pesca invited himself to join them, on the assumption that his wisdom and experience would be useful.

"The obvious choice is this one," Chagin said after studying the map for a moment. "Two days out for us, but twelve light-years closer than the second nearest system to this one. The third choice in about sixty light-years or so and not a very obvious jump."

"You don't seem to trust the obvious choice," Tarrel pointed out.

Chagin frowned. "Because it is obvious. Anyone looking for them would go there first."

"Do they have any reason to think that anyone would be following them?" she asked.

"No, certainly not."

"And is anyone who might be following them likely to cut in ahead of them and prepare an ambush?"

"I concede the point," Chagin agreed. "But that's exactly the problem. We're behind them now. They just had a leave, so they're not likely to stop anywhere for long any time soon. Can we overtake them now?"

"No, of course not," Tarrel agreed. "That's why we have to anticipate their move three jumps ahead and intercept them here."

The first officer looked at the place she indicated on the chart. "Yes, their steps from this next one are fairly limited. Unless they suddenly turn well out of their way, they will go here and then here."

"While we can cut directly across at top speed and intercept them in only five days."

"Can we do it?" he asked.

"We have to. I can't anticipate their move after that, not with three very likely choices," Tarrel said, then dropped her voice. "From this time on, I want one of us on the bridge at all times. Those first seconds after encountering a Starwolf carrier are ticklish ones. Under no circumstances can we allow something to slip, or they'll scorch us."

"Anything I can do, Captain?" Pesca asked.

"Just stay out of my chair, Wally."

That encounter was not at all likely to happen until they reached the system in question, unless the Starwolves did intercept their achronic message and pull Carthaginian out of starflight. Captain Tarrel counted the days, and she found herself half wishing that they would not find the carrier. If she did not find the Starwolves after a certain amount of time, she intended to take her ship back to Vinthra and turn the whole matter over to Commander Lake. He could wait for Starwolves to come into system in their own good time and then issue them a polite invitation to parlay.

They dropped out of starflight farther into the system than anticipated, a common variance—either too far in or out— after a long run at very high speed. Carthaginian engaged her forward main drives and decelerated rapidly, settling into a slow prowl as she began a continuous series of active scanner sweeps and transmitted her message. Starwolves were notoriously spooky and Captain Tarrel wanted to give them plenty of time to get used to the thought of being hailed by a Union battleship. She had no way of knowing just how far the carrier could be behind them, if at all.

"Minimum local traffic," the surveillance officer reported before he was asked. "Nothing unexpected."

"The System Commander is calling," communications added. "They have heard our transmission and request an explanation. No one sounds particularly upset about it, however."

"Invoke our diplomatic pass," Tarrel said. "Ask them to keep the local chatter and scanner sweeps to a minimum. No need to be pompous as long as the locals are willing to help. Our survivors might need to be rescued later on."

Her humor was appreciated by all but Lt. Commander Pesca, who was pale.

As it happened, she had almost guessed wrong. The Starwolves were there before her. The carrier appeared suddenly on scan almost directly behind them, passing swiftly over the Carthaginian before matching speed barely twice her own great length ahead of the battleship, clearly visible now on the main bridge viewscreen. Then she rotated slowly, until she was facing them, a vast black hull vaguely in the shape of an arrowhead, her short, slightly downswept wings protecting her main drives. Her color was an unreflective black, difficult enough to see against space, even at close range. There were no windows to betray her presence with their glow, although she did have her recognition lights burning as a courtesy. That was actually encouraging.

If there was trouble, Tarrel decided that the Starwolves could not have been more obliging in stationing their immense carrier directly in front of her missile racks. She doubted that those missiles could do the great ship any harm, but they might provide enough distraction to get her own ship to the vague safety of starflight.

"Message coming in," communications reported. "No visual."

"I'll take it at my station," Tarrel said.

"I should take it," Pesca offered in his excitement. "I am the linguist."

"You're also an asshole, and neither attribute qualifies you for this," she snapped, then addressed the communication unit at her station. "This is Captain Tarrel of the battleship Carthaginian. We wish to parlay on an urgent matter."

"This is Trendaessa Kerridayen," the response came, a strong female voice. "Just what seems to be the problem?"

Tarrel was surprised at that lack of concern. It made her wonder if the Starwolves found her battleship at all threatening. "Some large ship is moving through our systems, destroying every ship and station it finds. The situation is very alarming to us."

"So?"

No sympathy there. "So, we were wondering if the Starwolves were behind this, or if we have an alien threat to deal with."

"No. It is not Starwolves."

Tarrel was grateful that this was not a visual link, since she could not stop herself from making faces. "I have encountered this machine on three separate occasions. My opinion is that this is an automated weapon designed to seek out and destroy all power sources it encounters in space. It is also my opinion that a single Starwolf carrier could not fight it."

"Is that a fact? You seem to expect us to do something about it."

"This monster is efficient and absolutely merciless," she said. "We cannot fight it. Damn it, we can't even see it. Our military ships might be one thing, but this beast eats commercial ships and stations, both our own and the independents, without discrimination, and we can't protect them. System Commander Lake has empowered me to negotiate for your help, even to the point of declaring a truce between us."

"On our terms?"

"On just about any terms."

"My word, this thing does have you people rattled. I suspect that I would do best to call Commander Daerran to the bridge. That way, you only have to explain all of this once."

"I can wait," Tarrel agreed.

She muted the communication unit and leaned back in her seat, thinking that she had not started out at all well. She decided now that the Starwolf ship's odd manner had been deliberate, intended to keep her from presenting a prepared speech in the way she might have meant, possibly flustering her enough to say things she did not intend. She would have to be more on her guard.

"I thought that Starwolves didn't have last names," Pesca commented.

"They don't," she said. "That was the ship."

"The ship?" He was obviously greatly surprised. "Do you mean that their ships can talk?"

"They use sentient computer systems completely integrated into their carriers," Tarrel explained. "That way, their captains can circumvent the need to ever talk to knock-headed crewmembers."

At least that first tense moment of contact had passed, and the Starwolves were willing to talk rather than shoot first and ask no questions at all. She considered that a professional accomplishment, since one of her primary goals as the captain of a battleship was to avoid all fights that she had no way of winning. One of the greatest problems about being a Union captain was always being out-classed, not only in technology but also in raw size, and she was pragmatic enough to realize that Goliath won most of the time. There had once been a time when she had thought her seven hundred meters of battleship to be quite large.

"Captain Tarrel?"

She opened the line. "This is Captain Janus Tarrel."

"Yes, this is Commander Daerran of the Kerridayen," he responded. "My ship has played back for me the record of your communication to this point, and I agree that you have a most serious problem. Do you have reason to fear that your civilization, or at least large segments of your civilization might be in danger of destruction if we do not intervene?"

"Yes, I do," Tarrel insisted. "Very few of our worlds, or the independent colonies for that matter, are self-sufficient to any high degree. The destruction of ships and commercial stations could bring interplanetary shipping to a halt on a regional scale, causing technological collapse."

"Actually, the problem is rather more serious than I suspect your people are even aware," the Starwolf said. "Your interplanetary economy is a very fragile one at best. That is why we have always been very selective in the type and amount of shipping we capture or destroy."

"That's very kind of you," she remarked, trying unsuccessfully not to sound too critical.

"Do not mention it. If it had ever been our intention simply to destroy your civilization, we could have done that in a matter of weeks, at any time." There was a short pause. "Captain, would you be willing to come aboard the Kerridayen with any information you might have on this machine? I believe that Trendaessa should have a good look at what you know and we will see what she can make of it."

Captain Tarrel had to consider that very quickly. "Yes, I believe that I should come aboard. What is the recommended method for that?"

"We can receive your shuttle, or send one over to collect you," the Starwolf said. "The simplest thing in the long run would be to take your ship directly into one of our holding bays, so that you can have access to your own ship at any time you wish. But we can understand if you are not willing to trust us that much."

"Thank you, Commander. Perhaps it would be easiest all the way around to have you take Carthaginian into your bay. What should we do to prepare?"

"Just close down your drives, shields and navigational systems, and your main generators. The Kerridayen will position herself and bring your ship into the holding bay with her handling arms. I will see you in the bay in a few minutes."

Tarrel was not entirely pleased at allowing her ship to be taken aboard the Starwolf carrier, but she did not fail to recognize what a gesture of trust this was on both sides. The Union had laid too many traps and decoys for Starwolves in the past, a rare few of which had actually been effective. Commander Daerran was being rather gracious, not conceited, in his pretense that he and his great ship had nothing to fear. Such indications were very encouraging. She could see, however, that certain members of her crew were not so willing to trust. Chagin, for one, obviously thought that going aboard the carrier was one thing, but going aboard, ship and all, was quite another.

"We're safer there, even if things do turn out badly," she told him. "As long as we remain outside, their safest and quickest way of dealing with us is to shoot. Once aboard, we're completely at their mercy, and I do trust their mercy. They might keep the ship, but they will keep us safe and return us soon enough. But I don't see any reason why things should fall out at this point. You have command. No heroics, and no suicide attacks. You might be able to destroy this carrier from the inside by exploding the generators—and don't think they don't know that—but we might need every one of these ships to defend our worlds. What if more Dreadnoughts turn up?''

"I understand, Captain," Chagin assured her. "As you say, they won't want to do anything to scare us once they do have us in that bay."

"I'm supposed to go along this time," Pesca suggested brightly. "That is my primary mission objective now, you know. If we meet with Starwolves, I'm to listen to them and try to learn their language."

Tarrel turned to glare at him. "Wally, if the Starwolves use their own language around us so seldom that linguists haven't figured it out before now, then what the hell is the use of knowing it?"

Pesca looked shocked. "I never thought of that."

"Did you ever do anything to Sector Commander Lake that he sent you along on this mission just to be rid of you?"

"No, I really don't think so. I try to remember all the people that I've annoyed."

"Then you must be my punishment," Tarrel decided. "Very well, you can go with me. If the Starwolves think that most of us are just like you, they might just take pity on us and chase away the Dreadnought for us."

"That's not very nice," he complained.

"I am not a nice person," Tarrel insisted. "Chagin, have you ever known me to be a nice person?"

Chagin shook his head emphatically. "Never, ever."

The actual docking took place more quickly than the crew of the Carthaginian had expected. Kerridayen rotated herself and then dropped back until her starboard holding bay was directly above the battleship, leaving some members of her crew to reflect upon the size of a vessel capable of holding a Union battleship in either of two bays. The bay itself opened outward in the belly of the carrier, between and slightly ahead of her two sets of forward main drives, a great well of brilliant light in the dull black hull of the massive ship. Unfortunately, the view that could be had from any of the bridge monitors was not good. After a brief moment, a distant mechanical boom echoed through Carthaginian's hull as the Kerridayen's handling arms made contact with the battleship and drew her into the hold.

"Commander Tarrel?" Daerran called, only moments later. She took the message at her station. "Captain Tarrel."

"Excuse me. For us, Captain is the leader of a pack of fighters, while the Commander has the entire ship."

"For us, Commander is any person of command grade," she explained. "We use Captain for the commander of a ship out of tradition."

"I will remember that. I was going to say that we have set a docking tube at what appears to us to be your main airlock. But you do not have to worry about accidents, whatever door you might open. We have provided atmosphere within the bay."

"When do you want me to come over?"

"Any time you desire. Someone will be at the docking tube to escort you to the bridge."

Captain Tarrel put on her best dress uniform, told Pesca that she would have him court-martialed if he said so much as a single word, and took him to the main port airlock, with its wide double doors generally employed as a primary access at station dock. A quick glance out the window to one side of the lock had shown her that the docking tube was indeed waiting. She found, somewhat to her surprise, that the interior of the carrier was rather cool. This was enemy territory, the place that was death for humans to go; to her knowledge, she was the first Union officer ever to be invited aboard one of their carriers. Although the Starwolves rescued many from disabled ships each year, prisoners were usually kept very close to the bays and never saw the deep portions of the great ships. There was so much mystique woven about the Starwolves that she found herself honestly afraid to proceed, though she had thought herself too clever and jaded for such instinctive fears.

She was by no means prepared for her first sight of living Starwolves in their own element. Nine of them, wearing their black armored suits—which she recognized from their number and color as indicating that they formed a pack of fighter pilots—waited in the small lounge at the inner end of the tube. They were small people, all of them noticeably shorter than herself. Their appearance was vaguely human, although their vast, dark eyes and large pointed ears made them look more elfin. Their greatest obvious difference was the fact that they possessed two sets of arms, a second pair just below the normal arms and shoulders of her own race. She had heard stories of their lightning reflexes and their crushing strength. In spite of their small stature and delicate features, she could believe everything she had ever heard, although a more rational part of her mind argued that the black armor-plated suits made them appear more massive and menacing than they actually were.

At least they were courteous as they escorted her and Pesca to the lift—the fastest that she had ever ridden—and took them up to the Kerridayen's bridge. Commander Daerran was waiting to greet her personally. He was the first Starwolf that she had ever seen not in armor, dressed as he was in what might have been a uniform of white tunic and pants. He seemed at the same time to be smaller than the pilots who had greeted her outside the docking tube, as she had expected, but she could also see how heavily muscled his small frame actually was. Of course, it was not bulk alone that gave the Starwolves their tremendous strength and speed. Theirs was an artificial race, created completely by genetic engineering, and even their most basic biochemistry was entirely their own. The fact that they looked vaguely human was an arbitrary factor, for there was no actual genetic relationship between the two races.

"Captain Tarrel, welcome aboard," Daerran greeted her, his voice lighter and more musical than it had been over the com.

"Commander Daerran," she responded. "This is my special advisor, Lieutenant Commander Walter Pesca."

"A diplomatic liaison?"

"No," she replied vaguely.

"Allow me to introduce relevant members of my own crew," he said, leading them from the side corridor onto the bridge. "My first officer Kayell. And, of course, the present manifestation of Trendaessa Kerridayen."

Tarrel was rather surprised when the long, double-armed boom fixed to the ceiling of the center of the bridge pivoted around, a pair of camera lenses rotating in unison to focus on her. After that startling introduction, she almost failed to notice the first officer, a young male Starwolf. As a bridge officer, his white tunic had black bands about the cuffs. She was glad for the distinction, about the only way she had to tell one Starwolf from the other.

The bridge of the carrier was not as large as she had anticipated for a ship of such tremendous proportions. A single vast viewscreen dominated the front of the wedge-shaped bridge, with a line of various stations along the front. The middle bridge, with its large consoles for the helm and weapons station, was elevated above the main level by a series of steps to either side. And above that was the upper bridge, the Commander's station, where he could look down into every console on the bridge. Considering the telescopic vision of the Starwolves, he could probably read the data on the monitors at each station. Daerran immediately led them up to his own station. Trendaessa rotated her camera pod around to join them.

"Do you have your data on the thing?" Daerran asked as he lifted himself into his seat at the console, using the overhead bars.

Tarrel gave him a small optical disk, which he fed into a drive on one of the side consoles. The machine tried for a long moment to digest the disk, then abruptly spit it out again.

"Yo, incompatible format," Trendaessa remarked. "Kayell, will you run that disk down to the number three optical reader at the engineering station. Now, Captain Tarrel, why don't you tell us your impressions of what you saw."

At the same time that she listened to Tarrel's account of her three separate encounters with the Dreadnought, Trendaessa sifted through the various records that had been made aboard the Carthaginian at those times. She employed the three main monitors at the Commander's station to project visually some of the images she was compiling, almost as if she was thinking aloud through those monitors. She never looked at the monitors themselves, so she must have had some way of viewing those images directly.

"I suspect that your assumptions are basically correct," the ship said when Tarrel had concluded her account. "The Dreadnought, as you call it, is almost certainly only a machine, and not an especially clever one at that. Those times when it seemed only to be playing with convoy, destroying ships in an almost lazy manner, it was probably responding at a low-priority attack status. There was no need for it to be in any hurry."

"What manner of machine?" Daerran asked.

"A ship-killing machine, of course," Trendaessa explained. "It apparently scans large areas of space for the presence of artificial power sources and any machine that is intact and potentially functional. The attack on the station did show it destroying one larger ship that was not powered up, while shuttles escaped unharmed, so there must be some targeting priority other than just the sources of active power. My belief is that this is an automated weapon of unknown alien origin, designed to destroy a civilization's ability to make war by decimating the ships and supporting devices that make interplanetary flight possible."

"Did someone aim this damned thing at us?" Tarrel asked.

"That is possible, but I doubt it," Trendaessa said. "Most likely, this one was set loose and just never got turned off when the war was over, if there was anyone left to turn it off. The fact that it responded to your attempt to communicate is interesting. It was probably asking you if you were friend or foe. Needless to say, you did not know how to answer. Given much more information, which I doubt that I will be able to obtain, I might be able to learn the codes that identify a ship as a friend, or perhaps even tell it to shut itself down. It would probably take far less time to simply find a way to destroy it."

"Then you have not yet seen a way to destroy it?" Daerran asked.

"No, I am afraid not. That monster is protected by the most powerful shield that I have ever seen. My own shield can of course be set at the proper frequency and level of power that will make me invisible to scanners by simply absorbing the active scanner signals, and by containing all emissions from the ship itself. The Dreadnought has a shield powerful enough that it contains light, like a black hole, although gravity is not the agent of this process. It is not actually invisible; if it was between you and a planet of a very close star, then you would see that area blacked out by its shields. But it does not reflect or allow light to escape, and that gives it functional invisibility in open space. Scanner invisibility is much more useful. From a defensive standpoint, we are about even."

"And the offensive standpoint?" Daerran asked. "Can you see it, and can it see you?"

"I do not know. One carrier cannot see another that has its shields at stealth intensity, and I doubt that I could see this Dreadnought. I cannot know whether or not it could see me. Its shields are more powerful, and it might also have the technology to penetrate mine."

"And what about weapons? This energy-transfer weapon it uses does not seem especially dangerous to me."

"That is because we have never seen it used at anything more than its most basic level. We use a destructive achronic beam which cuts into the target before the power charge is released in a quick, strong jolt to destroy the object. The Dreadnought uses a benign carrier, and releases its charge in a relatively slow, steady stream. This benign carrier beam does not betray itself on scan, or visually, the way our own bolts do, so the weapon beams cannot betray the location of the ship itself. But I am very certain that the weapon can be stepped up quite a bit in intensity, once firepower is more important than absolute stealth."

"Then I doubt that our cannons would penetrate that shield," Daerran said.

"I doubt that even my conversion cannon would be able to penetrate that shield," the ship added. "I am not certain that I can fight this thing. For that matter, I am not certain that all the carriers together could fight it. It might be easy, and it might be impossible. We need more information."

"Do you have any recommendations?"

"Only to find it and see what we can see." She hesitated. "We need a decoy for it to attack, just as Captain Tarrel has so cleverly used decoys against it. Unfortunately, the only decoy that will serve our present need is myself. I must fight it, even knowing that I cannot win and that I will sustain some damage, for the sake of learning what we can."

"Is it worth damaging one of our few ships for the sake of information?" Daerran asked.

"Is it worth the destruction of a carrier, or worse, trying to fight this thing unprepared?" Trendaessa asked in return. "I am not concerned. I will withdraw before I am severely damaged."

Daerran leaned back in his seat, both sets of his arms crossed on his chest. "Get in touch with Home Base for advisement and tell them what you propose. If they agree, then we will attempt it. Tell them also that we will be moving to intercept the Dreadnought now, and to send their reply there. Do you have any clear idea where to look?"

"I do see the pattern in its movement," the ship confirmed. "This machine really is not very clever. I know exactly where to look."

Daerran nodded, then turned to Tarrel. "Captain, we have to release your ship to prepare the Kerridayen for battle. I can put your ship out here, or when we reach our destination. But I invite you to stay with us as an observer and adviser. I warn you that the ride will be rough.''

Tarrel nodded. ''Thank you. I believe that I would like to go along, but I would like to send the Carthaginian back to Vinthra now and have my first officer advise Sector Commander Lake of our progress.''

She hurried back to her own ship, knowing that the Kerridayen was delaying her own flight for her. She still needed to pack, uncertain just how long she would be among the Starwolves. And she wanted warm clothes; having asked, she had been told that they preferred a fairly cool environment to counteract the greater heat their fierce metabolism produced. She meant to compose a very hasty report, relay her instructions to Chagin, and send the Carthaginian on her way. The prospect of being aboard a Starwolf carrier during a major battle was an exciting and rather intimidating matter indeed. Lt. Commander Pesca ran to match her determined stride as they hurried down the long boarding tube.

She glanced at him over her shoulder. ''Are you planning to stay with me?''

''That is my assigned mission, Captain,'' he said. ''Is there some reason why I should not stay?''

''No, as long as you keep quiet and out of the way.'' She glanced at him a second time. ''How are the language lessons going so far, Wally?''

Pesca frowned fiercely. ''I have yet to hear a single one of them speaking their own language. Even their monitors had been converted to read Terran. They plan to keep their secrets.''

''Then is there any reason to come along?''

''They have to let something slip eventually,'' he insisted. ''Besides, you need at least one person about who has to do what you tell him.''

Pert boy!

Kerridayen moved into the system cautiously, her hull shields at stealth intensity. She made her changes of speed slowly, braking herself with her forward main drives as little as possible to contain their energy emissions. The Dreadnought's apparently slow changes of speed and direction during its previous attacks suggested that it employed very much the same tactic. The objective of this first round was to attempt to determine whether the alien ship could hide itself from Starwolf scanners—something they did expect—and see if it could see the Kerridayen even with her shields hiding her—something no one could guess. Whatever happened next would depend upon the results of this experiment. If the Dreadnought saw and attacked the carrier, they would have to fight immediately. If not, they would eventually have to show themselves. Trendaessa assumed that the enemy was here, but she could not be absolutely certain unless it attacked.

"Either the Dreadnought has been here already, or else this entire system has been closed down completely," Trendaessa said. "There is not a single drive or major power source in operation anywhere in nearby space. However, I do detect unexplained radiation residues, suggesting the explosion of conversion generators. I wish that I could tell you more, but active scanner signals would give away our position."

"Take us in closer toward the inhabited planet," Daerran said. "If we do not find the station, then we know that the Dreadnought has been here."

"Right now, we could use just one more of those drones I had a few days ago," Captain Tarrel remarked. She had been given a jump seat installed on the upper bridge, specially padded to protect her from the hard accelerations that the Starwolves considered normal.

"Yes, that is an idea." Trendaessa brought her camera pod into the upper bridge. "I could release one of my drones and have it run through the system. If the Dreadnought is here, it will snap at that bait."

"That would also give us the opportunity to observe its attack from a safe distance," Daerran agreed. He turned to Tarrel. "Captain, how long should we expect to have, assuming it can see us?"

"The first time, it found us within five minutes. In that case, I suspect that it must have followed us into the system, since it had not attacked anything there before our arrival. In the second case, it was on top of us within the first minute. Either we were very unfortunate about where we came out of starflight, or else it engaged its own stardrives to maneuver in quickly behind us."

"It probably saw you coming before you left starflight and

entered the system, and it was waiting for you," Trendaessa told her. "My own scanners are capable of that."

If nothing else, Tarrel was coming to have a greater appreciation about just where her side had always stood in the silent war they had been fighting with the Starwolves. Their technology made the best Union battleships seem very primitive in comparison. And yet the Starwolves themselves seemed to believe that they would find themselves helpless to deal with the Dreadnought. As Trendaessa had once said, it was stupid but powerful enough to have its way. Certainly the Union forces could never hope to fight that monster entirely on their own.

They made their pass of the single inhabited planet at speeds which were still a significant portion of the speed of light, coasting at that very fierce pace. Because of her speed, the Kerridayen did not actually come that close to the planet, but aimed her best optical sensors in that direction in the few seconds that they were passing near. She continued in on her trajectory, executing a series of wide parabolic loops about the local star to brake her speed without engaging her drives. At the same time, she was busy processing the information she had received.

"The Dreadnought has been here," she said. "I detect no station, no ships and no orbital power sources. There are some rather large pieces of scrap orbiting the planet, probably the remains of the station itself."

She directed a recording of the enhanced images she had received. The first was in motion, red-shifted on approach and then blue-shifted as the carrier had sped past, and it showed very little. She then displayed a small series of captured images from that sequence, further enhanced and magnified, showing a vague cloud of debris drifting in close orbit.

"I wonder if they had time to get out," Daerran said quietly.

"That depends upon whether or not a general evacuation order has been sent throughout this area," Tarrel answered. "If it wasn't for our present need for stealth, I could invoke my diplomatic pass and call down to the planet."

"We might get a chance yet," he said. "Trendaessa, is there any way to know how long ago that attack came? What about dispersal patterns for that radiation you detected?"

"One moment, Commander. Something is happening," she said, then lifted her camera pod slightly in a gesture of alarm. '*Val traron!* We are being fired upon."

Two words of Starwolf, and Wally was not there to hear it.

"What do we have?" Daerran asked.

"It is all very vague," the ship explained. "The weapon beams leave a very distinct trail of emissions after they have passed, probably leakage from their undischarged energy. My immediate guess is that the Dreadnought knows we are here, but she cannot scan us clearly enough to get a distinct weapon lock."

"Stand by your main batteries and ready your conversion cannon," Daerran said. "For now, try contacting that monster."

"No, wait!" Tarrel ordered sharply. Both the Starwolf and his ship turned to stare at her. "This might be your chance to get in one clean shot at that monster. Have your best weapon standing by. When you hail it, the Dreadnought might respond like it did for my ship. If it does, you trace the source of that transmission for a weapon lock."

"Whatever they say, humans are not all stupid," Trendaessa commented, with remarkable lack of tact for a machine. "Commander, this might be important, and we still collect the information we want if it fails. But if that ship has learning capabilities, which it surely must, then it might only work once. Either we try now, or we wait until we have several carriers ready to fire all at once."

Daerran looked up at Trendaessa's camera pod thoughtfully. "You still want to try this?"

"Of course. It is going to fail anyway. The Dreadnought is not going to lower that shield until we can give the proper code. But the blast of the conversion cannon against that shield might give scanner reflections of the interior. That is very important."

He nodded. "Charge your conversion cannon, then."

Before Trendaessa could prepare her most lethal weapon, one of the beams from the Dreadnought connected with her own shields. The discharge exploded like a storm of lightning over the surface of her shields for several long, tense moments—too long while her position was illuminated to her enemy—but the power couplings were finally able to handle the excess energy that was ripping through her shields. Once again hidden in stealth mode, the Kerridayen immediately shifted her position several kilometers down and one side, while a volley of new discharge beams lanced through the place where she had been only a moment earlier.

"Conversion cannon charged to eighty-five pèrcent," she reported. "Ready to fire on command."

"Transmit the code," Daerran told her. "If it replies, then fire on it the moment you can fix the source of its signal."

The Kerridayen transmitted her message, and the Dreadnought replied in a gesture that seemed almost automatic. Trendaessa identified the source, took the range and fired. The conversion cannon, already charged from a quantity of matter converted directly into a tremendous amount of energy, extended a narrow containment beam toward its target and released that energy in a sustained stream deadly enough to destroy a world. For a few brief seconds, the alien ship was engulfed in that blinding torrent of raw energy.

"No effect," Trendaessa declared only a moment after the firing of the conversion cannon ended. "The shield of that machine has some mechanism for shedding energy. It deflected the entire blast out into space. Needless to say, I did not get a scanner image of its interior."

"Has it opened fire again?" Daerran asked.

"No, I must have blinded it. But it will probably have its scanners cleared and recalibrated in a matter of seconds. I am taking advantage of the time for a close pass."

The Dreadnought opened fire sooner than Trendaessa would have liked; as the Kerridayen came nearer, her position was easier to determine. A pair of discharge beams connected with her shields in rapid succession.

"That was too much for my power couplings," Trendaessa reported. "I can no longer hold my shields at stealth intensity, and it can see us clearly."

"Cut off if it becomes too thick," Daerran told her. "It might step up the power on those beams any time now, and you are making threatening gestures."

"If I could, I would make rude gestures," the ship replied.

Unfortunately, the situation had become hopeless with the loss of stealth. Trendaessa stepped up her speed, but the beams were now discharging into her shields at regular intervals. The power load of any one beam was easy enough for her to bear, but the combined effects were beginning to tell. Since her close pass was not going to give her more than she already knew, she abandoned that tactic without consulting her Commander and began a very hasty retreat. She returned fire with the cannons of her rear battery, less in the hope of damaging the Dreadnought than to give her somewhere to shunt the tremendous load of power her shield projectors were trying to contain.

"The battle shields just failed," she reported. "All I have now are the main hull integrity shields. Those should bring us out of this."

"Time to starflight?" Daerran asked.

"Let me build my speed another fifteen percent or the acceleration will kill our passengers."

Tarrel glanced at the Starwolf Commander, but he did not even seem tempted to sacrifice her to save his ship greater harm. The Kerridayen was already accelerating so sharply that Tarrel was pinned to her protective seat, unable even to lift her arms. Her ears were ringing dully, and her vision was dim about the edges.

The release of pressure came suddenly at the same moment that the carrier took a particularly bad hit. They could actually hear the discharge boom and sizzle against the hull. Then the hull shields failed as well, allowing that energy to run directly through the systems of the ship. The monitors and console panels failed, while lights flashed dangerously. Trendaessa's camera pod began to droop, settling slowly to the floor.

Daerran spat some oath in his own language. "Trendaessa just went down. Engineering, get power to the drives any way you can. Helm, take us out of here the first moment this ship responds."

Perhaps the only thing that saved them was that the Dreadnought hesitated in its attack, an apparent response to the sudden loss of power on the Starwolf ship. The distance between them had grown steadily until it might have no longer been able to track the carrier accurately without generator and drive emissions to guide its scanners. Kerridayen's systems began to clear as the discharge faded. The main generators returned first, and that power was immediately directed to the main drives. The carrier moved away quickly on an evasive course, escaping another hit from the devastating weapons of the Dreadnought until she was able to escape into starflight moments later.

Trendaessa lifted her camera pod and looked about, her gesture one of confusion and possibly some embarrassment. "I must have fallen asleep. Did I miss anything important?"

"Possibly your own destruction," Daerran told her drily as he lifted himself from his station. "Engineering, get repair crews onto our power systems and put everything back into the grid. I want a list of every damaged system divided into those things we can fix and those things we cannot. Trendaessa?"

"Our worst damage is to our power systems," the ship answered. "We have no shields. The main drives are down to sixty percent, and I can get enough power to the star drives for only forty percent. We will not be going anywhere very fast unless we can replace quite a few power couplings. At least the generators are strong."

Daerran nodded. "Set a course for Home Base."

Trendaessa turned her camera pod to look at Captain Tarrel. "What about our passengers?"

"Just do it."

He walked over to join Tarrel, who was stretching in an attempt to relieve cramped joints. "How do you feel?"

"I should live," she said. "I just won't like it for a while."

"Captain, we have a problem," Daerran said, helping her to stand. "I need to take my ship and her information to our main base as quickly as we can get there. I would like to have you along, both as an advisor and a representative of the Union. But you will see and hear many things that you probably should not, and they might not allow me to take you home again. Are you willing to accept that risk? I can still have you put off."

Tarrel considered that briefly. "If I can do anything to help, then it would be worth the risk. Did we learn anything?"

"We learned that there are a few things that we should never try to do again. I hope that it was worth it."

—3—

Trendaessa Kerridayen took fourteen days to make her long, slow way home. Captain Tarrel had no idea of their course, nor did she ask. The location of the Starwolf main base was unknown in the Union, and she believed that it would have to remain unknown if she expected to ever be allowed to go home again. She was not even certain of the carrier's speed, although she suspected that they were limping along at a pace her own battleship would have found hard to match. The Rane Sector bordered the frontier with the old Republic, an area that was now believed to be Starwolf territory. Fourteen days of travel at the speed and direction she suspected would have taken them well outside of Union space.

The Kerridayen had been in a constant state of repair since her battle with the Dreadnought. Starwolves, as Tarrel discovered to her great surprise, did not sleep, and they were willing to put in some very long hours. Even so, there were fewer than three thousand of them aboard the ship, only two-thirds of that number active crewmembers, and they had a very large ship to maintain. For all their efforts, they made very little progress toward repairing their ship during that long journey home. The greatest part of the damage was not structural but to the ship's power grid and complex electronics; some of the damaged systems could not be replaced in flight, but would have to wait for a refitting in dock. Superficially the Kerridayen had been badly scorched—hard to see on her black hull—but she had been far more badly damaged than it seemed.

Kerridayen dropped out of starflight well inside the Alkayja system and began braking smoothly for her approach. There was none of the usual bravado and intimidation in her manner, such as she would have employed in Union space to remind people like Captain Tarrel that she was too dangerous for them to touch. This was her home, and here she was just a part of the regular local traffic. A small tender, painted bright orange and sporting powerful running lights, fell in just ahead of the carrier to escort her home, while Kerridayen herself ran with both her recognition lamps and the retractable main lights in her shock bumper burning. A Starwolf carrier was a very difficult ship to see, even considering her size, and she had to make her presence well known. It would have been better, of course, if so many of her lights had not burned out in the attack.

Alkayja station was rather more compact than the stations that Tarrel was used to seeing, particularly when compared to the kilometers of sprawling tubes and modules that formed the Vinthra Military complex. The main portion of the station consisted of two wide disks, each about twenty-five kilometers across. The thicker disk was lined along the outside with a continuous row of vast bays that allowed the carriers to dock facing in. The smaller disk above that was studded with bays for ships of a more conventional size. And the station was capped above and below with a flattened dome. Although it was a very visible white, Tarrel realized suddenly that the actual station shared certain similarities with the carriers. The flat, rounded domes on top and bottom offered armored protection against attack—just like the large, flat surfaces of the hulls of the carriers—with no sharp angles to catch a bolt that might have otherwise skipped harmlessly off that featureless surface. All machinery, pipes and ducting were within the shell, less vulnerable while keeping the exterior uncluttered. The station probably even had independent interplanetary drive capabilities.

Kerridayen's maneuverability was compromised from having too many of her field drive projectors burnt out, and so the immense ship had to be moved into a refitting bay by a team of tenders. Since the carrier weighed some fifteen million tons that had to be stopped once it was set into motion, that was a long and difficult process indeed. Half an hour passed just drawing her slowly up the full length of the bay, three kilometers deep, before she nosed into the bracket designed to receive her forward shock bumper. After that, bringing in the braces that steadied the ship's short wings and finally the two forward docking tubes was fairly easy.

"I hate that," Trendaessa said when it was done, lowering her camera pod to the floor. "I hate being towed. I hate being pulled and pushed. I hate being shot at. Why could I have not been built a freighter?"

"Freighters are stupid," Daerran told her. "Freighters are the cattle of the lanes. Do you want to be a cow?"

She lifted her camera pod. "No, not really."

"Send your data over to the station, and shut yourself down for a few weeks of convalescence," he told her, then turned to Captain Tarrel. "I would suppose that your stay with us is just about at an end. When you go out from this station again, it will probably be aboard another carrier. For now, we should go into the station and see what they have planned."

They took a lift down to the main starboard docking tube, which led them, after a walk of nearly a hundred meters along the nose of the carrier and into the station itself, to one side of the bay control station and the observation rooms to either side. It seemed that the station air, which also filled the tube, was something of a compromise. It was warmer than that within the ship, but still slightly cool by human standards.

Whether Commander Daerran had expected it or not, something of a reception committee was waiting for them outside the docking tube. Hasty introductions were made, but these were mostly between some three dozen people who already knew each other at least by name and reputation and Captain Tarrel was able to remember only the most important ones present. There were three other carriers already at the station, including one that was still in the late stages of construction. For reasons that she did not expect, she surprised herself by taking exception to the fact that the Starwolves were actually under the control of a human senior officer, a certain Fleet Commander Dave Asandi. He was a tall man and rather dark, reflecting like all other humans at the station a more direct Terran ancestry than herself, reminding her oddly of the Union's ruling Sector Families. The Fleet Commander's entourage of scientific and military advisors was a mixed group, with slightly more Starwolves than humans.

Kelvessan, she reminded herself, that being their name for their race in their mysterious language. A language that, for all the long-suffering Lt. Commander Walter Pesca had been able to determine, did not even exist. He was, for that matter, still in his own cabin aboard the Kerridayen, forgotten and not necessary for the business at hand. Now that she had discovered humans in the station, Tarrel wondered if he might be encouraged to defect.

It seemed that this group had been waiting for the Kerridayen to arrive with her important data on the Dreadnought and the observations of witnesses who had fought the machine. Their first serious strategy meeting was planned to begin immediately. Tarrel found herself walking beside Fleet Commander Asandi, who was openly curious about her. She had found the Starwolves to be very open, uncomplicated people, direct, honest and incapable of duplicity. The humans among them shared many of those same qualities, although it came across almost as a rigidly honest gallantry in them.

"I find you a very uncommon person, Captain," he said. From anyone else, such flattering comments would have put her on her guard against lechery and requests to borrow money. "You have repeatedly faced two of your most deadly enemies."

"You did not expect that of a Union captain?" she asked, speaking more directly than she would have among her own.

"Frankly, I did not," he admitted. "That is not to say that I question the courage of your officers. But the limits of your technology would not seem designed to inspire courage, but prudence."

Tarrel smiled. "To tell you the truth, I believe that the only reason I am alive now is because I have a very accurate sense of knowing when it is time to run."

"Your own people seem to value you highly," Asandi told her. "So that you may know how matters stand at this point, we now have a formal truce with the Union. You have been appointed special diplomatic and military advisor. And we are happy to have you. We will be carrying our fight with this Dreadnought into your own space, and we need you to smooth the way with local officials when our ships descend in force upon their systems. I have received a special communication detailing your new duties and special powers. I will add that you can expect any reasonable cooperation from us, including the right to see and to know certain things that we would otherwise have kept to ourselves."

She hesitated. "If you will excuse me for bringing this up,

but it does seem like the proper moment. Commander Daerran indicated that those very matters that you just mentioned might interfere with your ability to allow me to return home again when this matter is settled."

"He was right to broach that subject with you," Asandi explained carefully, after a moment's pause. "It involves certain assurances that he did not have the power to give you himself. He could not promise you something that the Council might then feel compelled to take away."

"I do understand," she insisted. "On less immediate matters, there are a few things I have been wondering about."

"Please speak freely."

"For one thing, I find it odd that a human would be the supreme commander of the Starwolf fleet. The Kelvessan seem to feel that they are people, not property, and certainly not machines of war."

"That might require a rather complex explanation," Asandi said as they filed aboard a tram to take them deeper into the station. Other members of the group continued their own conversation, allowing Asandi and Tarrel the privacy to speak freely. "In theory, the Kelvessan are in fact property and not people, and I am supposed to make their decisions for them. In practice, they make their own decisions among themselves. I serve as a liaison between the Kelvessan and the human worlds of the Republic, which supplies many of their needs. That is why my post has traditionary been led by a human. I am indeed not qualified to act as their military commander. I have never been in Union space and I do not fully understand the situation they face. They tell me what they need and what they would like to have, and I do my best to get it for them."

"But the Republic no longer exists," Tarrel insisted. "At least, that's what I have always been told. The Starwolves are fighting to restore the old Republic, which created them as a long-term weapon of last resort."

"That is partly true in itself," he agreed. "But the Republic has never ceased to exist. We are the Republic, admittedly only a handful of colonies smaller than a single sector of your Union. For that matter, those that you call the Starwolves are formally the First and Second Special Carrier Fleets."

"First and Second?"

He smiled wryly. "The First Fleet patrols your space. The

Second Fleet, considerably smaller, guards our own space from attack. They have not been needed since the early years of the war, but we keep a few carriers at hand just the same.''

The tram took them well into the interior of the station, and the entire delegation filed quickly into a large conference chamber, taking their seats to suddenly become a committee. Captain Tarrel herself began the discussion by relating the events of her first and second unexpected encounter with the Dreadnought, and her attempt to make contact with it afterward. Then she and Commander Daerran spoke of their observations of the Kerridayen's attack on the Dreadnought in an attempt to gain information. The scientists of the group took control of the discussion after that, analyzing and debating the data that the Carthaginian and the Kerridayen had collected. Tarrel did her best to keep up with the conversation from that point but matters became a bit thick for her education, especially when they began to explore regions of advanced physics that her own understanding of science told her did not exist. Secondary subspace refractions and achronic resonance seemed to be the topics of the moment, and she had only a vague idea of what those things even meant. She sat back in her chair, listening much but saying nothing as she waited for matters to return to subjects in which she could be useful.

"If you will excuse me for interrupting, it seems to me that your discussion has reached the point that it would proceed best in your laboratories,'' Asandi said at last. "Have you in fact reached some consensus upon just what direction your investigations should take?''

"We believe that we have some idea of how to modify our scanners to see through stealth-intensity shielding,'' Dalvaen, the Kelvessen research leader, answered. "We could have solved this problem long ago, except that there was never any need. Only our own carriers have the ability to cloak themselves; even our fighters cannot. As long as the Union never developed shielding technology to that level, there was never any need.''

"Then you can modify our present scanners?''

Dalvaen was hesitant to answer precisely. "We have a very sound idea that we are ready to prove through advanced computer simulations. If it passes the computer models, then we can attempt testing at scale. But I have no idea yet just how much modification of our present scanners this will involve. My suspicions are that these adaptations will be of a radical nature, requiring actual refitting of the carrier."

"Then we should let your people get to work immediately and discover just how much this will involve," Asandi said. "I will have appropriations cleared for anything you might require. But what about the question of weapons?"

The Kelvessan sat back in his chair, seemingly a gesture of defeat on his part. "Unfortunately, that is going to require some very serious thought before we can propose any answers. I am curious about modifying our cannons to operate more like the Dreadnought's own discharge beams. That shield might then be unable to simply deflect away the energy of our cannons, and we could overload the shield. We also want to look into the possibility of designing auxiliary shield projectors that could be carried within the holding bays and would step up the ship's own shielding capabilities to a level comparable to that of the Dreadnought, modified to deflect its discharge beams the way that our present shields deflect regular cannon bolts. Being able to look inside the Dreadnought's shields might tell us what we need to know. But I am afraid that we do not have any quick answers to this problem."

Asandi nodded. "I will send a message to the Union telling them to expect this matter to take some time. For us, it is time to get to work."

The meeting was adjourned, and Captain Tarrel was left to wonder what she was to do now. Commander Daerran had told her that she would no longer stay aboard the Kerridayen, since the damaged carrier would not be going out again for several weeks. But she did not yet know if they proposed to send her out again as an advisor aboard some other ship or if she was to stay there at the station until the Starwolves were ready to try their new weapons in battle, and she doubted that such a test would be coming anytime soon.

As she hesitated, Fleet Commander Asandi walked over to join her. "I was wondering if you would prefer to send that message to Sector Commander Lake yourself. Or perhaps I should first ask if you are satisfied that we are doing enough?"

"It sounds to me as if you really are doing your best," she assured him. "In as far as I was able to understand any of it, that is."

Asandi smiled fondly. "The Kelvessan really are such dear

people. They tend to forget that mere humans like ourselves are not as quick as they are, either in mind or body. If you wish, you might be more satisfied with their progress when they have something to show from their computer simulations. I have to admit that I probably don't understand any better than you just what they have in mind.''

"Do you suppose that I could look at their computer models as soon as they have something to show?" Tarrel asked as they stepped out into the corridor to return to the tram.

"Yes, certainly," he agreed without the slightest hesitation. "Then you would prefer to wait and send your message as soon as you are sure that we are on to something concrete?"

"No, I should have a look at my new orders and send a reply at once," she said. "I've been out of touch a long time, and I should be reporting in. I can send a more detailed report later. I suppose that I'll be sending a long-range achronic message through your own equipment?"

"We have a carrier standing by at the Vinthra Military complex that can receive and relay long-range messages. That might not seem very private, at least not for a diplomat, but it is the best we can do since your own achronic transceivers have a limited range."

"That should be just fine, really," Tarrel insisted. "I want Sector Commander Lake to send me a detailed report of every attack by the Dreadnought since its battle with the Kerridayen, unless they've been sending you that information already."

As it turned out, Lake *had* been giving the Starwolves detailed reports of those attacks, probably under the assumption that they had been making their own observations. And since they had, Captain Tarrel was able to read both sets of reports. Either the Starwolves saw more, or they wrote much better reports.

Things had gone generally from bad to much worse. After the fight with the Kerridayen, the Dreadnought had disappeared completely for several days before appearing halfway across Union space and beginning a new pattern of attack. This new pattern was much more difficult to predict; the Dreadnought now appeared to be making a large and apparently random change of location after every three attacks. Having met Starwolves once, it seemed to have decided to make itself a little harder to find, and it was apparently not quite as stupid as Trendaessa Kerridayen had expected. Captain Tarrel agreed with the Starwolves' own assumption that the single greatest factor in the Dreadnought's change of tactics was because the Union had been anticipating its movements and evacuating the traffic from the systems in its path.

She meant to make an issue of her belief in her message to Sector Commander Lake. One thing that she could not see in these reports, but anticipated just the same, was the pettiness of the Sector Families. The Starwolves were unable to stop the Dreadnought or turn its attacks, at least not fast enough for the Trade Companies and their masters who were losing property and profits to this menace, and no doubt chaffing under the terms of the truce. She was the only one able to see what the Starwolves were actually doing, and she had to keep the Union pacified by reporting that they were indeed doing their best. Her concern was really not so much for the Union; the Sector Families and Company tyrants could chew their misfortune raw and without salt for all that she was concerned. But she did not want their grumbling to discourage the Starwolves, who had every reason to let the Dreadnought eat the Union alive.

As far as that went, there remained a part of her that was still cynical enough to find it hard to believe that the Starwolves were willing to put themselves to such trouble for their ancient enemies, even admitting that the Union was in as much danger as they believed. She could agree that they had never wanted the collapse of Terran civilization, or they would have destroyed the Union themselves long ago. But she also suspected that they wanted to find some way to defeat the Dreadnought while the fighting could be done in Union space. The Republic apparently held only a bare handful of worlds, their only support, and the Dreadnought could run through them in a matter of days as matters stood now. Tarrel could see that her primary importance was as the grease that would keep the axle and the wheel from squeaking, and the duties and powers granted to her in diplomatic charter suggested that Sector Commander Lake had convinced the Union High Council to use her in that very capacity.

She composed her initial report and sent it out, then she allowed herself to be escorted to her apartment in the visitor's quarters of the government section of the station. She thought that the Republic must entertain visitors no more often than once in a thousand years, so she was glad to see that someone had been sent up to clean the place first. There was certainly no reason for complaint with these rich and spacious lodgings, except that she was not used to being treated like an esteemed dignitary; she was reminded of Victor Lake's apartments in the Vinthra Military complex.

Lt. Commander Pesca had been installed in the adjoining chamber reserved for the aide or valet, a promotion to another position in which he might prove his incompetence. He popped out of his own room as soon as he heard her come in.

"Captain, I've discovered the most amazing thing!" he declared, running over with enthusiasm. "I think that it might be some kind of big conspiracy. When they were bringing me here, I saw real people in this station. Humans. You know, like us."

"Since when did you pass the entrance requirements?" she asked peevishly, in no mood for foolishness. She was trying to make some determination about procuring food. "I became aware of that odd fact some hours ago. For that matter, I already know that there is no conspiracy, and that there are in fact more humans here than Starwolves."

"Well, what are they doing here?" he protested. "This is Starwolf space!"

"This is the Republic."

"But there is no Republic."

"Starwolf space is the Republic. Don't they teach you children anything in the Sector Academy these days?" She opened a cabinet and found a bar, but nothing she wanted. "Do they feed us around this place?"

"You can call for catering on the wall com," Pesca suggested helpfully. "They put up a menu on the monitor. The number is fifteen thirty-seven."

Trust Wally to know all the important things. She went over to the unit on the wall by the main door and put in the number he had given her, and she was rewarded with a menu. "How goes the linguistics?"

"Frustrating," he answered dismally. "They never will speak their own language."

"You might as well give that a rest for now," Tarrel said. "Terran is the official language of the Republic, or at least the station. I've spent my morning speaking Diplomacy. It's just like Terran, except that you sound like an educated ass and you get a headache from trying to figure out what you've said, much less what the other guy said. But that's easy compared to the language used by scientists. Just one question, Mister Linguist. What do you suppose a chicken would be?"

"A small bird from old Terra, as I recall. Khoran hens replaced them in popularity long ago."

Tarrel looked amused. "We really are in the Republic, aren't we?"

"What do *chickens* have to do with all of this?" Pesca asked.

"They seem to be on the menu."

When Kelvessan put their minds to it, they were enormously clever little problem-solvers. They had a computer simulation ready for demonstration only twelve hours later. Dalvaen, the director of the research team, explained that putting together the theories was a great deal easier than finding ways to implement those theories. At least this group was neither as large nor as formal as their first meeting had been. Fleet Commander Asandi collected Captain Tarrel and escorted her to the demonstration. Other members of the military staff and the Commanders of the carriers presently in port were also there, but that was about it other than the researchers.

"Do you trust these simulations completely?" Tarrel asked. "You really don't have a lot of information on which to base your models."

"It might seem that way," Dalvaen agreed. "However, we can infer how that shield works very exactly from the information we do have, because there is only one practical model which fits those clues. I would say that our model is accurate to within ninety-five percent, probably better. What we lack is the time to learn how to re-create the technology which projects that shield, or find the additional information we need to learn how to defeat it."

"Then, in military terms, we would say that the probability that your model is accurate is so high that it would not justify the time needed to obtain additional information and proofs."

Dalvaen finally seemed to understand her approach to looking at the problem. "Let me put it this way. The information that we have was obtained the hard way by yourself and by the Kerridayen. We will now exploit that information into advantages that will allow us to obtain more information about our enemy, which in turn will give us new advantages. Taking this in a series of steps, we will eventually be stronger than it is."

Tarrel nodded. "In other words, there are no quick answers. We have to do this the hard way from start to finish. Please, proceed."

Dalvaen indicated the main monitor. "For the purposes of this simulation, we have encapsulated the projection of a Union battleship, expanded in size to a length of nearly twelve kilometers, within a shield exactly like the one we believe the Dreadnought possesses. That ship is moving through the simulated star system you see on this monitor, presently unseen either visually or by scan. Our point of view on this monitor is that of the main screens aboard a carrier fitted with enhanced scanners. At the moment, we are trying to locate our Dreadnought with ordinary scanners. As you can see, we have no contacts."

He turned to a second monitor. "Let me show you something here. This is what we believe happens when light or scanner beams contact the Dreadnought's shield. The beam is not immediately neutralized at the point of contact, but captured within a layer of the shield where it travels like waves on the surface of calm water. The shield captures the beam and holds it until it can be absorbed."

"But the Dreadnought can use its own scanners effectively through this shield," Daerran pointed out.

"How can it?" Tarrel asked.

"There seems to be only one way to make that work. The Dreadnought's shield already pulses at a certain frequency. All shields do, since it is that wavefront pattern that deflects the bolts of cannon fire. At a high enough frequency and intensity, it will also break up active scanner beams. At an even more intense level, it has the same effect even on light. But the Dreadnought knows the frequency of its shield, and it knows the corresponding frequency for an achronic beam that will slip through the wave troughs. It is a shutter that opens and closes thousands of times every second. From the outside, it appears constantly closed. From the inside, constantly open. Does everyone follow me so far?"

"From a distance," Tarrel remarked drily, and several of the others seemed to agree with her.

"If the secrets of the universe were easy, there would be no justification for experts," Dalvaen explained. "Unfortunately, knowing all of this does not give us what we would like to have. Let me show you on the simulation what we have so far. This is an application of what Captain Tarrel did to get the only clear scanner reading of the Dreadnought we have so far. She hit it with so much energy that just enough of the proper frequency and intensity was bounced back by the Dreadnought's shield. We have developed a special high-intensity achronic scanner pulse which we propose to call an impulse scanner. When the pulse strikes the surface of the shield, it is absorbed in the same manner. But at that same moment, achronic resonance causes a signal of proportionally smaller strength and frequency to be bounced back.''

He set the simulation into motion. The carrier sent two pulses, and a target responded deep within the system.

"No scanner lock," one of the Starwolf Commanders observed.

"No, we do not receive a clear signal of the target," Dalvaen said. "All we get is a ghost reflection of the shield itself. It is perfectly accurate to location, size and distance, but it still gives us no detail about anything within the shield. It cannot, since the signal never penetrated the shield. It was easy enough to guess how to do this, since the Dreadnought did it to the Kerridayen after failing to find her on normal scan. You can find those pulses in the Kerridayen's records, but there was no reason for the ship's computers to consider it relevant information at the time.''

"Unfortunately, there are three deficiencies with this system. The first is that it gives you no information about the target itself. Because the pulse generates its response by interacting with the shield, it cannot reach through the shield to the ship within. Secondly, you will only want to use the impulse scanner very sparingly. The interaction of the pulse with the shield can be detected. The Dreadnought will sometimes know that it is being scanned, and the side of the shield reacting to scan indicates the general direction of the source of the scan. You can see it, but it will know to begin looking for you. The third problem is that there might not be a better way to do this, since the Dreadnought used the same system itself.''

"You used the word 'sometimes,' " Daerran observed. "Just how often does it become aware of the scan?"

"Our simulation is designed to respond to impulse scan by returning scan," the researcher explained. "The simulated Dreadnought returns scan only twenty-one percent of the time

However, we expect the real thing to be much more sensitive to scan by an unknown factor.''

"Could it see through normal stealth intensity shields, or would it get the same ghost reflection?" Daerran asked.

"The simulation tells us that it receives only the reflection," Dalvaen answered. "Perhaps it does not yet know what a Starwolf carrier looks like."

"It knows already," Daerran reminded him. "We lost our shields before it was over."

Fleet Commander Asandi nodded absently. "Very well, then. You have a working model. How soon can you design working hardware?"

"We anticipate two hard days of work, if we let the computers do most of the general design for us," Dalvaen said, having prepared his answer to that important question already. "The next question is, do we build a working model to scale and test it aboard a smaller ship, or do we go ahead with the fitting of a carrier?"

Asandi considered that only briefly. "We test it on a carrier. If it works, we're ahead that much. If not, we lose very little. How soon can construction and actual fitting of the device be completed?"

"That depends entirely upon the ship," the Kelvessan said, as if he already anticipated some problem with his answer. "This is a major refitting, requiring extensive opening of the hull around the nose and all through the ventral groove. We have to make major modifications to the scanner computers and rebuild the surveillance station on the bridge. We even have to go into the ship's core computer, and you know what that involves. Expect four to five weeks on an existing carrier."

"Existing seems to be the relevant word," Asandi observed.

"We could manage the conversion in half the time on the Methryn. Her hull is still open at every important point, and she was built with a number of modifications that make her computer grid more versatile. We can tie the new systems directly into the network. The parts can be installed as quickly as they can be made, perhaps nine days, and another week to close the hull."

Asandi turned to one of the Starwolf Commanders. "Is the Methryn ready to fly, Commander Gelrayen?"

"We were going to take our time closing up, perhaps another

four weeks," he replied. "By foregoing simulations and an extended trial run, we could do it. But I do not have to point out to you the disadvantages."

"We will discuss it," Asandi said, then turned back to Dalvaen. "Prepare designs for the Methryn, the Kerridayen and one of the flight-ready ships in port. We'll have a decision on which ship to refit first in a couple of hours at most. Could you join myself and the Commanders in my office in a quarter of an hour?"

Captain Tarrel was not completely certain what it all meant, except that a portion of her mind that was always devoted to business was thinking that, if the Union had this impulse scanner, the Starwolves would never again be able to slink about their systems unseen. All she could do was to remember everything that she possibly could of what she heard, for all the good it might do. The Union had trouble with the most basic achronic technology, so they could never reproduce this. She followed dutifully as Asandi and his flock of Starwolves made their migration through the station. Her presence had not, however, gone entirely unnoticed. When they entered the tram on the military level, Asandi joined her.

"You will tell me if you learn anything that you shouldn't," he said. "I have too much to worry about to remember to pay any attention to what you might be hearing. How many secrets have you dug up, by the way?"

Tarrel almost laughed, thinking that Asandi was good at pretending to be a kindly, doddering old fool. "Only one, really. We fool ourselves, back where I come from. The Union is completely out-classed. Your Starwolves could have made short work of us long ago."

"No, not really," he told her. "We have the technology, and you have the numbers. When we have pressed you to it in the past, usually without meaning to, you have been able to put together fleets large enough to pull down a carrier. Do you realize that you people have destroyed two-thirds of the ships we have ever built?"

"Just returning the favor," she quipped, although she was surprised to hear that.

"This is some fine war that we've been fighting," he continued. "We've been at it for thirty thousand years. Either side could end it at any time, and neither side wants to pay the price that would demand of us. I wonder if we might be able to keep the truce, once we get rid of this monster."

"Unless it eats us both alive," she commented.

The mood of the meeting in the Fleet Commander's office was a strained, brooding one. Commander Gelrayen sat somewhat apart from the others, looking remarkably like someone who had found himself in trouble and did not entirely understand why. He was a young Kelvessan, in so far as they all looked young. Perhaps it was fairer to say that he seemed less experienced than the others. While the others wore command white, he was in the solid black of the fighter pilots. She recalled that his carrier was still in the construction bay, and she realized that he had probably never commanded a ship in flight before.

"There is no reason to make an issue of this," Asandi declared as he took his own seat behind his desk. "This is not an emotional matter. We are here to discuss the merits of fitting the Methryn with the first of these pulse scanners. At issue, I suppose, is the question of whether or not a ship that has never even flown should become the spearhead of our attack against the Dreadnought."

"An inexperienced ship, and an inexperienced commander," Gelrayen added. "I might point out the Methryn might still be the best choice. If we have only one ship with an impulse scanner, it might be tactically best to have that ship stand off from a distance and supply information to the others. They could then remain invisible to the Dreadnought."

"Assuming that we move out now to attack the Dreadnought," Daerran said. "First we have to test the impulse scanner to see if it works, and to what degree. Then we have to do something about finding a way to make that machine vulnerable to our weapons. The Methryn would have a lot of work to do."

"Then you take the Methryn out," Gelrayen told him. "You have good, solid battle experience, but you need a ship. Your experience, and that of your crew, makes up for Valthyrra's lack."

"Captain Tarrel, what do you think?" Asandi asked suddenly.

She sat up straight, looking surprised. "Give the impulse scanner and anything else that comes along to the Methryn, and make Commander Gelrayen take her out to fight. He has no experience, meaning that he has no preconceived ideas of how a carrier should fight. You need your most inventive Commander running this ship, and inventiveness is the only thing that will make your new toys work for you."

"That is a very remarkable statement," one of the Starwolf Commanders said. "Could it be that, in your desperation to get help to your people as soon as possible, you have some motivation in having any carrier modified as soon as possible?"

"Are you accusing me of being devious?" Tarrel asked. "It is hardly in the Union's best interest to send out a carrier that is going to accomplish nothing except get itself damaged or destroyed."

"I am not questioning your honesty," the Kelvessan insisted. "I only wish to suggest that desperation might be influencing your judgement without your being aware. We are not trying to be stubborn. As you say, it does no one any good to send out a carrier that cannot accomplish its mission as well as one of the other ships."

Fleet Commander Asandi sat back in his chair. "I see no reason to question Gelrayen's ability to command. He has been a very capable pack leader for nearly a hundred years, with something of a specialty in dealing with unusual and dangerous situations. The Alcaissa Disaster alone—"

"You were responsible for Alcaissa?" Tarrel interrupted in surprise.

"Were you at Alcaissa also?" Gelrayen asked.

"At Alcaissa? It happened a decade before I was even born."

"Kelvessan tend to forget about time," Asandi told her discreetly. "The point is that he can handle the Dreadnought as well as anyone. But the fact remains that he has a carrier that has never flown and a crew that has never before worked together. Can they give him what he needs of them? Commander Gelrayen?"

He considered that carefully. "The crew might be new to each other, but they are by no means inexperienced individually. When I asked the carriers for crew and packs, they sent me their best. I see no reason to doubt them. As for my ship, I can say only this, Valthyrra is no longer young. Methryn has been under construction for sixty years, and her core was engaged almost from the first. She has been able to interact with people and other ships for at least five decades, and she has settled into her personality completely. But I cannot deny that she has no experience in flight, much less battle. She might be slow in anticipating what is required of her."

Asandi was watching the Kelvessan. "If the Methryn receives the pulse scanner, what would be your recommended course of action?"

Gelrayen already seemed to know what he would do. "I would like one day, possibly two for a trial flight. Then I would take the Methryn out to find the Dreadnought, test the impulse scanner from a safe distance and possibly play some slightly dangerous games. That first mission is to collect the information we need to find a weapon to fight that thing."

Asandi turned to Commander Daerran. "Do you think that the Methryn can tease the Dreadnought into revealing more secrets?"

"I cannot say," he admitted. "The Dreadnought might be able to keep the rest of her secrets from us until we do find a way to strip her shield. My suggestion is that we test the pulse scanner, and put Dalvaen and his people to work finding a scanner that will see through that shield."

"We need more information," Dalvaen said. "The information we expect to collect from the reflection of the pulse will give us our first detailed information on the actual composition of that shield. We might be able to infer the total output of power expended in maintaining that shield, whether the ship's hull is immediately below the shield or some distance within, even the number and location of shield projectors. We also expect to learn whether the Dreadnought possesses conventional drives or some other type, perhaps a non-reactive drive like a complex jump drive. Engaging any of those drives will affect the shield. In fact, the flare of conventional main and star drives require venting through the shield."

"That sounds like a tall order," Asandi observed.

"No, not at all," Dalvaen insisted. "We have a series of experiments that we need done, and recommendations on the best and safest way to get the Dreadnought to respond properly. The Methryn can do it."

Asandi turned back to the others. "I want Kelvessan input on this. You live and fight out there; let it be your decision. Consider this a vote, and give me your recommendation. Dalvaen, you seem to have indicated your judgment already."

"I am not a Starwolf," he reminded them. "I cannot say that

I should get a vote. But as I have said, this is something that the Methryn should be able to do easily enough."

"I understand," Asandi assured him. "Commander Daerran?"

He nodded in agreement. "Gelrayen should make a very competent Commander. He can make up for his ship's lack of experience with his own."

"Commander Schyrran?"

"I agree," she answered. "We could have the information for that next step Dalvaen spoke of by the time some other ship would only just be ready to go out."

"Then make your vote unanimous," the final Kelvessan added. "There seem to be more reasons for than against."

"Then I'll put in that order for an impulse scanner for the Methryn right now," Asandi concluded.

Captain Tarrel settled back in her chair, feeling very satisfied that Starwolves really did know how to do the right thing. In the Union, they would have only just gotten down to serious arguments toward a decision that would have been based as much upon personal ambitions, petty jealousies and prejudices as practical considerations. She had to admit to herself that her own judgement was based mostly upon her feeling that Gelrayen would make a very good Commander, but she was willing to place her complete trust in that judgement. If she could manage it in any way, and she suspected that it would not be hard, then she meant to go along.

—4—

Every time the Dreadnought changed its area of attack, every system in Union space seemed to tremble with fear of where it might appear next. In this matter, the independent colonies and the alien worlds were every bit as vulnerable as the Union itself. If anything, those worlds had the most to lose. An attack on one of the free colonies might mean the wreck of their ability to trade off-world, and eventually a loss of their independence. And for some of the smaller or less advanced alien races, just one attack could mean the collapse of their civilization. But if the Starwolves were unable to defeat the Dreadnought, or if it was able to defeat them, then all of known civilization was doomed anyway.

Part of the problem within Union space was the delay of information. News of an attack could spread only as fast as military couriers, and sometimes the commercial ships, could move through the lanes. No one except the Starwolves had effective long-range achronic communication, and their limited numbers of ships could not be everywhere at once. Usually only the sector capitals and a few other major worlds could expect a Starwolf carrier to pass through, and so most of the others were ordinarily aware only that they actually had been in danger several days afterward, and their current status could never be predicted. Some of the smaller or more remote colonies did not yet even know of the danger, as much as an attack on their system was likely to affect them.

Beyond that, the Dreadnought was not being selective. It

would appear seemingly randomly at one system, take out the next system or two possessing a station or any significant traffic, and move on. The relative importance of the system, or the amount of traffic it contained, seemed not to influence the judgement of the Dreadnought in the slightest, just as long as it found something to destroy. That certainly suggested that the alien machine had not mapped Union space to any great degree, or at least it was not following any map of targets of strategic importance. It was designed to be unstoppable, meaning that it acted on the assumption that it could simply fight in its own good time until its enemy was utterly destroyed. And since, at least at this stage, traffic would return to a major system within days of an attack, there was no reason to expect that it would not return, perhaps again and again to some place it had found rich in prey. Even if it was not planning ahead, no one doubted that it was at least keeping some record of where it had been and what it had seen.

The situation was hardly any more comfortable for the Starwolves, who now found themselves assigned the duty of guarding Union space. They were facing an enemy they could not see and could not fight, advantages that they had themselves always enjoyed in the past. The carriers were also under orders not to risk serious damage in a fight they could not win anyway. The best they could do was to find evidence of an attack as soon as possible and rush their warning to the surrounding systems in the hope of getting there before the Dreadnought. None of the carriers had actually encountered the Dreadnought since the battle with the Kerridayen, and so the Starwolves on patrol had not yet faced the question of what they would do with it if they did find it. Or face the question of how ready they were to fight to protect their old enemy.

Theralda Vardon, one of the younger carriers, was handling the situation as best she could. Her standard patrol route had been trimmed of every system unlikely to be attacked, and now she was running every six days a patrol that used to take her weeks. In most systems she would drop out of starflight for no more than an hour, just long enough to present the reassuring sight of herself to local scan and to exchange news, and then she would go on again. Once the Dreadnought appeared somewhere else, she would conclude her present round of patrols at the sector capital and give her engines a chance to cool. Fortunately the carriers had in fact been built for this type of abuse, even on an unlimited basis.

Once this was over, however, every carrier was going to submit herself for refitting as quickly as bays became available, for all that carriers were usually extremely reluctant to agree to the prolonged confinement of the bays. Some would probably have to wait. The refitting bays were very likely to be filled for some time to come with unlucky ships like the Kerridayen, in need of refitting whether they wanted it or not. The carriers that were still sound and capable of flight would have to take the others patrols until those ships were ready to go out again. No one willingly considered the possibility that there would be ships that might never fight again.

The subject of what would happen when the Dreadnought was destroyed was, however, an intriguing one to Theralda Vardon.

She brought the boom of her camera pod around and then forward into the upper bridge. "Commander Schyrran?"

He glanced up from his main monitor, as edgy as any of them about sudden interruptions, then relaxed. "What is it?"

"I was thinking that we are just taking it for granted that the war will resume once the Dreadnought is destroyed," she said. "I have realized that does not necessarily follow. Certainly the Republic will wish to see if the truce can be extended into a permanent peace. Does the Union have any reason to accept peace?"

"That might depend most upon just how badly the Dreadnought wrecks their interplanetary travel," he answered after reflecting upon that question briefly. "If they lose quite a few stations, especially the large ones, and a significant portion of their ships, they could be left hurting very badly. And if they lose their ability to make war altogether, they would have to keep the truce for quite some time. If the peace lasts for several years, they might actually learn that peace is at least as profitable as war, something we have been trying to tell them from the start. I wonder . . ."

"Commander?"

"If they do lose the ability to make war, we could actually take advantage of that," Schyrran explained. "We could keep their military reserves at a very low level by constant, selective raids. We might even be able to force a formal surrender on them."

"I cannot see Starwolves harassing an enemy that cannot fight," the ship observed. "And we might be at a disadvantage ourselves. We cannot guess how many carriers we will have left when this is done. They are presently fitting the Methryn with a special scanner that should be able to target the Dreadnought, but the news out of Alkayja is not otherwise encouraging and we must still actually fight that machine to destroy it."

"That is true enough."

"And we have so far talked as if we are very confident that we will find a way to defeat the Dreadnought," Theralda added. "As things stand now, even with this new scanner, I cannot believe that we will destroy it. We might yet be forced to abandon the Union and escape with what we can of Kelvessan and Terran civilization."

Schyrran seemed doubtful. "Before it comes to that, we would probably send one of the carriers as an envoy to the Aldessan. They will know of some way to destroy this thing."

"They might," Theralda agreed uncertainly. The Aldessan of Valtrys had done the actual genetic engineering to create the Kelvessan, who still spoke the Aldessan language and used their names. And the carriers were themselves Aldessan technology, not Terran. The Kelvessan looked upon the Valtrytians as their all-wise, all-knowing parent race; almost as gods. "Commander, we will be dropping out of starflight in two minutes."

"What, so soon?" he asked, meaning that in jest. The Vardon was making her patrol at such tremendous speed that most of her jumps were only a few hours in length. "How soon will you have scanner contact?"

"Coming up now, Commander," the ship replied. She was moving so fast that the effective range of her scanners in terms of distance corresponded to a much smaller amount of time than it usually did. Her achronic scanners had only just reached into the system when she suddenly whipped her camera boom around out of the upper bridge.

"All crewmembers stand by," she announced to the entire ship. "This is a class two battle alert. All on-duty personnel to their posts. All pilots and damage-control parties stand by. All nonactive personnel will remove to the inner sections."

"Trouble?" Commander Schyrran asked, while the bridge crew waited to hear the worst. The fact that Theralda had issued a class two alert meant that the ship was not immediately threatened.

"Trouble has been here," she explained. "There is no station in this system, just orbiting debris. Emission patterns indicate many destroyed ships concentrated in one area only a short distance out from the inhabited planet, so the system fleet must have put up a fight to buy time. I cannot yet say whether or not the Dreadnought has had time to move on. That will depend mostly upon the length of time since this attack, and it has not been very long."

"Recommendations?" Schyrran asked. Since this affair had begun, he had been depending far more upon her centuries of experience. Of course, their command of the ship was a joint one.

"I say that we should go straight in," she said without hesitation. "I must know how long it has been since the attack, and if the Dreadnought is still here. That will tell me whether or not I might be able to beat that beast to its next destination."

"Do you know where it is likely to go next?"

"I have reason to be very certain," Theralda said. "A likely target system is only eleven light years from here. The next closest targets are at least three times as far. I am sending my first achronic message out to the other carriers now."

A long moment passed as they waited for the Vardon to enter the system. Theralda brought her camera pod around sharply. "Commander, we have the first variation in the Dreadnought's pattern of attack. Locations on the surface have been hit as well."

"The poor devils would have never expected that," Schyrran commented. "What did it hit? Was there anything on that planet that would have attracted special attention?"

"Nothing that it has not seen before," the ship answered. "Comparing the locations of attacks with my maps of this planet—which is sometimes all I have left for identification—there is a pattern of high-energy installations that have been destroyed. Three planet-side military bases are gone, and almost two hundred manufacturing, mining and power-production facilities have been hit as well."

Commander Schyrran glance up at the viewscreen as the Vardon dropped out of starflight and began braking sharply. They had come in relatively close, although the planet was still too far away to be seen. "Then the Dreadnought has changed its tactics to wreck the planet as well as system traffic?"

"No, I would not say that it has wrecked this planet," Theralda insisted. "Two hundred or so major targets might seem like quite a lot, especially for a lightly populated colony. But out of the whole, that amount of damage is more like a threat or warning. What it all suggests to me, unfortunately, is that the Dreadnought is capable of a great deal more planned thought and subtlety than we first anticipated. Even so, I am not yet convinced that it is fully sentient."

"Sentience is not an indication of a machine's ability to plan its own strategies, even fairly complex ones," Schyrran pointed out. "A machine that is not self-aware can still be very dangerous."

"That is true enough," the ship agreed. "Even so, I still believe that self-awareness and even some emotional responses are necessary for a machine to be truly devious. That might be our advantage."

"If so, that machine must be programmed for deviousness," he said. "I do not know what else to say about a ship that develops one impression of its abilities and tactics and then abruptly changes. That is devious."

The Vardon had cut her speed considerably and was now making her final approach to the planet. At this range, she was finally able to make a detailed scan of the planet itself and the general area of attack. Now that she was able to get better information on some of the more subtle details, she began to realize that matters here were rather more complex than she had first anticipated. That also taught her a lesson on being more cautious, and she began to devote more of her attention to space about her, especially behind. That was no reassurance. If the Dreadnought was still lurking, she would not know until she was attacked.

Wondering what she could do to guard herself better, she recalled what she had seen in the reports on the attacks on the Carthaginian and the Kerridayen. She checked her files for the recognition code that the Kerridayen had used to hail the Dreadnought, modified that slightly and broadcast it in the achronic bands. When she received no response, she felt somewhat better about the situation. But not entirely.

"Commander, I have recognized a second change in the attack

patterns of the Dreadnought," she said. "Emissions and dispersal patterns indicate two separate attacks, over a full day apart. The main attack, the destruction of the station and most of the ships, occurred first. A second, smaller group of ships was destroyed some time later. I cannot say when the attacks on the surface took place, since dispersion patterns in atmospheric conditions are too irregular to predict. Because very few fires are still burning in the debris, I would predict that most if not all of the surface strikes took place during the initial attack."

"What would you make of that?" Schyrran asked.

She brought her camera pod back around. "Subtlety. I would say that the Dreadnought withdrew after the first attack, hid itself, and waited for more ships to come blundering into the system. It might still be lurking about, for that matter. The last attack was only a few hours ago. Because those emissions are fresh, I mistook them at first as the time frame for one single attack."

He looked up at her camera pod. "What is it thinking? If you were the Dreadnought, what would be your priorities?"

Theralda considered that briefly. "I have seen and fought a Starwolf carrier. I would consider the Starwolves to be the only real threat facing me in the performance of my mission, as far as they have been a threat. I might or might not be aware of how many carriers there actually are, but one of my greatest priorities would be the destruction of those ships. And I have only just realized where we might have been making a very serious mistake."

"What is that?"

"We have been treating the achronic channels as being entirely our own property, simply because it has been so for so long," she explained. "And we have been exchanging large amounts of information by achronic means, quite literally everything we know and plan to do. If the Dreadnought has been receiving and translating those messages, then it knows more about us than we would like. It will know our exact number, our general locations at any time, and all of our various facts and speculations about it, our enemy. It will even know that the Methryn is being fitted with a new scanner. And when she comes out to find it, then it will know that as well."

Schyrran crossed both sets of his arms on his chest, looking displeased about the situation. "Continue your reports as usual, but compose a message about your suspicions and send it on a very tight beam to Alkayja station. If that thing is listening to us, then we might be able to mislead it with false information."

During that time, the Vardon had braked to an orbital speed some distance out from the planet. She began broadcasting in the common Union commercial and military bands in the hope that someone on the planet could supply her with a more accurate timetable on the attacks. She was soon given to wonder if the Dreadnought's double attack had spooked the locals into being too terrified of their communicators to respond, for fear that the transmissions might draw the monster back. She might have spooked them herself; she had already met some resistance to accepting the idea that Starwolves were no longer enemies but allies. But she had not recorded a single scanner beam on her way into the system. As long as she used the Terran language and did not identify herself, they had no way of knowing who she was.

"Military shuttle AK-2110 D reporting," a reply came at last.

"Report your position, shuttle," she ordered sharply, encouraging them to believe that she was herself a Union military ship.

"We were evacuating from the station, and we were coming down to Forestan Base. When we saw that the base was under attack, then we decided to settle down into the mountains and wait."

"Then there was time to evacuate the station?" she asked.

"Hardly. I know of only two more shuttles that got away. There were pods all over the place. But there was a large munitions store at the station, and that went early on. I think the explosion took out most of the pods before they could get clear."

"But there was a second attack?" Theralda asked. She was certain of that, but she wondered if they knew.

"Yes, a small military convoy came in about five hours ago. They called down, just like you did, and the Dreadnought attacked while we were talking to them. Are your sure it's gone now?"

"It seems to be, and I have even hailed it," she responded. "You say that the last attack was about five hours ago?"

"Yes."

"Then listen to me. You can begin spreading the word that the Dreadnought seems to be gone, and it is unlikely to attack the planet itself again anyway. Try to get things up and running again as soon as possible. I would like to stay and help you, but I must try to race the Dreadnought to the next system likely to come under attack and order an evacuation.''

"You can't out-run that thing."

"I am the Starwolf Carrier Vardon," she said.

"Oh." That was followed by a very long pause that Theralda found vaguely amusing. "Then they will probably accept your word that everything is safe enough now.''

"If you cannot trust a Starwolf, who can you trust?'' she asked, knowing that it was unkind of her to tease humans in distress. "I am leaving orbit presently. Your own fleet should be here within a couple of days.''

Theralda shifted her attention back to her own bridge. Commander Schyrran had stepped down from his station and was comparing notes with the navigator and the first officer at the navigational station. They all looked up at her camera pod as the Vardon engaged her main drives and began to move swiftly out of orbit. She brought her pod closer.

"It has been about five hours since the last attack," she announced. "My own suspicion is that the Dreadnought left this system to proceed to its next target immediately after that. It had been waiting for Starwolves, and they did not come.''

"You said that you know where it is going,'' Schyrran reminded her.

"I believe that I do,'' she said. "And if it continues on for a third attack in this group, then it will hit Norden within a week at most.''

That was very bad news. While Norden was not a Sector Capital, it was still one of the most important and populous worlds in this Sector, a crossroad of trade as well as a center of high-tech industry. If the Dreadnought did hit there, this Sector would lose two major commercial spaceports, and orbital manufacturing complexes in addition to a large military station. And if the attack was not anticipated, the losses would likely include not only the system fleet but a very large portion of the Sector Fleet as well, as many as twelve hundred heavier ships, and perhaps another two thousand commercial vessels caught at the stations. A major shipyard would be gone as well, and that loss would effect this Sector's ability to recover quickly from its damages.

"Will you call ahead for support?'' Schyrran asked.

"I will, but I doubt that any other carrier will get there sooner than myself," she said. "Perhaps the damage might be less if I did not, but I still must proceed to the second system in this sequence and warn them that the Dreadnought is probably on its way. There is nothing I can help them to do otherwise."

He nodded his agreement. "But what about Norden? Are you thinking about trying to fight?"

"No, I cannot fight the Dreadnought," she admitted reluctantly. "Just the same, it very much goes against my nature to run away and allow that machine to have its way in a major system. That used to be my job."

Several hours later, and with her star drives coming dangerously close to overheating, the Vardon arrived at her next destination. She was unable to know the speed of the Dreadnought, but with every previous indication being that it moved fairly slowly, she should have expected to arrive well in advance of the mysterious ship. But since she now had some reason to believe that the Dreadnought spent some time after its initial attack loitering about, waiting for more prey to appear, that implied that the Dreadnought might be capable of moving very quickly between systems. Knowing the time of its last attack, she wanted very much to learn when it had actually arrived in the next system.

She would not, however, be able to wait around to find out. This next system was a relatively unimportant one, the local station and traffic load smaller even than what it had been in the system she had just left. She felt obliged to deliver her warning and press on to Norden, where the danger was far greater, and every hour that she saved in getting there would allow the locals to salvage that much more. They should at least be able to get their ships to safety. Given enough time, they might even be able to dismember and tow away the stations, which lacked the ability to move under their own power and were too sprawling to tow intact. The problem, of course, was that in a system of that size, traffic that could not be warned away in advance was going to be coming in constantly, and the Dreadnought was going to snap those up even if it could not find anything else. And whether or not it would again attack surface installations, and how much damage it might do, might depend upon getting the major power sources shut down in time.

And of course, it might also depend on whether the locals

were willing to listen to the advice of Starwolves. Commander Schyrran persisted in pointing out that pessimistic view, and Theralda could not deny that he might be correct. As far as either the Starwolves or their ships could determine, humans were largely motivated by greed, and could take some enormously ill-founded risks by weighing profit against danger as if the comparison was valid. The promise of profit did not reduce a risk, but humans could not always be convinced of that. If the local officials were unwilling to close to commercial traffic, much less haul away their stations, because of the threat of lost revenue, then they would find endless, and to them very valid reasons to question Theralda's judgement that the Dreadnought was coming their way.

Frankly, the Starwolves themselves could not care less. They would fight to the death to protect the innocent, but they were not in the business of protecting people from their own stupidity. They were, of course, such clever people by genetic design that they did not really understand stupidity. The Kelvessan were generally great magnets for information, with a thought process that was largely comparative. They had their own form of stupidity, usually reserved for when they missed some important detail, and then their mistakes tended to be both monumental and memorable.

Theralda Vardon went into that first system aware that she could find trouble but not really expecting it, and trouble was exactly what she found. She could not see the Dreadnought directly, but the fact that the planet itself was under attack and the station was already gone argued that it was there. She cut the very low-intensity scans that she had been using and was grateful for having been warned to maintain her shields at stealth intensity. There was nothing she could do here, so she kept her engines idle and settled into a long, gentle loop that would take her back out of the system fairly quickly, setting her course for her next destination. She did not dare to engage her star drives until she was well out of the area.

"Trouble again," she warned the bridge crew. "Our belligerent friend is already here."

Commander Schyrran looked up from his monitors. "Running the ship in a permanent class two battle alert certainly is convenient. It saves having to wait for the crew to prepare itself. I suppose that there is nothing we can do here. At least now that we know we are ahead of the Dreadnought, I suppose that we should just keep going."

"Yes, that was my thought," the ship agreed. "I am already bringing us around on the best course for Norden. And I do not even want to know what the Dreadnought is doing to that poor planet. This can all be very hard on a ship like myself, you know. I am used to being able to stomp anything I wish."

Theralda had no reason to expect that anything should be that easy, and she was right. The Dreadnought betrayed itself directly by suddenly sweeping all space around it with a powerful scan. Theralda had already wondered if its reason for loitering in that first system was to catch any Starwolves that might come along on a regular patrol, and it knew also from its fight with the Kerridayen that the carriers could cloak themselves with stealth-intensity shields. When that impulse sweep came around and registered on her passive scanners, she knew that it was looking for her. And if the Dreadnought was looking for Starwolves, there was certainly no difficulty in guessing why it wanted them.

The Vardon responded in about the only way she could, engaging her main drives to take her speed back up to a point where she could make a smooth, quiet transition into starflight. Her actual distance from the Dreadnought was over two light hours, since she had not penetrated very deeply into the system and was now looping around to head back out. Theralda assumed, or at least hoped, that she was out of the Dreadnought's effective range. Achronic-based weaponry could be fired across light-years without serious loss of power or definition; the problem was finding the target precisely after the first few hundred thousand kilometers. Given enough distance, a variation of even a millionth of a degree became a significant miss.

"Impulse scan contact," Theralda warned, although the members of the bridge crew had already noted her acceleration. "A second contact followed the first by several seconds, so I have to assume that I have been seen. The attack on the planet ceased at that same moment."

"Is it following us?" Commander Schyrran asked as he returned to the Commander's station on the upper bridge.

"I have no way of knowing," she admitted. "If it is, the best evidence will come when it begins shooting at us."

"You have us accelerating back to starflight?" Schyrran assumed. "Take us through quickly, but try to be discreet about our course. Head somewhat away and then change course five minutes into starflight.''

"Moving into starflight now."

The Vardon made a very smooth transition back into starflight. A carrier could make an extremely abrupt transition, due partly to its superior drives and acceleration dampers, but mostly because the Starwolves themselves were able to handle harsh accelerations that would have killed anyone else. But a forced transition, engaging the star drives while the ship was still well below light speed, caused a very turbulent dispersion of emissions from the drives that was easy enough to follow. The Vardon did not want to draw a line leading straight to her destination, especially if the Dreadnought would not have been going on to Norden otherwise.

Theralda brought her camera pod into the upper bridge. "I will not say that I like that. The Dreadnought was ahead of us with no more than a five hour lead, possibly less. That means that it is at least as fast as my own best speed, and I was running my drives to within two percent of risking permanent heat damage to the crystals. How can anything that size be able to move so fast? I wonder what manner of drive it uses?"

"Are we away clear?" Schyrran asked.

"I certainly hope so, but it seems a little early to promise anything." She lowered her camera pod slightly, a gesture of resignation or defeat. "I no longer know what to make of that machine or just what it might be capable of doing. We had assumed that it was slow because of the interval between attacks, but we now have every reason to believe that it loiters in-system after an attack to see what shows up, and that it actually travels at speeds a carrier would find hard to match. And that is probably only its cruising speed. I hesitate to think what it might be capable of doing in a pinch."

Schyrran nodded. "Do you know of any reason why we cannot relay that information on a tight beam back to Alkayja station immediately?"

"A tight beam should be safe enough."

"Then Norden is the next step. Get us there as fast as you can, and we should have two or three days from this point to get things ready before the Dreadnought shows itself."

"I will need sixteen hours at least to reach Norden," Theralda warned him. "My drives are hot. I knew that they would be, but

I was anticipating a few hours at least in this last system to let them cool. I will have to reduce power by at least thirty percent to keep drive temperatures from going up any more.''

He nodded. ''Do the best you can, but do not damage yourself. If you have a drive go down now, you could be out for months. It might seem like a harsh judgement, but a single carrier in good fighting condition is worth more right now than even a major system.''

Theralda did everything she could to keep her drives running at the best possible speed, keeping the phase rate for each of her two star drives calibrated for the greatest efficiency. She even tried shifting the frequency of her emissions in the attempt to convert some of that heat into a tremendous flare of visible light. In the end, she was finally forced to reduce her speed and keep it down, the one thing that she had not wanted to do. All such judgments were relative to the situation. Ordinarily, she would have considered her present speed to be fairly high, within her upper recommended limits. Now she felt that she was moving at barely a crawl.

More than anything, Theralda was feeling very helpless, and that was an unfamiliar experience for her. She was three kilometers of fighting machine and perfectly able to care for herself even without crew. Her speed was second only to that of her own fighters, and she had the power to destroy worlds. Now a thing that she could not even see was so much bigger, faster and stronger than herself that she could not hope to fight it. She hated to admit even to herself that she was doing nothing more now than making a constructive retreat, desperately struggling to stay ahead of a machine that would probably destroy her if it found her. The Union had come to the Starwolves, even proposed a truce that they would have never accepted otherwise, and the only thing she could do to protect them was to warn them to get out of the way of the engine of destruction following her. It was a lesson in humility. And frustration.

She entered the Norden system cautiously, not knowing what to expect, and so she ran with her shields at stealth intensity and her drives idle to reduce betraying emissions. Having made the run at much lower speed than she would have preferred, she almost expected to find that the Dreadnought had jumped ahead of her and was already attacking the system, or perhaps hiding silent and unseen to ambush her. Her first tentative scanner reports showed that the system was a scene of frantic activity, with hundreds of ships in flight at once, all seeming to be headed in different directions. But she could see no evidence of an attack. She opened a channel to the station. The response she received was unexpected.

"Attention Starwolf carrier." The message was over one of the achronic bands normally reserved by the ships for communication between themselves. "Attention Starwolf carrier. This is the carrier Maeridan."

"Khallenda?" Theralda asked in response, obviously mystified. "How did you know I was here?"

"Your drives are hot," the other ship explained. "You might just as well forget stealth for now, since you are leaving the widest trail of secondary emissions I have ever seen. Do you never look behind you?"

"More and more, these days," Theralda said. "So, when did you come into system?"

"Just a few hours ago. I caught the edge of your message and came running as fast as I could. The Karvand might be along in the next few hours. Are we going to have that much time?"

"I wish that I knew," Theralda replied, then hesitated. "Could you excuse me for a moment. The System Commander is answering my call. Better yet, you should join us. Then I will only have to explain all of this once."

"Would you find me a bother?"

"Oh no, not at all. I would consider it a pleasure." She shifted her achronic channel to the Union's short-range beams, remembering to speak the Terran language. "Commander? This is Theralda Vardon."

"Yes, this is System Commander Carrel," a man with a deep voice responded. "Do you have additional information on this Dreadnought? Is it really on the way here?"

"Yes, I left the Dreadnought eating a small system only sixteen hours ago. It might not be here for days yet. It might be right behind me. Or it might already be here, for all I know," Theralda explained. "Things have turned out rather differently than we first expected. The Dreadnought is a much more sophisticated machine than we first anticipated, and it has now changed its tactics by attacking not only stations and traffic but major installations on the planet itself. I have also found evidence that it lingers hidden in system for some time after the first attack to ambush ships that might be coming to investigate. My belief is that it is now trying to destroy all the Starwolf carriers it can find."

"What can we do?" Carrel asked, seemingly too surprised or appalled by what he had just heard to make sense of it.

"You can hardly evacuate the planet, but there is really no need. The Dreadnought has so far only attacked a relatively few planet-side targets. If you close down all major power sources and evacuate the large factories and all military bases, you should be all right. But it does seem to have a priority about military targets."

"I understand. I will have all planet-side factories and military bases cleared immediately, although I want to continue a cautions evacuation of some important materials."

"What have you been doing about the stations?" Theralda asked.

"The stations are being broken up into large components," Khallenda Maeridan reported. "Battleships are being locked into the hulls of the components of the military station and linked by computer to carry those segments away. I am carrying away the segments of the commercial station by locking them down to my upper and lower hulls."

"Is that a fact?" Theralda asked. "How is that working out?"

"Fairly well, actually. I have just returned from my fourth run. If you help me, we could have this entire system carted away in only three more runs each."

"Where are you hauling away your spoils?"

"There is a system with no inhabitable planet only two light years over where we have been unloading the components. I was able to transport a full load in little more than an hour, most of that acceleration and deceleration time. With any luck, the Dreadnought will never think to look for it there."

"That monster is damned clever." Theralda mused upon that for a moment. "We can put the station components there, but all the evacuated ships have to go somewhere else. If we leave a major emission trail all going to the same place, which is exactly what you will get from large numbers of Union drives, the Dreadnought is probably clever enough to wonder where everyone was going and if they could be caught."

"Then you will help us move our stations?" Carrel asked eagerly.

"Unfortunately, being your beast of burden is probably the most help that I have to offer," Theralda said, amused to think that they were chatting up like old friends, devoted allies that had recently been bitter enemies. She found it curiously easy to be sympathetic toward the Union; a very long lifetime of familiarity had led her to pity them.

She had kept the communication open, for the bridge crew to hear. Commander Schyrran was seated at his station on the upper bridge, looking very pensive. He glanced up at her as she brought her camera pod into the upper bridge. "What about your star drives? You will probably be moving your own weight again in station components. Can you manage that?"

"Yes, that should be no problem," she insisted. "For a two light-year jump, I hardly have the need to push that load to any real speed as long as I can get it moving. My drives are not damaged, and I have all the time they will take to strap down those components for them to cool. Moving that load the final fifteen percent or so up to transition will be the hardest part."

The Vardon settled herself into orbit quickly, then opened her transport bays and sent her own capture ships to manage the actual placement of the station components against her hull. Following the Maeridan's orders, the station personnel had divided the stations into sections of fairly precise length so that three long rectangular sections could be carried both above and below the long axis of the hull, while wider sections were fitted above and below the carrier's wings. The capture ships were narrow-waisted transports. With three pairs of long handling arms mounted to that long middle section, and powerful engines to move heavy loads; these agile little ships and their experienced pilots were perfectly suited to this task.

Under the expert guidance of their own capture crews, both the Vardon and the Maeridan were loaded for flight within an hour and a half. The crews of the capture ships were used to having to shift salvage quickly after a major battle, settling abandoned and disabled Union ships in the massive holding bays of the carriers. The station components were larger, but there were only ten of them to be settled against the flat outer hulls of the carriers. Large inflated shock cushions, that had already been fitted to the components, kept them from direct contact with the hull itself, and heavy straps of braided metal bands were used to tie them tightly to the ship. Having equal numbers and sizes of components above and below kept the carrier in reasonable balance while she struggled to carry her own weight in cargo.

The two Starwolf carriers moved out in nearly opposite directions, laying trails from their taxed engines toward false destinations with the intention of joining up later. The Vardon's star drives had cooled considerably in the time needed to load her for the flight, and now it was her main drives, hidden under her wings, that had to do the hard work of getting some thirty million tons of carrier and payload up to transition. She was easing her way as much as possible with her damping field, which converted the energy of acceleration that would have otherwise arrested her speed into additional acceleration. No ship would have flown much past half of light speed without energy dampers. They were as essential as the drives themselves. But dampers could only do so much. Even if she could remove all the energy of acceleration, Theralda still had to set that bulk into motion.

Carriers were built for abuse, and this did not stress their limits except in trying to meet the demands of time. Even the amount of dead weight they carried was not a danger to their frames. Integrity fields, like the shields that protected the ship from the outside, where projected through the frame itself, giving the carrier the strength to survive tremendous forces of compression and torsion. Theralda took twenty-two minutes to get herself up to transition, twice as long as what she would have normally considered a gentle run. Once in starflight, she was surprised to find that she did not feel the extra mass at all.

The Vardon arrived in the uninhabited system less than half an hour later, finding the Maeridan there only a minute ahead of her. The segments of the station that had already been brought through had been left in orbit over a rather dark, cold planet fourth out in the system, and the two carriers left the components they carried to be tied together with this first group. The unloading of the components took considerably less time than the more careful process of strapping them down to the hulls of the large ships, and the two carriers were on their way back to Norden in only about twenty minutes.

The complete transport of the commercial stations could be accomplished in two more runs only by having both of the carriers strap one segment more than they had hauled previously, braced by the components strapped onto the upper and lower hulls, actually across the nose of the ship. Neither of the two carriers were fond of that arrangement, since it completely blocked their forward batteries and left them essentially defenseless. The fact that they were already defenseless against attack from the Dreadnought was their only consolation, if it could be called that. It seemed better than making another trip, considering the time involved and the emission trails that they would be leaving.

While they were being fitted with their final load, they were able to witness the departure of the military station. Being a more solid and less sprawling structure, it could be transported intact by having battleships attach themselves to key points on the station's frame. These ships were then linked by computer, until they became in essence only the engines for a far larger ship made up by the station itself. The result worked, but it was not very fast, needing eight hours or more to get itself to transition speed. It would not be going into safe-keeping in the same system as the commercial stations, since spreading things about decreased the likelihood of any of them being found.

Because she had been delayed several minutes in getting away, the Vardon had to attend to the duty of making their farewells to the System Commander. "We will not be coming back, I am afraid. There is nothing we can do to help you now. We can do the entire Union more good by keeping ourselves intact and ready to fight when the time comes that we can do something about this Dreadnought."

"Yes, we understand that," Carrel agreed. "You have already saved our stations. No matter what the Dreadnought does to the planet, we can rebuild much quicker if we have access to those stations. But I think that we will not bring them back here until the Dreadnought has been destroyed."

"Perhaps that will be very soon now."

Theralda made her final run, feeling oddly alone and vulnerable now that the Maeridan was nearly ten minutes ahead of her. That was also a very new experience for her, and she thought that life would be much better when there were no more great, mysterious Dreadnoughts around to frighten honest, hard-working carriers. She eased herself down from transition speeds, grateful to be free of this duty. Her capture ships had been unable to return to their bays and had flown alongside her, and they now flew on ahead to assist in the unloading of the Maeridan.

"Is that how I looked?" Khallenda asked as the Vardon came nearer. "How are the humans taking it?"

"Stoically," Theralda said. "They just seem to be grateful to have had some warning. And they are very understanding about the fact that we are unable to stay around to try to protect them. I would have never thought that Unioners still possessed any nobler qualities. That makes it harder for me simply to run away and leave them."

"They were somewhat less understanding when I first arrived," the other ship remarked. "And I cannot forget all the times that I have seen them do to others what the Dreadnought is doing to them. A little shaking up might just do them some good."

"Perhaps . . . ," Theralda paused. "I just recorded a scanner contact."

"Are you sure?"

"I have been through this before. Blow yourself out of there." She turned her attention back to herself, putting her crew on alert at the same time that she brought herself around, away from the direction of that scan. "Commander, we might be doomed. I cannot dump this load. There is simply no way for me to cast lose the straps that are holding down those station components."

"What about the capture ships?" Schyrran asked.

"My capture ships are already on their way back, and the Maeridan is sending me her own since she is already unloaded. It all depends upon how much time we have."

Schyrran sat back in his head, both sets of his arms crossed. "That thing is a damned nuisance. How did it find us?"

"I suppose that it came into the Norden system, saw what we were doing, and followed me here during our last run. We did not have stealth engaged, so it probably executed an impulse scanner sweep just to be certain that we were alone here."

The attack came only a moment later. But the Dreadnought seem focused only on the orbiting station segments, blissfully ignoring the Maeridan as she made a very hasty escape out of orbit, letting the one moving target get away while it concentrated on targets that would be going nowhere. There were still times when the Dreadnought behaved like a very stupid machine, and times when it was only too clever. For the moment, it was content to chew away at the tight group of station components drifting in orbit.

Theralda was straining her main drives to work her way back up to light speed and the safety of transition into starflight. She had already dumped nearly half of her speed, and she would need at least six minutes altogether to work her way back up. Barely a couple of minutes had passed before the attack on the station components had ended, and she knew only too well that she was the next tempting target. She was still bearing her full load of components, and that meant that she could not even use her own main weapons. The capture ships had not yet overtaken her, and the Maeridan was far away. She was beginning to wonder what would happen to her if she engaged her star drives early. Ordinarily that would have been no problem to either ship or crew, but those segments might break loose and take large pieces of her hull with them.

Of all the ways she might have met her end, this was too embarrassing.

The first shot came in, and the Vardon's hull shook with the explosion. Theralda was already mobilizing her automated damage control when she realized that she had not herself been hit. The discharge beam had connected with the large segment over her left wing, and her evasive change of heading had shaken off the beam before it had eaten deeply into the mass of metal and plastics she carried. Theralda Vardon had become a turtle, slowed by the very burden that protected her. And that was just as well, since she was only able to engage her hull shields.

A second beam connected with the segment above her main hull, and she was able to shake it off before it cut through to her hull. It was not a perfect arrangement by any means, since some of the power from the discharge beam was getting through to her shields and leaking into her hull, giving hell to her major power systems and networks.

Theralda ordered the capture ships to move clear and make their own run into starflight. There was nothing they could do for her now that she was under attack. She would have to take this load along with her.

"Theralda, how are you doing?" Khallenda asked anxiously.

"Surprisingly well," she responded. "The components are protecting me from the worst of the attack. Keep yourself clear."

"I could come in close and shoot the straps."

"No, get yourself out of here. I can ride this through until I can make it into starflight."

At least she hoped so. The backs of her drives were unprotected by anything except their own retractable armored plates. Even a light discharge there would leave her unable to engage her drives, and the Dreadnought would have her. Fearful of this, she brought herself around in as tight a turn as she dared and began to rotate slowly, turning first her upper and then her lower hull toward her enemy. The components were being battered to pieces by discharge beams, large areas breaking up or burning fiercely, and too much stray power was getting into her own systems. But it was keeping those beams away from her vulnerable drives. She thought that she might still make it, although she would be in no condition to fight without some repairs.

"Khallenda, you collect our capture ships as soon as you can and meet me at Boulder," she said. "I am going to need help."

"What are you going to do?"

"Something drastic."

She engaged her star drives as gently as she could, kicking herself into premature transition at the cost of nearly sixty G's of acceleration past what her dampers were able to contain. The straps held and she carried the station components with her into starflight, the damaged sections shedding a cloud of debris.

—5—

Captain Tarrel decided that she wanted to go out on the first flight of the Methryn, and she was prepared to do all the begging and convincing she needed to be certain that she did. As it happened, the Starwolves had every intention of sending her. They had agreed to a truce with the Union which specified that they would do everything they could to destroy the Dreadnought, and they were apparently very sensitive to the accusation that they were not doing enough. And that accusation had indeed been made by certain elements within the Union, particularly those who had the most to lose, and who wanted the Starwolves to take a brute force approach with the Dreadnought by confronting it immediately. Some believed in the old myth, or perhaps more a fear in the Union, that the Starwolves were invincible. Others did not care what that battle cost the Starwolves, or else preferred to see both enemies of the Union fight to mutual destruction.

Janus Tarrel had known, even when Sector Commander Lake had first proposed a truce with the Starwolves, that it would come to this. Union attitudes both to others and to one's self were two-fold. The individual, such as herself, was supposed to be devoted, noble and willing to make any sacrifice toward the greater good; but greedy, cruel and suspicious when representing the interests of the Union to outsiders. Tarrel was wise enough to have figured out long ago that those attitudes were largely designed only to protect the status quo, and that she was not, herself, a part of that status quo and never would be. She was a willing servant, even protector of that system, for the simple reason that she was cynical enough to believe that it probably was the best of all realistically possible systems for human society. She did subscribe without reservation to the popular Union belief that all human society was best served by sticking together. She looked upon the independent colonies, and all would-be independents, as traitors. And, as the captain of a Union battle ship, she was willing to treat them as traitors.

At this particular time, she could not yet decide how those philosophies affected her own relationship with the Starwolves. They had agreed to do a very dirty job that was not necessarily their problem, and it was probably going to cost them dearly before it was done. She believed that they deserved some consideration for that. She also believed in the practical wisdom of allowing the Starwolves to wait until they were ready to fight with some assurance of winning. The Starwolves were the lesser of evils by far; they were only an annoyance, while the Dreadnought would apparently be satisfied with nothing less than the destruction of Terran civilization. It was better to keep the Starwolves than risk losing them by forcing them to attack too soon.

Responding to her own instincts, Tarrel decided that there were separate levels to her loyalty. As long as the Starwolves were fighting the Dreadnought, she would do anything to help them. But if she learned any secrets that would help her to fight them, even to destroy them, when this was over, that was quite another matter. She suspected, however, that her greater loyalty to the Starwolves would never be an issue. They guarded their true secrets very well, for they actually had very few weaknesses that she could ever hope to exploit. Their strengths were in things that she could never have and could not take away from them.

Her interests in being aboard the Methryn were therefore honest ones. The Methryn would be going out to hunt the Dreadnought in Union space, and she believed that the Starwolves would benefit by having her along. She could invoke the higest level of diplomatic passes, for the Combined Council itself had granted her extreme emergency powers in giving her the authority to override any Fleet or System Commander in any Sector. She could get the Starwolves any support and cooperation they needed. She had also been instructed to give them any Union secrets she felt would benefit the Starwolves in their attempt to destroy the Dreadnought. Of course, she was also given to wonder if the Union actually kept as many secrets from the Starwolves as it preferred to believe.

She certainly did not expect to be taken aboard the Methryn until the carrier was ready to go out, and so she was surprised when Commander Gelrayen himself came to collect her a week before their scheduled launch. She had seen little of this young Starwolf since the meeting in which it had been decided to fit his new ship with the scanner, and she had been curious about him ever since. Because Starwolf Commanders were chosen from among the pack leaders, he had very little previous command experience on the bridge of a full ship. In their last meeting, Tarrel had noticed that he did not yet seem entirely comfortable in his new role, but she had quietly predicted that he would learn quickly. She was curious to find out if she was right.

"Are you sure that I won't be in your way?" she asked. He seemed to have more trouble than usual with her use of contractions, something that seemed to be lacking from Kelvessan syntax logic. No Kelvessan would normally use a contraction, but they usually seemed to understand the use. He seemed to lack that much familiarity with the Terran language.

"No, not at all," Gelrayen insisted. "In fact, I would rather have you become a familiar element on the ship before we go out. With our collective inexperience, I want to eliminate as many uncomfortable elements as possible now. Would you like a quick tour of the ship? You can come back for your things later."

Captain Tarrel was not about to turn down that invitation, knowing that he might be too busy to make that offer except in his own good time. They descended to the observation deck level for the carrier bays, where Gelrayen was able to show her the work being done on the Methryn. A surprising amount of the hull about her tapered nose was still open, considering the fact that she was due to leave her bay in only a week. Tarrel could make little enough sense of the equipment she saw exposed within the hull, although she was impressed with the scale of that machinery. Components that she would have probably been able to hold comfortably in her hands from the ships she knew were larger than herself within the carrier.

"Those are the impulse transmitters, there in the shock bumper, one to either side of the main lights, and the primary cannon dead center," Gelrayen pointed out. "We call them cannons for good reason. At extreme range, that achronic pulse would probably knock a small ship right out of space. There are also side-directed cannons in the ventral grooves of the wing tips, that groove which runs the entire length of the ship where the upper and lower hulls meet."

"Why does a carrier have a ventral groove?" Tarrel asked.

"Mostly because of the size of the ship. The upper and lower hull are actually large pieces of armor built over the actual ship, and a ventral groove gives them room to flex. Also, the heating and cooling exchanges, the scanner receivers and the smaller remote cannons are protected from attack by being set back within the groove."

"And what about the shock bumper?" she asked. "It seems designed to be a separate component from the ship."

"Oh, that serves several purposes. The shock bumper is somewhat isolated from the rest of the ship, which cuts down on nuisance vibrations when aiming the cannons. The navigational shields are in the bumper, and that acts to reduce the shock of sudden large impacts against that shield. The entire assembly with the complete forward battery can be replaced as a single unit in a very short time. And it also gives the ship a bumper to push with. That comes in more useful than you might imagine."

"You are not worried about your secrets?" Tarrel asked. "This scanner is new technology for you."

"And absolutely worthless as a technical advantage in our affairs with the Union," he pointed out. "Our old scanners could locate your ships effectively enough, and you are unlikely to develop stealth-intensity any time in the foreseeable future. Besides, the objective is to avoid going back to war when this is over."

Tarrel was obviously amused. "If you expect a lasting peace between us, it means that one of us is going to be whipped so badly that we will no longer be able to fight."

"That is my expectation," Gelrayen admitted. "You first encountered the Dreadnought more than six weeks ago. I fully expect another two to five months before we finally destroy it, if we are lucky and very efficient. What is going to happen to the Union in that time? How much more damage will Union shipping and the military fleet take in that time? And how many of our own carriers will be sacrificed fighting the Dreadnought?"

"You do not encourage me," Tarrel said as she looked out across the vast expanse of the Methryn's smooth, black hull. She had been feeling very safe, thinking that she would be aboard a Starwolf carrier, even though she had been aboard the Kerridayen during its own fight with the Dreadnought. Methryn would be going out to find the enemy, sticking her figurative head into the mouth of a beast with a proven history of snapping.

"I do not feel encouraged myself," Gelrayen admitted. "Is this what it has been like for you people?"

"What do you mean?"

"Having to fight Starwolves when we possess all of the advantages."

Tarrel laughed, mostly because he was so sincere. "No, it was never like this. We always knew where we stood with the Starwolves, and how we could expect you to respond when we pushed. Your objective was never to destroy us, and that limited the scope of our war. This thing is merciless."

"Whoever designed it was merciless," the Kelvessan corrected her. "Would you like to go aboard and meet Valthyrra?"

"Yes, certainly."

He led the way to one of the two main docking tubes, a walk of some considerable distance just to board a ship. Captain Tarrel had to get used to everything involving the Starwolf carriers, operated on a very different scale, including the time it took to get anywhere. Since these ships were quicker and more agile than anything she knew, it was hard for her to think of them as being so incredibly large while she was aboard one in flight. Only seeing one in the enclosed space of a bay, standing at the nose and seeing that black hull stretch away into the distance, did its actual size become inescapable. Tarrel wondered how it even flew the way she knew it would and stay in one piece; she would have given a lot to have been in this bay six decades earlier and seen the ship's space frame standing alone.

"Do you know, I find myself feeling sorry for Valthyrra," Gelrayen commented as they walked the length of the docking tube. "Other carriers get centuries of light duty before they are given their first patrol. But Valthyrra has to go straight out from this bay and find the Dreadnought. This is no way for her to begin her life. But do not tell Valthyrra that I ever said such a thing."

"I understood that she is actually quite a bit older than I am," Tarrel said.

"She has been up and running for that long, but a carrier's life really does not begin until she leaves the construction bay and flies for the first time," the Starwolf insisted. "If you were locked in one place, unable to move and always seeing the same thing, would you consider that life?"

Tarrel smiled fondly. "Starwolves are secretly incorrigible romantics. Who would have ever thought? But I do see your point."

Gelrayen glanced at her. "You might not have been told; I do not know. The sentient systems aboard a carrier are not just a very big computer that you can turn on and have a person. They are given the means of developing a complete personality and a set of basic traits, but it takes time and a great deal of interaction with others before they become a complete personality like Trendaessa Kerridayen. Valthyrra still seems just a little remote and not always very spontaneous compared to other carriers."

"Have you been with her long?"

"No, I came aboard three months ago. We were supposed to have half a year together to get comfortable before we were to go out for the first time. It seems that I was chosen to be the Commander of the Methryn some time ago, but I only learned about it myself when I was transferred aboard."

"Why were you chosen?" Tarrel asked.

He seemed amused. "I was the Commander-designate aboard the Vardon, and Valthyrra must have been impressed with my record as a pack leader. But you will have to ask her yourself. I never have."

"Pardon?"

Gelrayen glanced at her a second time. "Carriers are allowed to make their own choices for their Commanders, including the Methryn. Theralda had already chosen me to be her Commander-designate six years ago. The Commander-designate is always chosen from among the pack leaders, of course. The two ships had gotten to know each other very well when the Vardon was in for refitting a few years ago, and I suppose that Valthyrra trusted Theralda's judgement on that subject."

They entered through the main lock and took the lift just within to the bridge, which was in fact not a particularly long ride from the point where they had come aboard. Captain Tarrel knew that they were indeed back aboard a Starwolf ship when she found herself suddenly pressed against the wall as the lift made its typically fast lurch forward. At least she had remembered to be certain that she was comfortably close to the wall when she had stepped aboard the lift.

They entered the bridge from the right wing, stepping slowly and carefully to avoid the various tools, cables and components scattered about the deck. Technicians and members of the Methryn's own bridge crew were all hard at work fitting the final adaptations for the impulse scanner, the work here involving the installation of a new surveillance console with an additional monitor and main keyboard. Images from the impulse scanner could of course be transferred to any monitor on the bridge, including the main viewscreen. Tarrel paused for a moment, having noticed that the main viewscreen was indeed engaged, but divided into a dozen segments to show images from various points within the construction bay.

Valthyrra, who had been watching the work on her surveillance station very closely, brought her camera pod around and rotated the dual lenses to focus on the newcomers. She seemed particularly interested in Captain Tarrel, who had considered it a point of honesty to wear her Union uniform. "Are you the enemy?"

"Not at the moment, no," Tarrel responded. "Right now, someone else has that job."

"Val, that is not entirely polite," Gelrayen warned his ship quietly.

"I know that," she replied with exaggerated dignity, then turned her camera pod back to the captain. "I have to admit that I am not entirely certain what to make of this. Making my first flight is going to be embarrassing enough without a representative of the enemy hanging out to see my mistakes. Are you going to spy on me?"

"Do you want me to spy on you?" Tarrel asked as seriously as she could, amused with the ship's rather remarkable sense of humor.

"Oh, would you? I would hate to think that I might have missed the war entirely." She turned her camera pod to Commander Gelrayen, who was waiting tolerantly. "The impulse scanner will be ready for static testing as soon as this console is rigged. It is already integrated into my computer grid."

Gelrayen nodded. "How does it feel?"

"I have not yet powered up the system, so I have not had a chance to get its feel. I am still worried about resonant scatter, however."

"We will not know if we actually have to modify the impulse cannons until we can get you out of the bay. Anything else?"

"At the moment, no. But I do believe that we should begin closing up the hull immediately. Nothing will be served now by keeping the plates off. Any modifications now will not involve internal components, and it might get me out of here two days early to start closing the hull now."

"Consult the construction chief and tell him that we both recommend that the closing of the hull should begin immediately," Gelrayen said, then turned to Captain Tarrel. "Would you like to see your cabin now? You can move yourself aboard while I attend to my ship for a while. The diplomatic guest suite here on the bridge level should be ready for use."

"Of course, Commander," Tarrel said. "That is probably the same as the suite I was given while I was aboard the Kerridayen. I do know the way, if you need to get to work."

As it happened, Commander Gelrayen wanted to get to work on the closing of the Methryn's hull immediately, and he suspected that the construction chief would not be willing, unless he presented his arguments and pleading in person and possibly brought along Fleet Commander Asandi as well. Captain Tarrel found the guest suite to be in the exact corresponding place it had been aboard the Kerridayen, proof that the Starwolves were fairly satisfied with the thirty-thousand-year-old deck plan of their carriers. Since it was in the collection of corridors immediately behind the bridge, that meant that she could be there in half a minute or less without having to bother with the lift. In fact, her cabin was hardly any farther away than that of the Commander himself.

She did not remember Lt. Commander Pesca until she was on her way back into the station to collect her things. He was unobtrusive enough, since she generally ignored him altogether, but she was still responsible for him and made a point of checking on him two or three times a day to see if he was making a nuisance of himself. The trouble was that she found him dull, inept and given to petty complaints—poor company compared to Starwolves—and she easily could have done without him. For one thing, he was not very likely to accomplish his mission of learning their secret language, all the more so because they probably knew exactly what he was trying to do. But Tarrel had no good excuse for leaving him at the station, and she thought it best to keep him close, where she could watch him.

"Pack your bags, Wally," she declared, finding him in the common lounge of their suite of apartments when she returned. "We're moving aboard the Methryn right away."

"Is the Methryn ready to go out?" he asked, looking surprised and curiously worried about her announcement.

"No, not for another week. But I've been invited aboard, and I'm not going to leave you wandering about here on your own."

"But is that a good idea?" he asked, still obviously concerned. "I mean, can't you do your work better here at the main base?"

"No, I can do my work better aboard the Methryn when she goes into Union space," she said, wondering what was bothering him. "If you don't want to go back into battle, I can probably make arrangements to have you sent home. But I'm not going to leave you here."

"No, I should go," he agreed grudgingly. "You might need me. Besides, I seem to be getting nowhere with their language."

"No, you never will," she told him. "They keep their secrets better than stones."

The first crisis had occurred by the time Captain Tarrel returned to the Methryn. Kelvessan were running up and down the docking tube, to the point that she spent half the walk through stepping to one side with her bags. A whole crowd of people was outside in the bay itself in what looked like furious inactivity, as if they very much wanted to do something but had no idea just what. None of that was very promising for the Methryn. Captain Tarrel did not know what the problem could be, but her first guess was that the scanner was somehow involved. She doubted that there was anything that she could do to help, except perhaps by staying out of the way. Her compromise to her own curiosity was to stay in her cabin and make herself at home for a couple of hours, time enough for the Starwolves to get over their initial panic and make some sense of the situation.

When Tarrel did finally present herself on the bridge, the crisis had settled itself to a state of desperate industry, which was probably to say that things were very much back to normal.

The work on the new surveillance console was continuing at an unhurried pace, as if nothing had happened, and that seemed to suggest that the trouble had not occurred here. Commander Gelrayen had left a message for her with Valthyrra, instructing her to join him on the floor of the construction bay.

As soon as she could see the interior of the bay, Tarrel had a much better idea of what was happening. Handling arms mounted on tracks on ceiling and floor had been brought in both above and below the ship to begin the work of fitting the remaining hull plates, suspended by the deceptively slender arms out of range of the artificial gravity that existed only at floor level. More plates were being held in groups by other handling arms, but the work itself appeared to have been suspended. Commander Gelrayen hurried over to join her before she saw him. He was not in Starwolf Commander's white, and she could not easily tell him from many of the dozens of other Kelvessans on the bay floor.

"We have a problem," he told her simply. "We have to send these plates back to the construction facilities. These plates were cast and shaped years ago, but this is the first time that they have ever been brought out into the bay."

"What is the problem?" Tarrel asked. "Don't they fit?"

"They probably fit perfectly," he told her. "Unfortunately, they have not yet been prepared for final fitting. Do you not see the difference?"

Tarrel looked closely, but the only thing that she could see was that all of the plates were shiny silver on both sides. "I suppose that the new plates haven't been painted yet. Can't you do that after they go on?"

"That is not paint," Gelrayen said. "The plates are bonded to a thick polymer coating that resists impacts and helps to insulate the hull against power discharge. And considering what we have to fight, we will need that coating. We fuse the sheets into a solid piece once it is on, and we can easily repair ripped and burned sections. But this much work has to be sent back to be done properly, and quickly enough to keep us on schedule."

"Can you still keep your schedule?" Tarrel asked.

He nodded. "Yes, we believe so. We began fitting the plates two days ahead of schedule, and that gives us two extra days to make up for our little mistake."

The main bay doors began to open, the internal atmosphere

held by containment fields, while smaller tenders waited just outside to carry away the hull plates. Considering the size of those plates, most of them almost sixty meters along each edge, this was the only door through which they would fit. Tarrel looked up to see one of the massive plates pass directly over her head, supported at one corner by a handling arm barely half a meter thick. For all the years that she had lived in space, she still had some problems with artificial-gravity environments.

"We might just as well go back aboard," Gelrayen commented. "There is nothing we can do to help here, except to get out of the way. Valthyrra will be powering up the scanners as soon as the bridge console is finished, and she told me to expect that within the hour."

Tarrel was interested to watch the tenders move along the length of the Methryn to collect the unfinished hull plates, but she did not necessarily want to be beneath while the plates were being taken away. They took the lift back up several levels to the observation deck, then crossed the docking tube back into the carrier. Tarrel was compensated for not staying below to watch, since the windows along the length of the tube gave her an excellent view of the tenders operating on their own level. Commander Gelrayen indulged her curiosity a moment, stopping to watch. The only problem with moving the weightless plates was maneuvering their awkward size through the tight areas between the Methryn and the walls of the bay.

"Will Valthyrra be able to fly this ship?" Tarrel asked. "I would think that she would need some practice to get the feel for anything this large and powerful."

"She has been practicing," Gelrayen told her. "She has spent the last week moving the Sharvaen in and out through the entire system by remote. She can establish a multi-channel achronic link with any of the other ships that gives her complete input of data and sensory devices and direct control over the other ship's major systems. So you might say that she really is getting the feel along with the practical experience."

"Can these ships actually feel?" Tarrel asked, surprised. "I did not use the word in that sense."

"Oh yes, they can feel," he insisted. "They have various motion detectors that allow them to judge degrees of accelerations and changes in direction, and they have stress, compression and torsional sensors throughout their frame and hull. They do not feel actual pain, but they know how different areas of the ship are responding to stress. They have a better feel for flying than any other pilot ever could.''

"So all of the concern was only about her actual battle experience?"

"Unfortunately, she cannot learn that from the other ships. Several of them have down-loaded their own experiences to her, but I am told that it is not quite the same. There are some things you can only learn by doing them yourself, and she can hardly take one of the other carriers into battle.''

The first of the tenders retreated from the construction bay, a plate of armor held in each of its short forward handling arms. Each of those plates was probably four or five times as massive as the little ship that was moving two of them out of the bay, lifting to pass over the top of the carrier's down-swept wing. A second tender started out from the other side of the ship, something that Tarrel had missed seeing so far.

"Will the Starwolves fight to the death against the Dreadnought?" Tarrel asked abruptly.

"No, we have already decided that," he admitted. "If we realize that we absolutely cannot destroy it, then we will retreat. Our concern then will be the evacuation of enough of Terran civilization, and our own ships along with this station, to start again. You might think that we are cold, but we must be practical. It is better to save something than lose everything."

The technicians had just finished closing up the panels on the new surveillance console as they returned to the bridge. Valthyrra rotated her camera pod around to look at them, obviously very pleased with the work. "The impulse scanner is installed and ready for the first level of testing. I want to begin bringing it into the main computer grid."

Gelrayen nodded. "Start getting comfortable with it, then. Anything else to worry about?"

The camera pod somehow managed to look uncomfortable. "Is there a very good estimate on how long the closing of my hull will take?"

Gelrayen regarded her suspiciously. "Probably a week. Why?"

"The Vardon is coming in a few hours from now, and she needs more that a square kilometer of new upper hull."

"That makes your poor nose look like a garden plot in comparison," he commented. "What happened to her?"

"Theralda is reluctant to speak of the matter," Valthyrra said. "She does relay important information regarding the Dreadnought, although it is all more in the area of bad news for us than good news, although still better for us to know. She says that the Dreadnought is now attacking planets, and that it is faster and more clever than we had first anticipated. She also warns us to use only tight-beam achronic transitions, since she believes now that the Dreadnought has been monitoring our wide-beam communications."

Gelrayen crossed both sets of his arms. "Wonderful! That monster knows everything we plan, then. It will be waiting for us when we go out now, you realize."

"We can hope that it has not overheard everything," Valthyrra suggested. "It is easy enough to miss a sweep transition if you are in the wrong place. Thirty-two percent of all such transitions are missed, especially at longer ranges. I am not speaking from personal experience, of course."

"Wait a moment," Tarrel interrupted. "Are your transitions usually in your own language?"

"Yes, of course," the ship answered.

"Then the Dreadnought understands your language?"

"I suppose that must follow, certainly. It is not difficult to figure out another language, if you can find someone foolish enough to speak it to you. You might try explaining that to your young companion."

Captain Tarrel laughed softly. "He can go talk to the Dreadnought, if he wants. But if he stays here, then we're all better off for letting him have something harmless to keep him busy."

"The Vardon will be here in perhaps eighteen hours," Valthyrra continued. "We will learn more about the matter then. She is very reluctant to use the achronic to any extent, and she seems honestly frightened. The scanner is fully integrated and nominally functional in as far as I have been able to test it so far."

"Very well, then," Gelrayen agreed. "Prepare the scanner for the second level of testing. Are you going to try rapid sequencing?"

"I thought I might. That is a key element in the grid."

"Take it easy, then," he warned, stepping back toward the middle bridge to allow members of the crew to take their stations for testing. Captain Tarrel joined him, and he leaned back against the wall with his arms crossed. "The problem is that all of these tests only tell us if we have installed it in the ship properly. We will not know if it actually works until we can take the Methryn out where she can maneuver."

"Can you take it out to test it now, before they're ready to put the hull shields back on?" Tarrel asked.

"I wish we could. Unfortunately, we will not know how well we are actually receiving because the receivers are calibrated to work surrounded by that great mass of metal. Besides, Valthyrra is running the ship off of station power. It would take hours to manually reconnect the power couplings and get her running."

"Oh?" Tarrel was surprised to hear that. "Is there some reason to keep the ship isolated from her own power? You certainly would not go to that much trouble for an ordinary docking."

"There is no need for her to generate her own power, as little as she can use. I suppose that keeping her in this state saves the time needed to change the couplings to station power if the technicians want to modify her power grid." He shrugged both sets of arms, a serious expression of his own helplessness to know the true reason. "As far as I know, she never has powered up her own generators."

"Then how do you know that the power grid works properly."

Gelrayen glanced at her impatiently. "Please, do not complicate my life any more than it already is."

A noise like distant thunder rolled through the frame of the carrier, a sound that made Tarrel think immediately that the Methryn had just taken a hit or some minor impact. Gelrayen seemed to think the same thing, and they both paused to listen intently. Tarrel realized that such a sound was more ominous here than it would have been on her own battleship, since any impact that would have carried through the bulk of this ship probably indicated a much larger blow than she first estimated. Her first thought was that there had been some accident with the tenders removing those massive hull plates, or even that the Dreadnought was attacking the station. She noticed first that all of the images on the main viewscreen looking forward from the nose of the carrier had gone suddenly black, and that sections of the main consoles were beginning to light up in a way that suggested an emergency.

"What do you have, Val?" Gelrayen asked cautiously.

She brought her camera pod around slowly. "The primary and two secondary impulse cannons in the shock bumper fired. There was no reason; they were not powered up nearly far enough to pulse."

"Something slipped?"

"Nothing on my end," she insisted. "The power levels should have held the impulse cannons in stand-by condition. I cannot see yet how the fault could have been at my end. The cannons discharged prematurely."

"No one is blaming you," Gelrayen told her, since she sounded almost as if she was on the edge of panic. "Forget the cannons for now; we should just consider ourselves lucky that it was only the three forward cannons. Tell me about the condition of the bay."

"I was not greatly damaged by the concussion itself, and my hull is open closest to the blast," she reported, calmer. "That suggests to me that the damage is not great. I was hit by a hull plate that got away from a tender during the concussion, but the plate defected off with minimal damage and has drifted away. I cannot say what has happened to the construction crew because I am blind to the front. Station control has called me, but I have not yet been contacted by bay control or the observation deck. Would you like to go outside and check conditions for me? I would appreciate it."

"Yes, I suppose that I should," he agreed pensively. "I would not expect any response from the observation deck, since those windows were only twenty meters or so away from the primary impulse cannon. Do what you can."

Although she had not been specifically invited, Captain Tarrel followed quickly as the Starwolf Commander stalked off toward the lift. Once the doors were closed, Gelrayen looked far more annoyed and concerned that he could have afforded to while his ship could see him. He was being protective of Valthyrra, trying to be attentive and commanding enough to make up for her own deficiencies. That made Tarrel even more concerned about what she had just seen.

"Commander, your ship was rattled," she told him. "Valthyrra was scared to death, and she nearly froze up."

Gelrayen frowned fiercely. "She was just concerned that she might have been responsible for damage and injury, all the more so because she knows how important time is right now."

"I certainly hope so," Tarrel said guardedly. "If that really is her reaction to danger, then you cannot take this ship into battle. She has a lot of growing up to do."

The first thing they discovered was that the docking tubes had been ripped away by the concussion. Gelrayen stepped through the airlock and out to the broken end of the tube, then gently propelled himself over the side. Tarrel followed his example with only marginal hesitation; there was no gravity in the bay except for the final two meters or so above the floor, and that final drop was small enough that even she made it easily. At least that gentle descent of over a hundred meters had given them both time for a good look about the bay.

As Gelrayen had predicted, the concussion from the primary impulse cannon had taken out the observation deck and the bay control room, although the nose docking bracket was built heavily enough that it had survived unharmed. The two secondary cannons had added their own power to the blast, and the concussion had swept along the length of the bay and out the main doors. At least the doors had been open at the time; the shock wave had been intense enough to blow out the containment field for a brief moment. There had been two tenders in the bay at the time. One, just coming in, had been kicked back out again. The second tender had already collected one of the immense hull plates, but that had been ripped from its hold by the concussion and had slid along the Methryn's upper hull until it too passed out the containment field. It had already been collected by the first tender.

Most of the bay crew had already gone to the construction facilities to help prepare the Methryn's armor. The dozen or so left had all been Kelvessan and hearty enough to survive more than this. Some had very minor injuries due to being tossed about by the concussion or else being hit by debris. There had fortunately been no one in the bay control room or the observation deck at the time; even Starwolves would not have easily survived that. All in all, things could have been worse. If the bay doors had been closed, the entire concussion would have been forced into the station corridors.

Of course, things could have also been much better.

Tenders continued to carry the hull plates out of the way, although a full hour passed before two of the little ships returned with replacements for the docking tubes which had been ripped away. These had simply been disconnected from another bay, but another hour passed before these new tubes were rigged in place and normal traffic in and out of the carrier could resume. By that time, most of the debris from the misfire of the impulse cannons had been cleared away. That was also more than enough time for Fleet Commander Asandi to arrive.

"Do you know yet what happened?" he asked. "I was told that the scanner malfunctioned."

Gelrayen nodded solemnly. "Valthyrra was powering up the system to see if everything was responding. She says that the cannons pulsed at a much lower power level than anticipated. They should have only been at stand-by status."

Asandi frowned at he stared up at the carrier. "I hope that this business does not involve a long delay."

"Valthyrra says not. According to her expectations, some minor mechanical changes and a primary computer control modification should correct the problem completely. She says that we should close up the hull and take the ship out just as she is, although she recommends certain design changes on the next impulse scanner we build."

"That sounds promising," Asandi agreed. "I still want to check everything through the research and design team first, though. Better a delay at this phase than having to bring the Methryn back in later to start over."

Gelrayen looked up at the new docking tube, which appeared to be complete. "I suppose that I should go back aboard. We have to get to work on finding out just why those cannons fired prematurely."

"Tell Valthyrra that we really do not need these delays," Asandi declared. "Her first battle damage, a result of shooting herself in her own construction bay. This is not a promising beginning."

"Send Dalvaen and his friends in research over and have them tell us why their cannons discharged this much energy at stand-by level," Gelrayen responded.

As it happened, Dalvaen had already taken his team of research scientists and engineers onto the Methryn's hull to look at the impulse cannons, and they had their answer soon enough. The projection coils in the cannons were cooled to very low temperatures within a matter of seconds by solid-state coolers, and the designers had seriously underestimated the increase in efficiency from the super-conductor coils. Power levels that should have held the cannons ready to pulse on command, instead caused them to discharge. That was by no means bad news. Any system that could deliver the same performance on half the power input was an advantage to any ship, and especially so to a fighting ship. Valthyrra simply had to reprogram the automatic systems in the scanner control to feed a reduced power curve to the cannons.

The Methryn had been somewhat more damaged by the concussion than she had first thought, although that damage was still not serious. She was designed to take far worse punishment than she had just received, and the damage was mostly limited to some of the more delicate equipment exposed by the missing hull plates. Wiring and major power leads had been ripped loose from several shield projectors, scanner receivers and perimeter cannons set in retractable turrets within the ventral groove. None of the machinery itself, however, had been damaged, and everything was easily repaired by reconnecting or laying down new wiring.

If no one else was pleased with what had happened to the Methryn, it did at least put Theralda Vardon in a better mood. If nothing else, it encouraged her to hope that everyone else would be too impressed with Valthyrra's embarrassment to pay much attention to her own stupidity. She was quite mistaken, especially so if she had ever believed that the sight of a Starwolf carrier coming into port with the wreckage of a Union commercial station still strapped to her hull could be ignored. Her crews had actually cut away large parts of the station components already, given the amount of time they were allowed, but nearly every piece of the station she carried had been fused to her armor in several places by the Dreadnought's discharge beam. And with her shield projectors gone, the wreckage of the station components offered the best protection she had against attack.

Fleet Commander Asandi took one look at her and walked away shaking his head, muttering that the survival of known civilization was in the hands of idiots. Captain Tarrel was beginning to find it all very educational. She had discovered that not only were the Starwolves capable of making mistakes, sometimes they were also just plain unlucky.

"What I regret most, I suppose, is that it happened when we were actually doing so well," Theralda remarked during an open conference between the carriers. "We were finally doing something constructive, even if we could not fight the Dreadnought itself."

Although Fleet Commander Asandi had already gone aboard the Vardon to view the damage, Daerran had joined Tarrel and Gelrayen on the Methryn's bridge for the conference. Valthyrra had channeled images of the Vardon to her main screen as well as the monitors at the Commander's station on the upper bridge where the group was gathered. It was hard to tell that a Starwolf carrier was actually hidden beneath that wreckage. Theralda had removed only the segment that had been strapped across her nose. Tenders and crews working in suits were working to remove the wreckage as quickly as possible, although the process made some think of old stories they had read about sailing ships, and the removal of barnacles.

"Could you just run through your observations about the Dreadnought step by step," Commander Asandi suggested.

"Well, the first thing we discovered was that the Dreadnought has begun attacking major surface targets," Theralda began. "The damage that I observed was relatively limited, although the Dreadnought does identify and destroy all surface military targets. I have also found evidence that the Dreadnought lingers in system for a time to see what might come along responding to calls for help. That suggests to me that the Dreadnought moves more quickly between systems than we have first anticipated, and that it is capable of more sophisticated planning than suspected. My personal suspicion is that it is loitering about waiting for Starwolves."

"But I already knew that it was waiting in system," Tarrel added. "When I first encountered the Dreadnought, it attacked the convoy my battleship was escorting hours before it struck the station."

"We had not forgotten that, even if Theralda had," Trendaessa Kerridayen remarked.

"There is additional evidence that the Dreadnought is more than just a simple automated weapon," Theralda continued.

"When I entered the system where I first encountered the Dreadnought, I was discovered when it made a routine impulse scanner sweep. It was looking for Starwolf carriers running with stealth-intensity shields, perhaps as a result of its battle with the Kerridayen. It definitely is more clever than we had assumed, or at least hoped. And being that clever, it is certainly capable of intercepting our achronic transitions and being prepared for what we plan to do."

"We have to make plans for that possibility," Asandi agreed, "Anything else?"

"Just more evidence of its intelligence," she continued. "It followed me to Norden within hours, rather than loiter in the last system it attacked. A change in its usual methods. And when it came into the Norden system and saw the Maeridan and myself carrying away segments of the commercial stations, it followed us to see where we were going before it attacked. Those might all be automatic functions, but they are also evidence of a higher level of sophistication than we had first expected. But, when it did attack, it went after the station components rather than myself or the Maeridan, which gave me time enough to get away. That does not suggest careful planning, and that brings us back to assuming it is an automated machine rather than sentient."

"I suspect that your assumptions are very accurate," Asandi agreed. "Perhaps the Methryn can answer those questions more accurately in a couple of weeks. But we do have to be prepared for the fact that we are indeed fighting an enemy that is not just far more technically advanced than ourselves, on a scale of power far beyond ours, but clever enough to anticipate us."

—6—

The wide door at the rear of the Methryn's upper right fighter bay opened, revealing the open doors of the construction bay more than half a kilometer behind. Captain Tarrel stood well to the front of the bay with Commander Gelrayen, waiting for the arrival of the Methryn's first pack of fighters. The packs were the most well-known of the Starwolves; the pilots in their black armor the only Starwolves that most people of Union space were likely to see. Certainly the packs were the most infamous, the most feared and also the most romanticized of all Starwolves; some believed, without really stopping to think about it, that Starwolves were all pilots.

Since coming aboard the Kerridayen, Tarrel had discovered that most of the massive carriers kept only ten to twelve packs each, ninety to a hundred and eight pilots. Of the carrier's complete crew of about two thousand, only half were active crewmembers and most of these existed to serve the packs. The ship largely took care of itself, employing a small army of remote units. Each pack was commanded by a pack leader, that being in fact the most commonly-used name, although the official rank was that of Captain. The pack leader always ran in the center of the standard V-formation of the pack, with four fighters sitting to either side in each wing of that formation.

Tarrel had been told that the pack leaders held the rank of Captain, the same as her own, because the packs were intended to operate fairly independently once they were in space and their leader needed the authority to make major strategic decisions without the time-consuming process of consulting the carrier.

For that same reason, the senior officer of the carrier itself was not a Captain but a Commander, ranking higher than the Captains who served under him in the packs. That was supposedly how the Starwolves had received their name, since each carrier was in principle an armored and highly mobile base for a group of wolf packs. Curiously, the Union itself had first given them the name of Starwolves.

"They should be coming around any moment now," Gelrayen warned.

Captain Tarrel was content to wait, using her time to inspect the bay itself. The bay was many times wider than it was high, giving the illusion that the ceiling was much lower than it actually was. And it was rather low by her estimate; she would not want to fly a relatively large fighter a hundred meters and more down the length of the bay with only twelve meters or so between floor and ceiling. The fighters would land near the front of the bay. Where she now stood, she could see the nine white lines painted on the floor of the bay, with a corresponding set of handling arms on ceiling tracks above. A massive framework called a rack waited to receive the fighter once it was down and secured. The rack had a double function preventing the fighter from being thrown around the inside of the ship by sudden turns, and serving as a launching platform for the fighter. When not in use, the fighters were carried in their racks to a separate holding bay.

"Will the packs be of any help to you in fighting the Dreadnought," she asked.

Gelrayen shook his head. "No, not at all. I would not even dare to send them out, since even a minor hit from the Dreadnought's discharge beams would be the end of a fighter."

"Then you could easily do without them now," she observed.

"I suppose. We are just so used to thinking of the packs as the carrier's defense that we will feel better for having them. And you never really know just what you might find useful."

The arrival of the pack was sudden and rather alarming. The first of the black fighters suddenly whipped around the station in a swift turn, through the outer doors of the construction bay, and directly into the Methryn's landing bay at a speed that Captain Tarrel would have considered sufficient for an attack run. It dropped its speed quickly once it was inside the landing bay, extending its slender landing gear, its long-legged stance meant to accommodate its down-swept wings. The fighter drew itself to an abrupt halt only three meters from where they stood beside its rack, hovering for a moment before lowering itself slowly to the deck. The second fighter was already on its way in by that time.

The landing of all nine fighters in the pack was accomplished in less than a minute. The handling arms came in to pin the fighter to the deck, a needless precaution aboard a carrier that was not in flight. Once the engines and generators were shut down, the fighter was lifted so that its landing gear could be retracted and it was then moved forward into its rack. Members of the bay crew hurried in to lock the fighter into the rack and slide forward the boarding platform.

Gelrayen himself tended the middle fighter, ascending the boarding platform as the canopy was raised, helping the pilot to release the seat straps and remove his helmet. Tarrel recalled that he had been a pack leader himself until only a few months earlier, and that, like all Commanders, he still missed flying with the packs and probably always would. As he helped the pack leader remove his helmet, a lone Starwolf fighter slipped relatively sedately into the bay and settled to the deck behind the lead fighter. This arrival was clearly a last-minute addition, since Valthyrra was only just bringing out its rack after it had landed, while two extra members of the bay crew hurried to assist the pilot.

Gelrayen returned a moment later, followed by the pack leader in black armor. "Captain, this is pack leader Teraln. He is to be the Methryn's new Commander-designate, although the real purpose for his existence is to do all the things that I wish I could be doing for myself."

"I'm Captain Janus Tarrel," she introduced herself. "There is no real purpose to my existence at the moment, but I'm supposed to be useful in the near future. Are the packs only now beginning to transfer aboard?"

"We should all be here within the next couple of days," Teraln explained. "My pack transferred here with five others aboard the freighter Fyrdenna Lesdryn. The other four should already be on Alkayja station."

"The first four arrived on station nearly two weeks ago," Gelrayen said. "Listen, I need your help. I will be giving every moment I can spare to this ship until this business is over. Will you watch over the packs and make certain that they get settled comfortably?"

"Yes, certainly," Teraln insisted.

The pilot of the lone fighter walked over to join them, a female Kelvessan in full flight armor of command white. Tarrel was surprised to see that, since she had believed that only the pilots flew the fighters. Since her hair was somewhat ruffled from being inside the helmet, she somehow looked even younger and more delicate than most of her kind. Gelrayen was watching her with great interest and some mystification.

"Kayendel, reporting aboard as first officer," she announced formally, although she did not salute. Starwolves, at least in Tarrel's experience, never saluted, perhaps because they could not decide upon which arm to use.

"I already have a first officer," Gelrayen commented. "Not to reflect upon your welcome here, of course. Is there something going on here that I should know about?"

"Because of my previous battle experience with the Dreadnought as the first officer of the Vardon, I have transferred positions with the Methryn's original first officer," she explained. "Fleet Commander Asandi and Valthyrra Methryn herself approved the transfer."

"Oh, well. No need for anyone to bother me with little details," Gelrayen commented sourly.

"This all happened in the past thirty minutes," she said. "I was unaware that you had not been consulted. Perhaps I should not have come aboard so quickly, but I thought that I might be needed."

"No, you are needed," he assured her. "Especially if you have had some experience with the Dreadnought. The more of that I can have aboard this ship, the better I will like it. For the duration of this mission, I want you to be near the bridge at all times. Take one of the visitor's cabins behind the bridge."

"Yes, Commander."

They looked around as Valthyrra lifted the fighters in their racks and began moving them in a neat parade toward the storage bay. The members of Teraln's pack gathered about in a loose group, having collected their things from the storage compartments of their fighters.

"We will have more packs coming in here any moment now since we have only two bays operational," Gelrayen observed. "I should at least make certain that the packs get settled in their cabins."

"I should go settle into my own cabin and then present myself on the bridge," Kayendel added as she began to gather up her rather large bundles, which a member of the bay crew had brought her.

"I think that I will go along," Captain Tarrel added. "Would you like for me to take one of those?"

She tried to lift the case that was still on the ground, only to find that it probably weighed as much as herself. Kayendel took the case in her one remaining hand, although she was already carrying bundles at least as large in her other three hands. "I really should have warned you that these are all my worldly goods, all quarter ton of them. Did you hurt yourself?"

"No, I could have lifted it," Tarrel insisted. "I just wouldn't want to carry it far. I haven't seen much evidence of Starwolves doing the things that make them legendary, so I forgot about your strength."

They had started toward the side of the bay and the lift that would take them to the bridge. Kayendel carried her load easily, as if so much weight was still of small consequence to her, even though she also wore her armor. Tarrel had sometimes felt tempted to dismiss much of what she had always been told about Starwolves as mythical, the product of fear and exaggeration. They were not cruel and they did not engage in strange practices. They were very pleasant and intelligent, but in some ways very innocent. But certain claims about their tremendous strength were probably true.

"You can certainly tell that Commander Gelrayen came up from the packs very recently," the Kelvessan remarked. "Theralda Vardon warned me that a new Commander will find every excuse to stay near the packs and the fighters for a long time afterward."

Tarrel pressed the button to call the lift, but one was waiting for them. Valthyrra Methryn had probably anticipated the need. They entered and began their long ride to the bridge. Kayendel took the sharp acceleration of the lift with complete ease, in spite of her burden.

"I obviously don't need to ask if you are getting tired," Tarrel observed. "Just how strong are you, anyway?"

"Oh, I would never want you to think that I am just showing off," Kayendel said. "I am really not as strong as some of the pilots; part of the reason I did not stay with the packs."

"Please brag a little."

She smiled. "We do have to exercise regularly, just to live with these muscles. I can lift about four tons with either set of arms. Using both sets of arms and putting my back into it, I can move about ten."

Tarrel frowned. "I used to be proud of that ninety kilo bench press."

The Kelvessan watched her pensively. "If I can speak freely without fear of being insulting, I must admit that you are not at all what I expected. I was prepared to dislike having you aboard my ship."

"Is that a fact?" Tarrel asked, quietly amused.

"In the last seventy years, I have probably had port leave on more Union worlds than even you have ever visited," she explained. "Until now, I have never had much reason to think that your people were either very interesting or well-mannered."

"It was probably the circumstances. I suspect that you Starwolves tend to forget just how frightening you can be, stalking about in that heavy armor. It makes you look twice as big."

Kayendel looked confused. "Our armor keeps us cool in your warm environments. But I suppose I know what you mean. Actually, we try to keep your people afraid of us. There are many times that we do not have to fight because our reputation keeps us safe."

The lift stopped in the corridor outside the left wing of the bridge, and they followed that corridor back behind the bridge itself, past the various meeting rooms, to the block of visitor's cabins. Kayendel selected a cabin that was adjacent to, but smaller than the suite that Captain Tarrel had been given.

She looked around in great curiosity. "This is a remarkable thing. You can live on a ship all your life, and yet there are places aboard where you have never been."

"This is not the Vardon," Tarrel reminded her. "But since everything seems to correspond, I suppose that I know what you mean. Of course, the size of this ship has a lot to do with that. There isn't a corner of my own little battleship that I don't know intimately."

Kayendel set down her cases and bundles in a neat row. "Perhaps, but I have lived aboard a carrier all my life. You would expect to get to know any ship intimately in ninety years."

Tarrel stared. "Just how long do your people live anyway?"

"About three hundred standard years," Kayendel explained as she opened the chestplate on her armor and began shutting down the cooling system. "Sometimes a little less. Sometimes quite a bit more. Around here, anyone less than a hundred is still considered young."

"I'm beginning to envy you people," Captain Tarrel remarked, then realized that the Starwolf was in the process of removing her armor. "Do you want me to leave?"

"Only if you want to," Kayendel told her, unconcerned. "That depends upon how you react to naked Starwolves. I was hoping that you would take me to the bridge and introduce me to Valthyrra Methryn. You know her already, and I doubt that Commander Gelrayen will return any time soon. He wants to spend some time with his packs, I am sure."

"You arrived aboard in a fighter," Tarrel observed. "And you have fighting armor."

"Our suits are all very much the same, even for those who never fly with the packs," the Kelvessan explained. She unbelted the middle section of her suit, disconnected the leads and pipes connecting the top half with the bottom, and stepped out of the lower part. Not only was the lower part a single section, it stood upright on its own. "But as first officer, I am also the ship's helm and I can fly her manually. Of course, you can hardly ever convince a ship to allow you to fly her, so we keep a fighter of our own to stay in practice."

She separated the top half of the suit and pulled it off, also in a single piece. Fully naked, she looked far less human that Tarrel had anticipated. Large, bony hips, and a chest and back that were massively muscled to support the structure of her double set of arms, were joined by a middle section that was only a slender tube, her single pair of small breasts being her most human feature. The bones of Kelvessan looked deceptively light, but were in fact precipitates of iron, capable of bearing tons of stress. Without the unifying factor of clothing, even Kayendel's facial features appeared far less human. There was some subtle difference to her cheeks and mouth, suggestive of an animal's delicate muzzle, and her eyes appeared unnaturally large, like those from some cartoon drawing. Her pointed ears peeked out through her typical Starwolf's mane of soft brown hair. Tarrel was surprised to note that Kayendel's hair was actually not as long as it appeared, but simply grew in a strip down the full length of her spine.

"I am told that we actually look far less human than we first did," she said, seeming to know what her companion was thinking. "We were also originally less than half as strong. We evolve in steps about once every ten thousand years."

Kayendel opened one of the cases and took out the uniform of a command officer, white tunic and pants, with cuffs trimmed with a black band, and began dressing quickly.

"The Starwolves don't use a real uniform with emblems of rank?" Tarrel asked.

"Why should we bother?" Kayendel asked. "Most of us stay aboard the same ship our entire lives, so we know each other by sight. And yes, we really can tell each other apart quite easily."

Captain Tarrel tried not to laugh. There were indeed only a very limited number of physical differences between Kelvessan, including size.

"There are compensations for being Kelvessan, but precious few. Races of artificial origin do not have much sense of identity, and about all that we have ever been allowed to do is fight. Perhaps you can understand why we hope very much that the war does not resume," she continued, pulling on her boots. "Well, I suppose that I am ready to present myself to Valthyrra. I have been told that even Commander Gelrayen has reservations about her adaptation."

Captain Tarrel did not comment, recalling how the ship had seemed almost about to panic with fear and guilt after the misfire of the impulse cannons. She knew that she might be attaching too much significance to the incident because she did not think of machines as being given to panic. But she was certain that she would find it hard to trust a helm officer of her own ship who had behaved in that manner.

"Main conversion generators are fully operational," Valthyrra reported as she began the process of powering herself up for flight. "Main scanners, shields and environmental support are all on-line. Main drives are standing by. All systems ready for flight."

Commander Gelrayen had been pacing the bridge, checking

the readings on the monitors at station after station. Everything was actually going very well. The Methryn was leaving the construction bay a full day ahead of her proposed schedule, in spite of the problems she had encountered. Her long, tapered nose was fully plated, and her scanner was as ready as it was going to get, short of full testing. The Methryn finally had a full crew, although she carried almost no non-active personnel, and a compliment of ten packs. She had never flown herself before, but she had done this often enough with other carriers by a remote link. If she could fly another carrier, it seemed reasonable to expect that she could fly herself without the slightest difficulty.

"Do you feel ready to go?" Gelrayen asked.

She brought her camera pod around. "Yes, I feel ready."

He nodded. "Contact bay control. Tell them to release the braces."

Captain Tarrel was watching from the Commander's station on the upper bridge. Although a jump seat had already been installed for her, Gelrayen had insisted that he would not be able to sit through this first flight. Kayendel was at the helm station on the middle bridge, standing ready at her manual controls if Valthyrra had any trouble controlling the ship.

"Docking braces are released," Valthyrra reported. "The ship is standing free to maneuver."

"Back yourself out of the bay under field drive," Gelrayen told her. "And be very, very careful."

"I see no reason to worry about my embarrassing myself," Valthyrra assured him.

The Methryn began to push herself straight back, drifting completely free the moment her shock bumper slipped away from its docking bracket. The field drive was a non-reactive drive, so low-powered that it was effective only for steering the ship and for precise maneuvering in close proximity, such as moving through dockings. She backed out of the construction bay much farther than she needed, just to be completely certain of her clearance, then turned and began to move away. System control granted her consent to free flight, and she engaged her main drives cautiously to move out of orbit into open space.

"The ship is clear and away," Valthyrra reported. "All major navigational systems are in perfect order. Navigational shields and standard scanners are functional. Main drives are phasing properly. Acceleration dampers are at high efficiency. I am ready to begin additional testing.''

"Very well, then," Gelrayen agreed. "Begin a series of low-speed tactical maneuvers. Keep our passengers in mind."

The Methryn began her series of rapid turns and dodges, leaving Captain Tarrel grateful to be strapped into a well-padded seat. Because the Starwolves had better acceleration dampers, the ride was seldom any worse than it often could be aboard her own battleship. Union crewmembers wore their own armored suits, protection against both high G's and sudden decompressions from a breached hull. The only difference was that the vast Starwolf carriers made routine accelerations greater than she cared to consider. The present series was only moderate, even by her own standards.

Commander Gelrayen ascended the steps to the upper bridge, ignoring the shifts and jerks that kept Tarrel pinned to her seat. "Comfortable?"

"I wish I had my flight suit," she said. "If these straps break, don't expect me to stay in this seat."

"Our seats and straps are designed to hold through two thousand G's more than we can take ourselves," he told her. "We will have to build a suit of armor for you, to give you better protection when the time comes to fight. If you want, we can put you off for the duration of these tests."

"Perhaps you should," she agreed. "You don't have much time to complete these tests, and I get the impression that you're holding back for my sake."

Valthyrra brought her camera pod into the upper bridge. "Actually, I will not be doing anything more energetic than a basic test of all my mechanical systems. I hardly see any point in stress-testing my frame and drives, since everything is new. Besides, I might actually break something, and then where would we be?"

Gelrayen looked up at her impatiently. "Are you paying attention to what you are supposed to be doing?"

"Of course I am. I keep one aspect of awareness on the bridge at all times, but all the rest of me is very hard at work."

Tarrel looked very confused. "I beg your pardon?"

The camera pod moved slightly closer. "My conscious mind has multiple simultaneous aspects, as well as dozens of subconscious aspects for monitoring the ship's automatic functions."

"How very convenient," Tarrel remarked. "Can Starwolves do that also?"

"We do not have the need," Gelrayen said. "Besides, our brains are much smaller than those of a human, and separated into several bony compartments as protection against accelerations. We have nothing to spare. We do, however, have a built-in mathematical function that operates independently."

Valthyrra rotated her camera pod around to face the main viewscreen. "I register some fluctuations in the right inboard drive. I am making adjustments in power distribution until mechanical modifications can be made. Ready to proceed with high-speed maneuvers."

"Are you satisfied with that drive?" Gelrayen asked.

"Yes. That drive is not a problem; it is just not running as efficiently as I would like."

"Then begin your high-speed tests. Just be prepared to back off that drive if it gives any trouble."

"That drive is not a problem," Valthyrra repeated in curiously hurt tones.

After all that this ship had been through in the past couple of weeks, she was probably becoming a bit defensive about having her abilities questioned. Captain Tarrel could sympathize, but something about that simple, plaintive protest led her to suspect that Valthyrra still had some work ahead of her in developing a complete personality forceful and decisive enough to effectively command this ship. For the moment, however, Tarrel was distracted from her thoughts, as the stress of the Methryn's maneuvers returned, more forceful than before.

"We will be climbing to transition under evasive maneuvers," Gelrayen told her. "The jump into starflight will be the hardest part, but relatively brief in duration. That will be the end of it."

"I have to get used to it," she insisted. "I do know one thing. After flying with Starwolves, I won't be afraid of childbirth. It can't be as rough as this."

Gelrayen looked mystified. "I had not thought of you as maternal. Were you considering children?"

"No, never. So I never had any real reason to be afraid of childbirth. I suppose you people have your own way of doing that."

"No, but I have never heard that it is painful."

"I am taking myself on into starflight," Valthyrra announced, bringing her camera pod back into the upper bridge. "This ship is behaving so well, I am almost disappointed with the lack of excitement."

"I doubt that," Gelrayen remarked. "But do what you think best, esteemed one. We might as well test all of your systems quickly, so that we will have more time to go back to the bay if something does not work. Signal the other carriers to prepare themselves for the test of your impulse scanner."

The Methryn made the transition into starflight flawlessly and went on to execute various directional changes, about the only thing she could do in starflight that was not potentially damaging to the ship. After about an hour of maneuvering, she was prepared to make a very quick, deep penetration into the Alkayja system, normally a very aggressive approach. The other carriers that were in port at that time, at least those which were not presently in the refitting bays, had moved out into the system on courses of their own choosing and were running quietly with their shields at stealth intensity. Under other circumstances, not even another carrier would have known they were there. The Methryn's task was to find them, using her scanner, and also discover to what extent the other ships were able to identify her own location by her impulse emission traces.

"We are out of starflight," Valthyrra announced, as if there was really any need. "Scanner is at stand-by state. Ready to begin testing."

Captain Tarrel watched as best she could, although the Methryn's sharp deceleration made that difficult. She was pushing back on the arms of her seat, trying to relieve some of the crushing pressure that was thrusting her forward into the straps. A suit with a solid chestplate did a lot to distribute that stress, which felt worse at the moment than the downward pull. The carrier always kept her artificial gravity one or two G's above that of any acceleration, so that her Starwolves could continue to walk about only by the means of their tremendous strength and accurate balance.

"Any time," Gelrayen told Valthyrra.

He had returned to the main bridge and was standing behind the surveillance station, where he could observe the process on the impulse scanner's own group of monitors.

"I will supply a system schematic on the main viewscreen,"

Valthyrra told the bridge crew. "Beginning a rapid sweep of the full system."

Tarrel watched the main monitor, which showed the complete Alkayja system, ships in-system that registered on normal scan, and a scale of relative distances. Valthyrra did not have to actually sweep the entire system with a single beam, but leveled herself with the plane of the planetary orbits and fired a rapid, low-power achronic pulse with every impulse scanner along her ventral groove. This should have allowed her to see in every direction at once, with the greatest range ahead and to the sides. Instead, the scanner schematic slowly fuzzed completely out.

"Trouble?" Gelrayen asked, glancing up at her camera pod.

She rotated around to look at him. "I was completely blinded by scatter. Even the normal scanners were obscured."

The scanner image cleared slowly, then failed again as she tested the impulse scanners a second time.

"Do you know the cause?" he asked.

"No, but the fact that there was scatter from every scanner is an ominous indication that it is not simple mechanical failure. The problem was a very broad band of secondary achronic radiation, which blanked out normal and scanner receivers in a uniform wash of emissions. In other words, I could not see for the glare."

A third test gave the same results.

Commander Gelrayen was obviously displeased. "Do you have any ideas about the cause of this emission glare?"

"The first indication is that the emission coils continue to radiate uniformly across the achronic range for a brief time after the main pulse, which is emitted along the predicted tight band. This might be an extension of the problem we experienced in the bay." Even her camera pod looked bemused. "I believe that I just invented self-jamming scanners."

"The power that holds the coils at stand-by level causes the coils to emit radiation for a short time?" Gelrayen asked. "Can you predict the amount of time that the coils will continue this emission?"

"Yes, the process repeats itself very precisely each time," Valthyrra said. "I will try re-writing the firing program to cut power to the scanners for the duration of that interval."

"That was my thought exactly."

"That is an imperfect solution, since it closes down the cannon entirely for that interval," Valthyrra added. "Ready to repeat testing. This time I will engage only the main scanner."

This gave the same results, if to a lesser degree. It was still enough to leave the impulse scanner completely useless, and it still blinded the normal scanners.

"Take us back to the bay," Gelrayen told her. "The sooner that we get the experts to work on this problem, the sooner we can try again."

Lt. Commander Pesca was not in his cabin when Captain Tarrel went to check on him, and he did not return for several hours. She had wondered about him briefly during the Methryn's test run, since there were no acceleration seats in their cabins and the bunk was a poor substitute. Either the Starwolves had remembered him and taken him somewhere for safe-keeping, or else he had survived well enough and he had gone out into the ship in his quest to learn the secret Kelvessan language. Tarrel's ability to be concerned for him was limited to the hope that he would do nothing to embarrass them both.

She was busy enough herself before long. As soon as the Methryn was safely back inside her bay, the first officer Kayendel took Tarrel down to one of the carrier's workshops where automated machinery, under Valthyrra's very precise guidance, fitted armored suits. This was Tarrel's own turn to get naked, and quite a number of Starwolves came to witness that as measurements were taken for her new suit. Being career military, she was used to being undressed even in social settings; she was not used to being put on exhibition for the curiosity of four-armed aliens who used to be her mortal enemies, but she endured it gracefully. Valthyrra set the machines to work, promising to have the suit prepared by the next day.

Captain Tarrel returned to her own cabin, and was reading when Pesca did finally present himself. He looked rather worn and somewhat beaten up, as if the Methryn's test flight had been harder on him than it had been on her. She suspected that he had not been adequately protected during the accelerations.

"Are you keeping yourself out of trouble?" she asked without looking up.

"Actually, I've been looking for trouble," Pesca said. "Unfortunately, the joke was on me."

She glanced at him over the top of her book. "Didn't they warn you about the test flight?"

"Well, they did," he admitted reluctantly. "I've flown in couriers so often, I wasn't worried. I spent the first part of the test flight on the floor in various parts of the ship near the fighter bays. Then the Starwolves found me and put me in one of the fighters."

"Did you learn anything from the controls?"

He shook his head. "No, the power was completely shut down. Besides, I passed out again."

Tarrel was interested to know that he had passed out, while she had taken those stresses very much in stride. "What did you do after that? Or did the Starwolves let you sleep?"

"Actually, they took me up to the group of cabins shared by their pack," he explained. "I was hoping to have a look at the books they keep. They do keep books, but every last damned one was in Terran."

"There probably aren't enough Kelvessan in existence to justify the printing of books in their own language," she speculated. "Anything of their own would be kept in the computers, and Valthyrra Methryn has absolute control over those. At this rate, you're going to get yourself flattened in some back corridor of this ship before you learn a single word. Valthyrra Methryn wants to measure you for a suit anyway, since we didn't think to bring our own."

"Have them look in some hold where they throw their loot," Pesca complained. "They've stolen at least a dozen of everything the Union has ever made."

Tarrel was inclined to laugh. "Now, now. The Starwolves are our good friends, and the only damned thing that can save our butts. You can go back to criticizing their habits once they destroy the Dreadnought, but not one moment before."

She sent him immediately to present himself to be fitted for his suit, although he seemed curiously reluctant to go for reasons that she could not imagine, as if he considered the suit a threat aimed at him personally. But she was beginning to find his presence increasingly troubling. Since their arrival at Alkayja station, and especially since coming aboard the Methryn, Pesca was becoming increasingly suspicious and sullen. Perhaps it was only his frustration at failing to learn the Kelvessan language. The Starwolves were conspiring against him, and he knew it.

What she found alarming was the degree of his resentment, which seemed to be turning quickly to hate and paranoia. She considered once again whether it would be best to put him off the ship. The Starwolves would take him home soon enough, and he would have human company until then.

Perhaps that, she thought, was the root of his problem, something that she had even seen in the past. Some people simply reacted sharply to a prolonged stay in an all or mostly alien environment, even aliens as human in appearance and habits as the Kelvessan. Then again, she reminded herself, the Starwolves might appear far more alien to Pesca's eyes. She honestly liked them and enjoyed their company, but Pesca was still very loyal to Union ideals. He had been brought up to hate and fear Starwolves, and a sudden change of policy was not going to influence his deep-seated prejudices that quickly.

The testing of the Methryn presented Tarrel with far more interesting problems to consider, and she forgot about her companion soon enough. Dalvaen and his engineers had come back aboard the carrier the moment she settled into her bay, and they had the answer to the problem quickly enough. The supercooling of the impulse scanner emitter coils was indeed the problem, as it had been before. Just as superconductivity had caused the cannons to fire prematurely, it was also causing the crystals that those coils influenced to continue to radiate achronic signals even after the coils themselves were no longer under power. The answer was simple. The solid-state super-coolers were removed, and the power needed to fire the impulse cannons was increased to the previous level.

The Methryn was ready to go out again only a few hours later. For the purposes of this second test, she had remained isolated in her bay while the two functional carriers and the Starwolf freighter that were presently in port took themselves to separate portions of the system hidden by stealth-intensity shields. In that way, Valthyrra could not have the slightest idea of where to look for them, and her ability to locate those three ships would be entirely dependant upon the effectiveness of her impulse scanners.

The Methryn backed out of her bay, this time with much greater speed and certainty, and moved slowly into the system to begin her search. If this test was not successful, she would begin to fall behind the schedule that she had been given to keep.

If it was successful, she would not be returning to the station but would turn her long nose toward Union space. Captain Tarrel was once again at the Commander's station on the bridge, while Gelrayen watched from the surveillance station below.

"The ship is clear and away," Valthyrra reported. "No contact on normal scan. Are those ships out there?"

"They should be," Gelrayen told her. "I do not sense them, so they must have their drives shut down and their major power systems at low level."

"Pardon?" Tarrel asked, mystified, although she had not meant to ask that question out loud.

In fact, she did not know about the hyper-sensitive hearing the Starwolves enjoyed. Seated at the helm station just below, Kayendel had heard her and turned to look up over her shoulder. "We have the ability to sense the size, direction and range of drives and large conversion generators, and without the lag of real-time. It saves us the trouble of having to consult our scan when we fly. We always know where all the ships around us are, even carriers running under stealth."

"Well, you learn something every day around here," Tarrel remarked. "That must mean that you cannot sense the Dreadnought, or all of this business would be unnecessary."

"Exactly. Either its shields defeat even that, or else it uses a type of drive that we cannot sense. We had wondered if it could be a jump drive, but we are supposed to be able to sense even that."

"You would be able to sense its generators at least," Tarrel speculated. "It must be the shield."

That completely upset any hopes she might have had about the possibility of Union warships with stealth-intensity shields. The Starwolves seemed to have answers for everything, except the Dreadnought.

"We are well away from the station," Valthyrra reported. "I am ready to begin the first level of testing."

"Have at it," Gelrayen told her.

The Methryn leveled herself with the plane of planetary orbits and sent out a low-level pulse from all of her perimeter impulse scanners. A long, tense moment passed before they knew that the system schematic on the main viewscreen was not going to simply fuzz out in a backlash of radiation as it had before. Then, one by one, three additional contacts revealed themselves to the impulse scanner. One had been sitting idle, well above the planetary plane, where a perimeter scan had been expected to have trouble finding it.

"The target ships were supposed to report the moment that they detected my impulse beam," Valthyrra said.

"They have not?" Gelrayen asked.

"No, at least not yet. That might be some indication that I use a less powerful beam than the Dreadnought. Then again, once it locates a ship with a general scan, it might be locking on a tighter beam to make a more detailed identification."

"Try locking onto a single ship."

Valthyrra turned slightly, aiming the beam of her main impulse scanner at the most distant target.

"No response from target at low intensity," Valthyrra reported. "Scan indicates that this ship is a Starwolf carrier. I do get a response at medium intensity. The ship identifies herself as the carrier Baldaen."

Gelrayen looked up at her camera pod. "What do you make of that?"

"I suspect that she is trying to trick me," the ship insisted. "That scan indicates a ship that is much too light to be a carrier. There is no muffled return from contact with the heavy plate armor of the hull. I still believe that ship to be a freighter."

"Tell her that and find out what she says," he suggested.

Valthyrra paused. "She admits that she is a freighter. My interpretation of the impulse scan is accurate."

"Congratulations," Gelrayen said, and everyone seemed relieved. "Do you feel that the impulse scanner is operating efficiently enough to conclude your testing now?"

She rotated her camera pod fully toward him. "Yes, I do."

"Then contact the station and tell them that the tests have been concluded successfully, and that we will not be returning," he said. "Tell them that the Methryn is going out to hunt."

—7—

Captain Tarrel found herself again in familiar territory. The Rane Sector had borne the first series of attacks by the Dreadnought, and chances were good that the Methryn would find it there again. A Starwolf freighter, taking a patrol run to help support the limited carrier fleet, had found the Dreadnought taking apart a lesser system and had been forced to run after being fired upon from a distance. Since the Dreadnought had attacked a system two sectors over only two days earlier, there was reason to believe that it had only just changed its location according to its habit and would strike at least one more system in the immediate area before moving on. Since the Methryn had nearly crossed the gulf separating Union space from the Republic, she was actually the closest fighting ship at hand.

Because the Starwolves had no time to spend on being subtle, they were admitting to a lot of things that they probably would have otherwise wanted to have kept somewhat more secret. Given all that she had been able to infer so far, Captain Tarrel was fairly certain that she could have taken her own ship, set a course out from the Rane Sector, and found herself in Republic space in two or three weeks, even if finding Alkayja and the Starwolf base would not have been so easy. She had serious misgivings about what she should do with that information. The Starwolves were letting slip these clues for the sake of sparing her own people from the destruction of the Dreadnought as quickly as possible; they could have spent extra days to make this journey, giving the sense that the distance was greater, or swung around wide to approach from a different direction.

That left her with the uncomfortable feeling that she owed them a very great favor in return. Knowing the location, size and capabilities of the secret Starwolf base was a major tactical advantage, one that could possibly be exploited as the first step in their eventual destruction. And they knew what she could do to them with that information. But, because the Starwolves had willingly surrendered that information for the sake of protecting the Union, it seemed to her that they were due some equal consideration. At least the decision was entirely her own to make. She doubted very much that Wally Pesca could have found his way back to Starwolf space even if she had told him where to look, and he had no way of knowing much that she did.

The problem for now was finding the Dreadnought and learning some more of its secrets, which they fully intended to exploit. The Methryn changed course immediately for its last known location, increasing her speed even more to try to close the distance between herself and her enemy before it could get ahead of her. The Methryn fully expected to be engaging the Dreadnought in the next two or three days, perhaps as little as four hours if she found it still loitering in that first system.

Tarrel tended to forget that they were not actually going into battle, and that the Dreadnought, unless they were unexpectedly very lucky indeed, would not be destroyed in this round of the contest. All the Methryn proposed to do was to use her impulse scanner to learn more of the Dreadnought's secrets, its size, its power capabilities and the true nature of its drives, even if she had to present herself as a target just to get in close. In a way, it hardly seemed fair to Valthyrra Methryn. She was the newest ship in the Starwolf fleet, sleek and proud. And yet she was certain to come away damaged from this encounter, perhaps seriously, just for the hope of securing information.

Commander Gelrayen called a last tactical council on the Methryn's upper bridge, even though his group of experts was very limited in both size and experience. Janus Tarrel was there mostly on the basis that she had seen the Dreadnought more often than anyone else, human or Starwolf. Kayendel had also fought the Dreadnought, acting as helm aboard the Vardon. Valthyrra herself completed the group by rotating her camera boom into the upper bridge.

"What do you think?" Gelrayen asked her bluntly.

Valthyrra lowered her camera pod slightly. "Seriously? I believe that my objective should be to obtain as much information and sustain the least damage that I can, with information being the priority. I keep thinking that I can only play this as it comes, but I suspect that I will have to get in close to the Dreadnought and give it a sustained shot from my three forward cannons before I will see inside that shield.''

"Is there any hope of catching it by surprise?'' he asked. "Could we hit it with those cannons from a greater distance if we knew where to expect it, possibly catch it with its shields at a lower intensity? If we just found out where to find it using a very low-intensity sweep, without giving away our own presence, we could hit it with a high-intensity beam before it could react. I am thinking of our success with the last testing of the impulse scanner.''

"I haven't heard that the Dreadnought ever reduces that shield,'' Tarrel said. "Part of its advantage as a weapon is that it's able to maintain a battle-ready status at all times.''

"I fear that Captain Tarrel is correct,'' Valthyrra agreed. "All the same, I still recommend that very tactic as our initial course of action. Certainly I will find it easiest to scan the Dreadnought before it begins shooting at me. I have little hope that the sensors for the impulse scanner will survive for very long once that discharge beam begins hitting my hull.''

"Yes, there is that,'' Gelrayen agreed thoughtfully. "Then what we are facing is an engagement that will be very short in duration, simply because our own usefulness will probably deteriorate badly after the first minute or two.''

"I've seen a carrier try to engage the Dreadnought once before,'' Tarrel said. "I would give you no more time than that, once it opens fire.''

"Could we get it to chase us, now that we can keep a careful track of its location?'' Kayendel asked.

"It hasn't seemed prone to giving chase before,'' Tarrel remarked. "It moves in slowly and takes out everything within range.''

"Well, it has not been given much incentive to chase,'' the first officer pointed out. "That situation might change once it knows that our impulse scanner works. If we could maintain contact at a certain distance, we could prolong our useful time for scanning that machine and minimize the effectiveness of its weapons.''

"All the same, I would not anticipate that we could encourage it to give chase to this ship," Tarrel insisted. "Twice already it has allowed damaged carriers to move out of range, although it could have given chase and destroyed them both easily. Chasing would mean allowing itself to be distracted from its main goal. It's probably programmed against chasing."

"I have to agree with that," Valthyrra added. "Even given that we cannot predict anything absolutely, the Dreadnought's past performance gives us some indication of what we can expect. I do not expect that I could encourage it to chase me."

"You seem to have a great deal of insight into how we can and cannot deal with this thing," Kayendel remarked candidly.

Tarrel smiled. "That's my advantage as a Union captain. I'm used to having to operate from a position of disadvantage. Starwolves are not."

"Then what do you expect?" Gelrayen asked her.

"Well, you're overlooking one important fact," she began. "We already know that the Dreadnought makes routine scanner sweeps, just so that Starwolf carriers running under stealth cannot sneak up on it. The Methryn has the same stealth-intensity shields as any other carrier, so are our chances of sneaking up on it any better?"

"No," Valthyrra admitted bleakly.

"Then, if sneaking is out, you can only make a very quick approach under stealth and try to be on top of it before it has a chance to see you coming," Tarrel continued. "If you were the Dreadnought, loitering in system before or after an attack but not presently in battle, where would you be?"

Valthyrra brightened, lifting her camera pod. "I would stay in close to where the action is, or was. The inhabited planet is the focus of all traffic in and out of the system."

That really was the best course of action they had. Very much depended upon whether or not the Methryn's scanner actually could penetrate the Dreadnought's unusual shield. Although that scanner had a proven ability to receive some impressions of a Starwolf carrier running under stealth, the shields of the Dreadnought were of a much higher intensity. They had little reason to expect that this attempt would be successful. But the Starwolves needed more information on the physical structure of the Dreadnought before they could fight it, even if they had to risk an entire carrier to obtain that information.

The problem was that they were very likely to get no return for the price they were prepared to pay.

Now that they were nearly five days behind the Dreadnought, they did not expect to encounter it in this first system. All the same, the Dreadnought had demonstrated a talent for doing the unexpected, based partly upon the fact that it was more clever than they had first thought and partly because most of their other guesses had been equally limited. After the Vardon's report, they had no way of knowing if the Dreadnought might still be loitering somewhere in the system even after this amount of time. There was even the possibility that it had intercepted the communications to the Methryn and was preparing an ambush at that very moment. Theralda Vardon had certainly believed that it might already know about the Methryn's modifications, a matter that had been discussed freely through the achronic channels when they had believed the Dreadnought too stupid to notice. Valthyrra was inclined to agree.

With the possibility of battle just ahead, Captain Tarrel wanted to be prepared for a fight and the sharp accelerations that would involve well in advance. While they were still a short distance out, she returned to her own cabin to put on her armor. Valthyrra's automated equipment had completed it on schedule, exactly like the armor worn by the Starwolves except for having only one set of arms and certain structural modifications to allow for her physical differences. She was somewhat surprised to find that it had been constructed in command white, although it was the color of a ship's commander.

She was also surprised to find that Lt. Commander Pesca was in his own cabin. He was almost always off somewhere, wandering about the ship and talking with Kelvessan in the hope of learning their language. He was trying to meet every member of the crew. The Starwolves had discovered very quickly that he could not tell any of them apart. He seemed to have a bad memory for people. He would come up to each of them as if they had never met before, even if it was their third or fourth encounter, and the Starwolves would pretend to be someone different each time. If Pesca ever paid attention to such details, he would have been beginning to think that there must be four or five thousand Starwolves aboard this ship, when in fact there were hardly a thousand due to stripped ranks and the lack of any non-active personnel.

In all the years that Captain Tarrel had been fighting Star-wolves, or at least trying to avoid them, she had never anticipated their possession of such a mischievous sense of humor.

Commander Pesca looked miserable. He looked somehow like a kitten that had been left out in a cold rain, forlorn and weary and badly in need and want of comforting. Tarrel noticed that especially, not because she was able to feel any sympathy for him but because of her complete lack of pity. That was what surprised her. Since she had become a senior officer, she had always been very parental toward those who served under her, especially her junior officers. She knew that Pesca was in trouble with his obsession to learn the Kelvessan language, and that he was having a very xenophobic reaction to being trapped in alien company. He deserved pity, and yet she could not find it in herself to pity him. She realized that she had been ignoring him so far, rather than face the question of just what it was about him that bothered her. Perhaps he was simply too stupid and self-centered to develop any honest social graces, like a child who was too dull to be able to stop acting spoiled.

"Put on your armor and find yourself a safe place to ride," she told him. "The Methryn is looking for trouble."

"The Starwolves locked me on one of the escape pods," he told her.

Oh? How very clever. "The escape pods have good acceleration seats, I'm sure. I can have you put off, but probably not before this first fight."

"I'm not getting my work done," he said, a vague and rather hopeless complaint. She took that to mean that he was not ready to be put off.

"Then what's bothering you now?" she asked. "You've been in battle before. You were there aboard the Carthaginian, and the battle between the Dreadnought and the Kerridayen. You're practically an old hand at this. And the objective of this mission is to survive. The Methryn will turn away as soon as she learns everything she can. The ship will survive, whatever else that thing does to her."

"Yes, but something can go wrong," Pesca reminded her. "I just realized that I'm not ready for that. There's so much I haven't done."

"What, made a will?"

"It's not funny, Captain," he complained, then put on the

most dejected face he had. "You might laugh to hear this, Captain, but I've never . . . well, you know. I just thought I had more time, but I don't like to think that I might have lived my entire life without doing it."

Tarrel did not laugh, simply because she was not surprised. It was the old line about going into battle and being afraid to die a virgin. Either he really was a virgin and he meant this, or else he was naive enough to think that he could try such lines on his Captain. She could believe either case. "I'm sorry, Wally. There are only Starwolves aboard this ship, and I don't expect you to have any luck propositioning them."

"We're not all Starwolves on this ship," he suggested with an amusing lack of subtlety. "Since the two of us are alone among aliens, it just seems to me that we should stick together."

This time she nearly did laugh. "Wally, I have absolutely no interest in sticking to you that closely. I'll give you two warnings. First, its safer to proposition Starwolves. Second, if you don't straighten up and act like a good little trooper, I'll have you put off this ship at the first opportunity. And if you ever get familiar with me again, I'll ask the Starwolves to confine you to quarters until I can have you brought up for misconduct. Understand?"

Pesca looked pale enough to faint. "Yes, Captain."

"I'm not picking on you," she told him. "That's just the way the rules work for everyone aboard ship, although maybe it's less formal when you work behind a desk."

"Yes, Captain."

She returned to the bridge, hoping that she was not late. The armor was somewhat heavy, usually an irrelevant matter since even such weight was of no consequence to Starwolves compared to the value of added protection and durability. But it was heavy to her, and she did not want to be caught in the corridors once the Methryn began two or three extra G's of braking. She was appreciative that Commander Gelrayen was willing to surrender his seat to her, knowing that he welcomed the excuse to remain on the main bridge. He was still a pilot at heart; he wanted to be in the middle of things, not sitting on high and giving occasional directions to a ship that flew herself.

"We are ten minutes out," Valthyrra told her as she walked carefully onto the bridge, still getting used to the weight of her armor. "What about your young friend?"

"He's afraid of dying a virgin," Tarrel commented sourly.

"There is nothing wrong with virginity," the ship said. "I am a virgin, and I expect to stay one for a very long time. Monks die as virgins, and they are called holy. To be more specific, I was wondering if he is preparing himself for our transition out of starflight."

"He was when I left him. If his sense of normal caution should become overwhelmed by baser instincts, it might do him good to spend some time on the floor. Or even the wall."

"He seems to be having a hard time of it," Gelrayen said, joining them at that moment. "I have told the crew to be gentle with him. His behavior is becoming rather odd."

"I can have him put off the ship, as soon as we find someone to take him," Tarrel offered. "I think it would be better for him if he does go. He seems to be a paranoid xenophobe."

"Is he?" Kayendel looked up from her helm station. "Why would he want to become a linguist if he is afraid of aliens?"

"Some morbid fascination to the unbalanced mind, I suppose. Half of all mental health professionals I've ever met were worse off than most of their patients."

"I am bringing the ship up to full battle alert," Valthyrra announced. "We have to be ready for anything. If this is the time, then we must move very quickly and get away."

Captain Tarrel obediently hauled her armored self up the steps to the Commander's station, allowing the Starwolves to attend to their last-minute duties. She was just a little annoyed that she was unable to wear her armor with the complete disregard of the Starwolves; they made it seem easy to look grand and powerful in their suits. The armor itself was only half the weight, covering the pressure suit, pressurization equipment, and a self-contained atmosphere designed to satisfy Starwolf needs for up to ten hours using a carbon dioxide converter system and solid oxygen supplement canisters. The heating was a simple wire mesh inside the pressure suit, and cooling—a more important matter under most circumstances—was a solid state unit assisted by a micro-circulation network. The power, enough to supply auxiliary weapons or to run a companion's damaged suit, came from a self-contained total conversion generator.

Her greatest problem with the suit was getting herself into the seat at the Commander's station. In order to have the consoles with their controls, keyboards and monitors as close as possible, the station was enclosed. The seat could only be reached using the pair of bars built into the overhead console; it was a simple enough matter for a Starwolf to lift himself and his armor into that seat, even under hard accelerations, but not for her. Once she was in, her armor settled very comfortably into the seat, and the alternate set of straps attached directly to the chestplate. She set her helmet in its own rack, close at hand in case the hull lost pressure.

"Beginning deceleration from starflight," Valthyrra announced a short time later. "Six minutes to sublight transition."

Changes of speed within starflight, although actually far greater, were far less stressful than those below light speed. The reason was simple enough; matter cannot be taken past the speed of light, but the acceleration dampers let the ship cheat by never allowing its bulk anywhere near that speed. Once the ship was moving through space faster than light, its relationship with the universe was altered and changes of speed and direction resulted in a greatly reduced energy of acceleration.

"Have you been looking at the system map?" Gelrayen asked.

Valthyrra brought her camera pod around. "Let me put it up on the main viewscreen."

She cleared the current image and installed a map of the system ahead as it appeared in her library, correcting the orbits of the seven planets by mathematical interpretation and laying in her own approach path. Like most of the systems in Union space, it was moderate in population, industry and importance. But if the Dreadnought had taken it by surprise, the damage could have been devastating.

"Captain Tarrel, do you know this system?" Gelrayen asked, looking up at her.

She found the button that released the pressure on the straps and leaned forward in her seat to look down over the front of the console. "I've been here a few times, but I really don't know all that much about the system. I don't recall anything unusual."

He turned to Valthyrra, who had the advantage of knowing what every other ship had seen and filed. "Mining, both metals and hydrocarbon. The debris in this system is very rich. And there is a very large gas giant, which has two very large moons heated by gravitational stress, that have actual seas of hydrocarbons. Most of the plastics and other hydrocarbon products for the Rane Sector come out of the bulk processing plants in orbit here."

Captain Tarrel made a vile face; it helped to keep her from saying certain things out loud. She remembered this system only too well now. Those orbiting bulk processors turned raw hydrocarbons into the base material for the making not only of regular plastics but hydrocarbon-based ceramics, many other synthetic materials and a variety of solvents and combustion fuels, so that only the finished products had to be shipped out of system. The Dreadnought would have ripped apart more orbital hardware here than it would have found in any ten normal systems, and the economy of the Rane Sector could well feel the effects for a century to come.

"Captain Tarrel, you seem to recall where you are now," Valthyrra said, having witnessed her reaction.

"I do indeed," she agreed. "You just don't think about such places as being that important until you realize what will happen when they're gone."

"It could be even worse," Valthyrra said. "My files indicate that two million people lived in orbit here. That is the reason why Starwolf attacks have been so selective here for centuries."

"I doubt that any of them got to safety," Tarrel said, settling her armor back into the seat. "The facilities for rapid evacuation just aren't there. Station life is so completely free from hazard."

Valthyrra called their attention back to the viewscreen. "If that is the case, then we must expect that major attacks took place on the second planet, the only inhabited world in this system, and at the stations on the moons of the fourth and fifth planet. This was a very slow-firing star in its early development, allowing gas giants to form close in, where lighter gasses are generally swept farther out by solar wind. Some two-thirds of the orbital facilities were located around the fourth planet, which had larger moons and warmer conditions as well as relative proximity to a belt of debris very rich in rare elements."

"What about the inhabited planet?" Gelrayen asked.

"Very little interstellar traffic was going in and out of there," the ship explained. "There was quite a lot of specialty manufacturing, but most of that went out to the stations for shipment out of system. Most of the planet was colonized to feed the stations. As large as stations can be, it is still much easier and cheaper to farm planet-side."

"And what if it is still in system?" Gelrayen asked. "If you were the Dreadnought, where would you be?"

"We have discussed the subject once already," Valthyrra answered. "As it happens, that is more difficult to predict. Most of the system traffic and a large portion of the orbital hardware was at the fourth planet. We must now assume that those stations are gone and the personnel dead. A rescue mission is probably expected to press on to the only place where there is still anyone alive, the second planet."

"Is that what the Dreadnought will decide?" he asked.

She made a curiously hopeless gesture with her camera pod. "I do not know what the Dreadnought will think. That depends very much upon the level of sophistication of its ability to plan, and we know now that we cannot predict that. If the stations and all traffic in-system was destroyed, then it would probably look to the inhabited planet. There would still be power sources there to draw its attention, if not its fire."

"Commander," Tarrel called to him. "Will you have any back-up on this? I know that a Starwolf freighter has been here once before."

"Yes, another carrier arrived several hours ago and is standing by some distance outside the system."

"And what about that freighter?" Tarrel asked. "Even if the Dreadnought has not been—or no longer can—follow your transmissions, would the presence of a Starwolf ship in this system encourage it to go into hiding in the hope of ambushing another?"

"Yes, that is a valid concern," he agreed. "Until you brought that up, I had been very certain that we would not find the Dreadnought here. Now I am given to wonder."

They could speculate on that matter for a long time, but the moment came at last when the Methryn had to take herself out of starflight. Guided by their discussion, she dropped down from starflight well inside the system, using a minimum of power to brake below threshold and then coasting at nearly light speed. The carrier was running with her shields at stealth intensity and her normal scanners were silent, containing any emissions that might have betrayed her presence. She cautiously began a quick, very low-intensity sweep with her impulse scanner.

"No contact on first sweep," she announced to the bridge crew. "Scanner sweep did indicate a great deal of debris, including some very large pieces, above the fourth and fifth planets. There are also some two dozen intact and functional ships in this system, mostly of Union military class. It seems that we are not the first to arrive.''

"The Dreadnought might still be hiding somewhere," Gelrayen cautioned her. "Continue your sweeps at a higher level."

Valthyrra Methryn needed only a few minutes more to feel very certain that the Dreadnought was no longer in this system. Her own impulse scanners had detected nothing, and she had registered no contact by an impulse beam from any other ship. The Union fleet was involved in some indeterminate work in the wreckage above the fourth planet, unaware even yet of Methryn's presence. Since there was no indication of danger, Valthyrra suggested that they have a brief word with the Union forces before they continued their hunt for their enemy.

The Methryn settled silently into orbit over the massive gas giant, after a brief run back into starflight followed by a sharp braking maneuver that left Captain Tarrel rather breathless in spite of the suit's greater protection. Valthyrra kept her shields at stealth intensity, wanting to see what the Union fleet was doing before they knew that she was about. Old Starwolf habits that were not even her own kept her cautious.

She moved in very quietly behind the largest area of debris where almost all of the Union ships were engaged in, as far as she could tell, mapping and cataloging the pieces of wreckage. It seemed like the silly, pointless sort of thing that the Union would consider very important in a crisis. But that debris was more interesting than she would have guessed, and it soon demanded her full attention. In the past, the Dreadnought had been very thorough in making certain that anything it destroyed was ripped to pieces, but some of these sections of station and factory components were still very large. A few were larger than herself, and scores of sections were as large as any Union battleship or bulk freighter, two or three hundred meters across. There was, however, no question of survivors in that wreckage. Every section was torn and twisted, and burnt black by tremendous discharges of power. The fact that there were no bodies drifting in space was an ominous indication of what had happened to anything organic caught in the storm of energy that had raged through these stations.

"Another change of tactic," Valthyrra reported. "The Dreadnought was in a hurry. It killed, but it did not take the time to obliterate."

"It might have been overwhelmed by the very volume," Tarrel suggested. "It would have taken hours to have eaten these stations bite by bite, the way it did the first time we met. Just destroying the first completely would have given them the time to evacuate all the other stations and get every ship out of system."

"When it attacked the Vardon, it seemed to lack any awareness of tactical priorities," Valthyrra reminded them. "Does it seem to you that this monster is getting smarter?"

"Actually smarter, as opposed to simply showing us more of its abilities?" Gelrayen asked.

"Exactly," the ship agreed. "I am reminded of myself, sixty years ago when I was first brought on line. I was dull, remote, and completely unaware of anything going on around me except my programmed function. I was aware of myself, but I did not even know what that meant. It was the need to be able to do the things required of me that forced my development."

Gelrayen considered that for a brief moment. "Are you suggesting that the Dreadnought is a child, or perhaps a weapon that had never been activated until it drifted into the Union and the presence of ships and stations triggered an automated response to attack? Then it actually would be becoming smarter as it learned how to plan."

"That might well be," Valthyrra agreed. "Or perhaps it was simply shut down to dormant levels for so long that it has needed time to remember how to think and plan for itself. Very much would depend upon how old it actually is. Our suspicion is that it is ancient because we have no idea who built it, and that it has been bounding around space for a very long time. It might also be very new. I remind you that the Union does not explore outside its own territory, and the Starwolves never have the time."

They watched the main viewscreen for a moment as the Methryn moved slowly through the wreckage. Blackened and battered pieces of metal hundreds of meters across drifted past, most of them rolling in an oddly calm, stately manner from the impetus of the force that had ripped them apart. Gelrayen walked over to stand beside Kayendel at the helm station, then looked up at the camera pod.

"What are your thoughts on the subject?" he asked.

"I believe that it was a mistake not to seek the advice of the Aldessan of Valtrys when this affair first began," Valthyrra answered without hesitation. "They might very well know who built this machine, and how to shut it down. But the ships were not consulted."

Captain Tarrel smiled to herself, impressed with the censure that the ship was able to convey in her words. Valthyrra Methryn was probably very correct in her belief that development in a sentient machine corresponded to need. She was coming along very smartly.

They came upon the first Union ship suddenly, a small cruiser drifting alongside one of the larger pieces of station wreckage. It had actually been facing away at first, but it reversed itself very quickly in what certainly seemed to be a very startled gesture. Tarrel was given to wonder if its very aggressive stance was as obvious to the Starwolves as it was to her. She could understand the alarm of the little ship's captain, suddenly finding himself nose to nose with the largest and most deadly ship that he had ever seen, and why he continued to respond to what he perceived to be a threat.

"Valthyrra, do you still have your shields at stealth intensity?" she demanded.

"Of course. I consider that to be a correct response to a situation that is possibly threatening, and I wondered what they were doing."

"I would suppose that they're probing the wreckage at close-range scan for survivors," Tarrel told her. "You forget that human instruments are nowhere near accurate as your own. And you had better make contact with the Fleet Commander before you do have a threatening situation you never intended on your hands. That cruiser is about to fire at you."

"The Fleet Captain's battleship is approaching now," Valthyrra said. "In fact, I am being surrounded by no less than two dozen ships."

"Then I suggest that you begin talking very politely."

"Can I just shoot them?" the ship asked. "I have never shot anyone in all my life."

"Valthyrra, behave yourself," Gelrayen warned. "This is serious. Stand ready to run if things turn nasty."

"I am not certain that I have room to run, with all of this debris. I should probably just put up my best shields and push my way through." She paused. "I have an audio-only channel with the Fleet Captain."

"This is Fleet Captain Cullan," he began, proud and belligerent. "I demand to know your business here."

"This is the Starwolf carrier Methryn. I have been fitted with a special scanning device and I am following the Dreadnought in an attempt to learn some way of fighting it."

"You damned murderers don't fool us," Cullan shouted back. "We know that you're behind these attacks. This is all some great plan of yours, wrecking our systems and pretending to be chasing some great, invisible enemy. Some of us have decided to do something about this, and we might as well start with you."

"I am sending the packs to the bays," Valthyrra announced privately before returning to her communication. "Captain Cullan, you are badly mistaken on three important points. First, the Starwolves are not behind these attacks, and there really is a Dreadnought. Second, if we had wanted to destroy you in this way, we could have done so at any time. We do not need sneaky plans. Third, you do not have the firepower to confront me. If you do not get out of my way immediately, I will release my packs."

Captain Tarrel rolled her eyes. "Valthyrra Methryn, you are the very soul of discretion and tact."

"It is good to know that I have a soul," she responded, turning her camera pod. "Starwolf rule number one. No one threatens a Starwolf and gets away with it."

"Then will you get me a visual channel and let me handle this in my own way?"

Valthyrra turned her camera pod to Gelrayen, who nodded. Captain Cullan came up on the main monitor of the Commander's station a few moments later. He looked exactly like Tarrel had expected, arch-conservative traditionalist, old and thin and going through life looking as if he had just eaten his shaving cream and could not get the taste out of his mouth. Sector Command tried not to promote these types to captain warships; they believed their own propaganda and were too prone to make egotistical decisions in the field that cost the Union dear. Which was what was about to happen here.

"Captain Cullan, this is Captain Janus Tarrel," she began quickly, giving him no chance to talk. "I am the Union's special diplomatic envoy and military advisor to the Starwolves. I carry a special diplomatic pass and I am calling upon you to honor it or face immediate charges of insubordination and high treason. You are employing Union warships against direct orders."

"The very soul of discretion and tact," Valthyrra remarked softly.

"You seem to have gotten very cozy with your Starwolf friends in a hurry," Cullan observed disdainfully, noticing her armor.

"You either wear the best protection you can get on this ship or you end up plastered to a wall," she answered. "I can tell you beyond any doubt that there is a Dreadnought, and that it is not a Starwolf weapon. I've fought the Dreadnought twice myself, and I was aboard the carrier Kerridayen when she fought it and was severely damaged. I've seen Starwolf carriers with their hulls ripped to shreds from trying to fight that thing. And now this ship is going out to draw its fire in the hope of finding a way to fight it."

"I have no way of knowing that I can trust you," Cullan responded, although he no longer seemed quite so sure of himself.

"Yes, you do," Tarrel insisted. "Every ship's captain and System Commander has been told who I am. You know damned well what your orders are. You and your friends aren't as smart as you seem to think, because you don't know what's really going on. You've already bought yourself a court martial, since I am going to report this. Right now, I'm trying to save your damned life."

Captain Cullan suddenly looked very surprised and turned away after muting the channel, leaving Tarrel to wait.

"Tactical re-enforcement," Valthyrra reported. "They were keeping most of their ships behind us, away from my forward battery. The carrier Maeridan just moved in behind them. Discretion and tact were losing ground."

"You have to hit an idiot like that right between the eyes or he doesn't even hear you talking," Tarrel commented sourly.

"We are in no danger," the ship insisted. "They carry a light compliment of very ordinary weapons, and my defensive battle shields can turn aside anything they have to throw at me. If they do attack, I will simply push through them."

She shook her head impatiently. "Cullan has not attacked, and he has not returned to his monitor. I believe that he has just collapsed into complete indecision. Let's make the decision for him and push on out of here very slowly.''

''That sounds fair to me,'' Gelrayen agreed.

The Methryn turned toward an opening through the wreckage and the smaller ships surrounding her, then began to move forward slowly with her running lights engaged. It was a move that was as bold as it was casual in appearance. Captain Tarrel had guessed right, knowing her own people better than the Starwolves or their ships ever could. Whatever Captain Cullan and his cronies had been telling themselves, she had been certain that most of the junior captains were not as willing to believe Cullan's rather simplistic conspiracy theory. They were certainly hesitant to join in deliberate mutiny on such an insubstantial excuse.

''We are free and clear to run,'' Valthyrra reported. ''I am taking the ship out of orbit and beginning the climb to threshold. We might as well press on to our next projected target system.''

''Yes, we should stay on top of it,'' Gelrayen agreed. ''Is the Maeridan away as well?''

''Right behind us.'' Valthyrra brought her camera pod closer. ''Khallenda Maeridan wants to follow us. She says that she will stay well out of system while we do our work, but she would still be there to come running if we got into trouble. I can even share impulse scanner images with her. After she corrects the image from her own perspective, she will see as well as we can.''

''If you both like the idea, then I agree,'' Gelrayen said as he ascended the steps to the upper bridge. ''Captain, we owe you something for that.''

Tarrel shook her head. ''I should have warned you when I heard that our ships were in the system. We've been at war for so long that suspicion of Starwolves has become almost an instinct. Hell, my first job was to make sure that the new threat wasn't Starwolves. Small minds are going to react to their fears.''

''Well, I hope that is the end of it,'' Valthyrra said as she brought her camera pod into the upper bridge. ''I would hate to think that the first enemy I ever engaged was the wrong one.''

—8—

The Methryn dropped out of starflight well inside the system, keeping her speed nearly to that of light, in a manner that was becoming standard in the task of stalking the Dreadnought. The only difference was that this time she expected to find it. Unless it had broken its latest pattern and moved on to its next target, or had moved at random, then it had attacked this system the day before and was still lurking about to see what else might show up. If it indeed was waiting here, then Valthyrra Methryn knew that it would sweep space at unpredictable intervals, looking for Starwolf carriers like herself that were running under stealth. She had to find it before it found her.

On the Methryn's bridge, the tension was like a storm threatening to break at any moment. Captain Tarrel was again at the Commander's station on the upper bridge, watching the preparation for battle with the calm objectivity of an observer. The Starwolves were all experienced and professional; they knew what to expect and what was expected of them. The concern was for the ship herself, for they knew beyond any doubt that the Methryn would certainly take a beating in the coming battle. Tarrel wondered if, like herself, they were worried whether Valthyrra Methryn was ready for this battle. The ship was like a half-grown child, sometimes very mature and complex, sometimes uncertain and fearful, occasionally sullen or defensive. She had handled the situation with the Union fleet well enough, but that had involved an enemy she had no reason to fear. The Dreadnought had a proven ability to hurt her, and there was no way to predict how she would react when she was actually fired upon.

When the time came, Valthyrra would have to be calm, clever, and brave; qualities that she had never had to demonstrate in her life.

She tried a new tactic, one that she had discussed with her Commander and Helm as a suitable alternative for her present situation. Taking the risk that she could slip in during the interval between the Dreadnought's routine sweeps, she kept her impulse scanners silent as she made a quick run toward one of the larger planets in the system. She began braking fairly hard at the last moment, knowing what the stress was doing to her human passengers, and began her first low-intensity scanner sweep just as she was looping in for a tight orbit. Then she swung abruptly out from the planet, engaging her main drives until she had matched speed for a more or less synchronous orbit.

"Contact," she announced. "The Dreadnought is here, sitting off a short distance from the inhabited third planet. I have moved quickly to place this gas giant between it and myself. I have detected no impulse scanner contact so far."

"Do you suppose it did not detect your own sweep?" Gelrayen asked.

"If it had, I believe that it would have reacted immediately with a sweep of its own." She rotated her camera pod to glance into the upper bridge. "Commander, will you attend to Captain Tarrel? She was not able to stay with us through that braking."

"What did you pull, twelve G's?" he asked as he hurried up the steps.

"Fifteen. Telemetry from her suit indicated that she went under fairly early on, so I took advantage of the situation."

Captain Tarrel had passed out in her seat, which had been inclined about halfway in anticipation of this event. For the same reason, the supply of drugs that had been selected was close at hand. Now that they had found the Dreadnought, she could be given the drugs used by the Union that gave humans a higher tolerance to stress, allowing them to recover almost immediately if they did pass out. For the moment, simple smelling salts brought her back instantly.

"Vile stuff. Take it away," Tarrel commented, making a face. "How goes the war?"

"Valthyrra found the Dreadnought," he told her, giving her the additional drugs. "It apparently did not sense her scanner pulse, and she was able to put the planet between us before it could discover us. We are waiting now to begin our next move, once we know what to do. Any ideas?"

"Based upon past experience, run like hell comes immediately to mind. The trouble is that hiding from the Dreadnought does us absolutely no good, beyond offering the chance to choose our own time and method of acting. Is there any way to sneak in closer before it knows that we're here?"

"There is none that I can envision," Valthyrra said, bringing her camera pod well back into the upper bridge. Kayendel had joined them as well.

"Two thoughts come to mind," Tarrel mused. "We do something that hints of our presence without giving it away absolutely, and then we see if we can lure the Dreadnought into coming here. Or we can use the Maeridan as bait. If the Dreadnought chases her, we might be able to slip in behind. Is she blind to the rear, I wonder?"

"I am not," Valthyrra said. "I would not expect that plan to work. I would have to use my impulse scanner to track its position, and it will become aware of that too soon."

"Then we should bring it here," Kayendel declared. "Valthyrra, correct me if I am wrong. Like most gas giants, this one probably has a very large and powerful magnetic field, which serves to hold in an invisible cloud of ionized particles that will interact with a ship's shields and cause stealth to become ineffective."

"Yes, I have already dropped my own outer shields altogether," Valthyrra agreed. "I was looking like a distant thunderstorm with all that discharge over the shell. Anticipating the point of your question, the answer to that part is also yes. If the Dreadnought comes through here, we will be able to see it from static discharge even if the ship itself remains invisible. That probably offers the best chance we will ever have to get an extremely short-range scan."

"Before it turns around and kicks our ass," Tarrel added. "The only real alternative is to wait for it to make a regular scanner sweep and then move in on it quickly. But that doesn't work, does it?"

"If we detect the sweep, then the sweep detects us," Valthyrra agreed.

"The other plan is best," Gelrayen agreed. "What do we need to do?"

Valthyrra was already considering that. "Supplying the bait should be simple enough. I will simply have one of my drones hide itself on a small moon and begin making random achronic noise. The Dreadnought will have to come here to see what it is, something that it can only destroy at very close range. The only real problem is hiding myself. Where does a fifteen-million-ton fighting ship hide itself?"

"Anywhere it wants?" Captain Tarrel asked innocently.

"Cute."

A solution to the second problem presented itself very quickly. Once Valthyrra had a look about with a very short-range scan, she was able to find any number of small shepherding moons in the gas giant's band of rings. One of these moons, an irregular rock about twenty kilometers across, had a very convenient hole like a very deep impact crater that was just the right shape to hold a Starwolf carrier. Her construction bay at Alkayja station had been smaller. The Methryn was able to back into this, ready to move forward just enough to expose her main battery and her sensitive forward scanner array. The moonlet did posses a trace of gravity, just enough to pull the carrier slowly to her left. Since the rate of fall was only about a tenth of a meter every minute, her field drive was able to counteract that pull.

A drone was prepared and sent on its way to a much larger moon just outside the disk of the ring, at present less than ten thousand kilometers away. By the standards of the Methryn's scanner, that was very short range indeed. Better yet, the most direct approach path between that moon and the Dreadnought's present position lay only three thousand kilometers out from the Methryn's cubby hole. Valthyrra hoped that static discharge against that very high-power shield would give away its position as it passed through.

"Something about this situation bothers me," Captain Tarrel commented. "This entire plan seems very unorthodox."

"The stupid idea is a favorite Starwolf tactic," Gelrayen told her. "When nothing else works, try something stupid. You always surprise your enemies, and you often surprise yourself."

"I'm beginning to understand why you people were never able to win the damned war."

"My drone has begun its first series of broadcasts," Valthyrra reported. "It is repeating a brief sequence on a low-power signal, very much like a transponder or a distress beacon. In fact, I have it using Starwolf codes. If the Dreadnought knows our language, as certain of my siblings have suggested, then it should find that bait irresistible."

"I thought that you were going to be more subtle," Gelrayen said, looking up at her camera pod. "Just random achronic signals."

"The Dreadnought is in the business of breaking things, and random signals would already sound broken. It has destroyed a small mining station in these moons already, and it might think that a transponder came from that wreckage. This is designed to look like a surveillance drone trying to transmit data out of system using the gas giant as a shield."

Captain Tarrel leaned back in her seat. "Now I get the feeling that you're trying to get this complicated."

The camera pod rotated quickly. "I am trying to be subtle. In my experience, subtle and complicated look very much alike."

"The logic aboard this ship is amazing," Tarrel said, and sighed. "If it thinks it knows what it is, won't it just leave the thing alone and see what happens? If it looks like it belongs to Starwolves, a Starwolf might come along and claim it."

"Oh, I never thought of that." The camera pod dropped slowly, then lifted brightly. "Well, I still believe that it will work. The Dreadnought will have to be curious. What else does it have to do with its time?"

"Oh, that's logic again! It's a machine. It has an untapped bounty of machine patience."

"I'm a machine, and I can be very impatient."

Tarrel had to think about that for a moment. "You know, I suspect that you've just invented a trap for catching yourself. What are you going to do if this doesn't work?"

"Something else."

It took a while, but Captain Tarrel finally realized that she was being teased by a machine. Unfortunately, that thought did not occur to her for another three days. It amused Valthyrra to play harmless games of subtlety with Tarrel, who obviously doubted her ability to be clever.

"Passive scanner contact," Valthyrra warned, again very serious. "I have identified static discharge against a high-power shield approaching from six thousand kilometers. No visual contact with any ship."

"Is it the Dreadnought?" Gelrayen asked.

"Well, that is the only invisible ship I know. It is definitely moving toward the drone."

"How did it get here so quickly?"

"I have three theories about that," Valthyrra offered. "It might have been built to handle routine accelerations of two or three thousand G's, or else it might employ some type of drive that either negates or avoids all energy of acceleration. Or it might have become aware of the drives from that unshielded drone the moment it left my bay, and has been under way to this location for some time."

"Warn the crew to prepare for immediate battle," Gelrayen told her. "Have damage control parties standing by throughout the ship. Surveillance?"

"Impulse scanners and passive receivers standing by."

"Weapons?"

"All power is diverted to the main battery," the weapons officer on the middle bridge responded. "Conversion cannon is at pre-stage warming."

"Helm?"

"Manual controls are at stand-by status," Kayendel reported.

"Captain Tarrel?" he asked, glancing toward the upper bridge.

"I'm counting all the ways that things can go wrong," she answered as she tightened the straps. "Standing by to pass out."

"Your confidence is reassuring. Valthyrra, do you have visual contact of any form?"

She responded by sending a highly magnified image to the main viewscreen, although the only thing it showed was a light shower of minute sparks as the Dreadnought's shield reacted with ionized particles charged by the gas giant's magnetic field. But at least they had direct visual evidence of its presence, and not just in that discharge of sparks. The Dreadnought itself, or rather the light-absorbing cloak of its powerful shield, appeared as a vast black shape passing before the stars. It was a curiously frightening vision, for Captain Tarrel even more so than those times when she had not been able to see it at all, like the shadow of a ghost.

"The Dreadnought is at closest approach," Valthyrra reported. Even she spoke softly, as if fearful of being overheard. "No scanner contact yet, so I assume that it is not aware of my presence. Stand ready."

"Whenever you think best," Gelrayen told her.

Valthyrra moved out of her hiding place on the moonlet, rushing forward with a quiet, steady acceleration from her main drives. At these distances, relatively small increases in speed covered a great deal of distance in a hurry. The carrier moved in a sweeping, graceful glide, actually meant to minimize her reliance upon field drive for navigation.

"I will probably have only the one chance, so I should make the most of it," she reported. "I am going to throw as much power as I can into a forward impulse sweep."

Being in the shadow of the planet was a mixed blessing. It was essential to her decoy and it allowed her to see the fairly small flashes of discharge against the Dreadnought's shield. On the illuminated side of the planet, she would have been able to track the Dreadnought with far greater accuracy as its black shadow passed over the bright bands of the gas giant. At least she could locate it easily enough by the discharge flashes of its shield. She had not warned the others that she had actually not been completely certain that there would be any visible static discharge, knowing that it might have been absorbed into that light-eating shield.

She dropped in quickly behind the Dreadnought, then moved cautiously forward until she followed at only fifteen kilometers, five times her length and only slightly more than its own. As far as she knew, this was as close as anyone had ever come to the Dreadnought. Even at this range, all she could see was a featureless black shape passing before the stars. One portion of her multi-layered mind was aware that at some point in the next minute or two, that vast machine was going to turn and begin ripping her apart. She was new, still bright and shiny, and she did not want to submit herself to the damage she expected to take. But the rest of her mind was very much on business, aware that her time was very limited. She aimed every impulse cannon that could be brought to bear and fired, standing ready with her primary attention to the scanner receivers, her main drives and defensive systems, and a very close electronic eye she kept on the Dreadnought's response.

"I have the results of my first close-range impulse scan," Valthyrra said. "Nothing. Absolutely nothing. I cannot see through that shield. I would have to be able to match frequencies to get a scanner beam through, and I cannot do that at random."

"Well, we expected that," Gelrayen remarked, then looked up. "Hold on. Are we running like hell?"

"No, the stupid thing still has no idea that I am here. I wonder if it really is blind to the rear. It seems like such a waste, sitting here right on the monster's tail and not able to do anything about it."

"We could try shooting it, I suppose," Gelrayen mused. "What would happen if we gave it our conversion cannon at this range?"

"It would probably do it no more harm than when the Kerridayen shot it at somewhat longer range, considering that shield," the ship replied. "But the backwash would, however, fry us."

"Yes, I had forgotten about that. Stupid idea."

"I thought Starwolves like stupid ideas," Tarrel called from the upper bridge.

Gelrayen glanced in her direction. "We have to draw the line somewhere."

"Would anyone want to listen to a good idea?" Kayendel asked. "Since we seem to have the time, what about keeping an impulse beam on that shield and changing frequencies rapidly until you have a match?"

"That might just work, if I can find that frequency before the Dreadnought turns around and kicks me in the nose," Valthyrra agreed. "Even if I get through that shield, I will probably only get a moment at best . . . Hold on."

"Trouble?" Gelrayen asked, noticing that the Methryn still had not run.

"Someone is shooting at the Dreadnought, and it is not me."

Actually, it was not particularly hard to figure out just what was going on. Her passive scanners did not detect the approach of any ship, just a series of high-power bolts just like those from her own forward battery. The shots were actually going somewhat wide. It was, of course, the Maeridan, but she was still too distant to target accurately on the visual reference of the black shape of the Dreadnought's cloaking shield moving over the brightly colored bands of the gas giant. A hail of short-duration bolts was coming down at random over a radius of about twenty kilometers. Valthyrra was faced with the need to consider raising her own battle shields to protect herself from her own sister ship. Like the Maeridan, she had her own outer shields at stealth intensity, so that the other carrier would have been able to locate her only by visual identification, and her dull black hull was designed to defeat that. Considering how relatively tiny she was compared to the Dreadnought, she could easily be overlooked.

"What the hell does Khallenda Maeridan think that she is doing?" Valthyrra asked herself. "She was supposed to keep herself hidden unless I found myself in serious trouble."

"She probably thinks that you are," Kayendel reminded her. "I suspect that you must have set that drone to broadcast a Starwolf distress code. Your own, no doubt."

Valthyrra rotated her camera pod to look at the ceiling. "Damn my hull! Of course. I forgot that she was sitting out there waiting, and I did not think to warn her to ignore that distress code. She is trying to rescue me, and that drone led her right here."

"None of us thought of that," Gelrayen told her. "Do not blame yourself."

"I have just received scanner return," Valthyrra reported, returning to business. "The Dreadnought has just taken the Maeridan's range by scan. I do not believe that it is aware of me, since I detected no direct scanner pulses aimed in my direction."

"If you try to warn the Maeridan, you will give away your own position," Gelrayen warned her. "Do you want to try backing away from that monstrosity first?"

"No, I like it best right where I am."

The Dreadnought opened fire on the Maeridan, although it seemed to be having some trouble getting the carrier's range by impulse scan alone. It was firing a series of sustained bolts of moderate power, obviously hoping to lock with the carrier's shields and force an overload that would cause the carrier to lose her stealth capabilities. The Maeridan was responding by throwing everything she had in the direction of the Dreadnought, making herself an easy and obnoxious target. Her intention, no doubt, was to give a damaged Methryn a few moments to collect herself and get to safety any way she could.

Of course, Valthyrra Methryn was alive, well and ready to employ one of those complicated plans that so annoyed Captain Tarrel. She opened fire with all sixteen of the larger cannons in her forward battery, directly into the back of the Dreadnought's shield. She could not hope to do any damage. Rather than the usual short, rapid bursts from her cannon, she maintained a steady fire as she tried to match frequencies with that shield, each cannon searching a different band of frequencies. Long seconds passed, and with each instant she feared that the Dreadnought would discover her before her experiment proved itself. Then one of the cannons found the right frequency and penetrated the shield. In only a fraction of a second she had matched the frequencies of all the other cannons with the first, and she poured all the raw power she could channel inside that shield.

The result was spectacular. The Dreadnought's shield collapsed in a sudden, blinding flash, and for a single long moment the immense machine stood fully revealed before them, obscured somewhat in the flare as the Methryn's powerful cannons continued to rip across its bulk. Surprisingly, its hull did not seem to be a massively armored shell like that of a carrier, as they would have expected, but a maze of machinery of tremendous size. If her conversion cannon had been ready, even at partial power, she could have destroyed it at that very moment. The Dreadnought began to turn slowly and then that black shield was up again, locking out the Methryn's destructive beams and cloaking the alien weapon in the blackness of space.

Valthyrra knew when it was time to leave, and this was certainly the time. She pivoted herself about sharply until she was facing back the way she had come, then engaged her main drives in a single, sharp burst of speed. But the drives failed after only the first instant, leaving her drifting at a speed that was not taking her away from her enemy fast enough.

Valthyrra was so surprised by that sudden loss of power that she brought her camera boom up sharply, cracking the pod against the ceiling. "*Rashah ko ve'ernon! Val traron de altrys caldarson!*"

If she had been able, Captain Tarrel would have taken notes for Walter Pesca's language lessons.

"Are we hit?" Gelrayen asked anxiously.

"No, damn it all," the ship snapped, cursing in Terran now. "I just ran out of fuel."

"*Varth!*" Gelrayen exclaimed. "Valthyrra, you happen to be a new ship. You could not have run your entire supply of water through your conversion generators in just the last few days."

"No, I have twenty tons of distilled water in my main tanks," the ship said. "Unfortunately, no one back at the station ever thought to switch me over from my reserve tank to the main line. Right now, all I have is just enough power to hold my shields at stealth intensity for a few minutes more, and some field drive maneuvering left over. The line has to be switched manually. It is not something I can do for myself.''

"Oh, this really is stupid," he commented, then turned to the engineering officer. "Gheldyn, do you know where to find this reserve tank and switch the line over?"

"Yes, I believe that I do," she answered, with slight uncertainty.

"I will deliver your lift as close as possible, then talk you through it over your suit com," Valthyrra told her, and Gheldyn hurried to the waiting lift.

"Val, this is going to take time," Gelrayen reminded her. "What do you propose to do with yourself until then? Can you call the Maeridan back to cover us?"

Valthyrra brought her camera pod back around. "No, I sent her away. For some reason, the Dreadnought has not attempted to open fire or even to track me by impulse scanner. I might have hurt it more than I thought, or else it has some programmed priority to secure any damage before continuing to fight. I can still see its shadow following my original escape path. It has not yet noticed my change of course."

"Well, where are you going now? We seem to be descending back into the ring."

"I am taking us back to that moonlet where we were. I intend to back myself into that cubby and sit there until I have full power."

Commander Gelrayen did not have to think about that for very long. "Val, is that really a good idea?"

"No, but it is the best idea we have."

Whether it was a good idea, a bad idea, or just, plain stupid, this was what Valthyrra intended to do. It seemed like a long-term solution to what sounded like a fairly simple problem, but no one felt like taking her to task over the matter. Her plans seemed complex, unorthodox and rather extreme, as Captain Tarrel had pointed out, but they did work fairly well. She had taken on the Dreadnought and actually seemed to have gotten the better of the argument, and she was the only carrier who'd managed that. It was hard to fault her after that.

She was still able to track the Dreadnought as its shadow passed over the stars and minute sparks discharged against its shield, which led her to wonder why, with a very large and colorful planet just below, it did not see her own black hull. Of course, both ships were right on the very edge of the plane of the ring. Her shape might not have been quite as obvious as it passed just above that clutter. Then she realized that the Dreadnought was blind. That shield swallowed light, so there was nothing coming through for visual identification. The only thing it seemed to have was its impulse scanner, and yet she knew that it employed that only at rare intervals. It had to be using some type of common scanner, passive and active, although less effective than her own because of the difficulties of seeing through that shield. It had not used impulse scan since her attack, which led her to wonder if she had damaged it more than she would have expected.

She reached the moonlet, braking very gently with her field drive, both to spare her very limited power resources and to avoid detection as the Dreadnought passed only sixteen hundred kilometers above her. As it happened, both ships were actually moving opposite the orbit of the planet, so that the use of braking thrust actually increased the Methryn's speed to match that of the moonlet.

"Gheldyn reporting," said the chief engineering officer. Valthyrra kept the message on bridge audio so that the others could hear.

"What do you have?" Valthyrra asked.

"A problem. All of the tubes are here, but the actual line leading from the main tanks to the pump, and the distribution grid to the ship's conversion generators was never built. I have several hours of work here, if I try to do it myself. Perhaps half an hour or less if you send me an engineering team to assist. I could certainly use another pair of hands."

"Where would you keep them," Tarrel asked quietly, finding the thought amusing even under the circumstances.

"I anticipated the need, and a damage control team will be there to assist you any moment now."

"I will be as quick as I can," Gheldyn promised.

"Did you know that line was not completed?" Gelrayen asked.

Valthyrra brought her camera pod around. "I knew that it would have been done in the last few hours before my launch, and I do not recall it happening. Considering our situation, I had good reason to suspect that it might not be. Anticipating the other part of your question, that is also why I wanted some place where I could hide for some time."

They noticed then that Captain Tarrel was easing herself down the steps from the upper bridge. The actual weight of the armor was less a problem to her than the fact that she found it more awkward then she had expected, at least descending the steps when she could not see where she was going. Once on level ground, she was able to carry herself fairly well.

"Do you feel safe?" Gelrayen asked.

"I was given to understand that this ship could not generate the power to send herself anywhere if she had to," Tarrel answered. "I thought that I had better move about a little while I can. And I'm dying of curiosity. What did you do to the Dreadnought? I was blinking too much to see anything."

"It lost its shield for a moment when my cannons matched frequency and were able to penetrate," Valthyrra said. "That serves as an important lesson on the virtue of stupid ideas. It was a risk, but it worked. If I had had power for my conversion cannon, and a little more time, I could have destroyed it."

"Remind me never to play cards with any of you people," Tarrel commented. "The gods smile upon fools and Starwolves with stupid ideas."

"They also play their little tricks," Gelrayen added. "Valthyrra, I hope that you were able to record what you saw."

"I did get a good contour scan of what I could see, which was unfortunately only about twenty percent of the Dreadnought's total area," she answered. "The fact that it began to swing around before the shield went back up was the only thing that allowed me to see more than just its tail end."

"I could sense its conversion generators while that shield was down," Gelrayen said. "Apparently the shield itself is able to suppress even that psychic response."

"Psychic? Are you trying to tell me that you Starwolves are mind-readers? I had assumed that your ability to sense high-power systems was a function comparable to ordinary scanner." She paused a moment, thinking about the matter carefully. "No, pardon my skepticism, which was misplaced. Nothing you could tell me about Starwolves would ever surprise me again."

Gelrayen wisely treated the matter as settled. "I did not, however, sense any drives in operation. Is that because they simply were not engaged at that moment?"

"No, not entirely," Valthyrra said. "I simply did not see any main drives or star drives of any conventional sense. In fact, I saw nothing that I would consider an external drive of any type. Of course, that is not a surprise."

"No?" Tarrel looked surprised.

"We had already guessed that the energy flare of conventional drives could not be contained within that shield," the ship explained. "I do not have to remind you that our own shields must have openings for the drive flare, or the wash will overload and burn out the shield itself. That is part of the reason why our packs almost always attack a ship at the drives first."

"That, and to take the ship mostly intact," Tarrel added.

"Yes, there is that. If the Dreadnought had conventional drives in any sense, it would have had shield vents. If such drives were vented through the shield, the Starwolves would have been able to sense them, and shoot through those vents."

"Do you have any better idea of just what sort of drive it must possess?" Gelrayen asked. "Would it be a highly refined jump drive?"

"That is my best guess at this time," Valthyrra said. "I cannot believe that even the most powerful field drives would be able to take a ship into starflight, unless it also employs an acceleration damper of almost flawless efficiency. It might also use a type of drive unlike anything we know. All I do know now with any reasonable certainty is that it does not use conventional drives."

"Well, it's a shame that we weren't able to destroy it while that shield was down," Tarrel remarked. "Do you think that we might be able to use that same trick again?"

"That depends upon how well the Dreadnought learns from its mistakes. We might be able to set up some variation of that same trick that might fool it." She paused, lifting her camera pod slightly as if listening to some distant sound. "Gheldyn, do you have any estimates for me?"

"Another five minutes at least," the engineering officer responded over the bridge audio.

"Do the very best you can. We are running out of time." She turned her camera pod back to the others. "The game begins again. The Dreadnought seems to have recovered from whatever I did to it and is moving through the outer edge of the ring detonating some manner of concussion discharges."

"Trying to shake us loose?" Tarrel asked.

"Perhaps. Those concussions are creating some very intense plasma shock waves that would react sharply with my armor, producing a very clear signature on passive sensors. They are not a direct danger to me, however."

"But if it finds us, we should be able to run," Gelrayen added.

"I certainly hope so," the ship agreed. "If I pull myself well back into this hole, the moonlet will shield me from any shock wave unless both the concussion and the Dreadnought itself were somewhere in front of the opening. We might just be able to ride this out."

"Famous last words," Gelrayen remarked to Captain Tarrel.

She nodded. "I think that I'm going back to your seat before anything else happens."

Tarrel took herself back to the upper bridge and strapped in for battle, fairly certain that it would come without warning. She could not believe that they were going to get out of this one. The Dreadnought was a weapon that possessed tremendous abilities, and she doubted that the Methryn's one lucky shot had damaged it all that much. For that matter, she did not entirely trust Valthyrra's belief that it was only trying to chase them out with concussion discharges. It knew, within a relatively specific area, just where they were hiding, and it probably meant to destroy everything along that portion of the ring to have them.

She strapped herself into the seat on the upper bridge and watched as the Starwolves continued about their business with a frustrating lack of concern. For the first time in what seemed like a long while, Tarrel was reminded of the rumors and legends about Starwolves that she had lived with all her life. They were said to be nothing more than coldly efficient weapons of war, incapable by design of either compassion or fear. Since meeting them, she had laid aside all of those old beliefs and suppositions. There was certainly no reason why they would be risking their lives and their ships to protect Union worlds, except compassion. But she wondered now if their calm reaction to danger was something they had by design, or if it was something they had learned with experience.

Their first warning that the Dreadnought was close was the sound of the concussion discharges, rolling along the hull of the ship like distant thunder. The lack of an atmosphere meant that they were hearing the passing of the shock wave itself, and the absence of air also allowed the shock wave to travel farther before dissipating. Just the same, if those shock waves were still rolling through, then their point of origin must be very close.

"Gheldyn, we really do need to be going," Valthyrra said.

"Another minute," the senior engineer answered.

"We really do not have a minute," the ship insisted. "You also do not have a complete main line."

Captain Tarrel decided at that point that they were in serious trouble. The next concussion thundered in, this one strong enough to shake the immense carrier. Valthyrra was turning her camera pod from one station to the next, where members of the bridge crew waited patiently at consoles controlling systems that still lacked the power to respond.

"Gheldyn, are you accurate in your estimate?" she asked at last.

"Yes. We are making the final connections now."

"Then I am going to move the ship quickly, even if it uses all the fuel elements left in the lines. You keep working straight through this, since I am going to need that power immediately. This tactic will not get us out of danger, but it will buy you that time."

"I understand," Gheldyn promised her.

"Commander, I am going to do something stupid," she said, turning toward Gelrayen. "Stupid times demand stupid gestures. May the gods pity us one more time."

Before he could reply, another concussion struck the ship violently. The moonlet was caught on the leading edge of a powerful shock wave and sent tumbling slowly by the force of that explosion, and the Methryn was carried with it. Only the fact that Valthyrra had maintained the hull integrity shields at battle intensity saved the carrier from damage as her wings and upper hull were dragged along the interior of the cubby. After the first few seconds, the moonlet settled into a predictable roll that Valthyrra could match.

"Scanner contact," Valthyrra reported. "It knows where we are. I no longer have any choice."

The ship engaged her main drives at full power without bothering to first move clear of her hiding place in the moonlet, hurtling herself out into open space and well beyond the Dreadnought. Even then she did not let up, switching from one conversion generator to the next to pull every remaining bit of water from each line in the distribution grid. By the time the last generator gave all it had, barely half a minute later, the Methryn was nearly two million kilometers out from the gas giant and drifting at a third the speed of light. Captain Tarrel had reacted to an abrupt twenty-seven G's of sustained acceleration predictably. When she did come around, she was going to regret it. The stress drugs had her stirring weakly almost immediately.

"Gheldyn?"

"I still need just a moment."

"Hurry," Valthyrra insisted, then lifted her camera pod toward the main viewscreen as it shifted to show the image behind the ship. "Stupid idea to buy time, part two."

The moment that the Methryn had left cover, Valthyrra had re-established contact with the drone that she had hidden earlier, ordering it to keep pace with her. Although she did not yet know it for certain, she had every reason to believe that the Dreadnought was somewhere behind her, in spite of the fact that it had never before pursued a fleeing ship. She had made herself particularly annoying, if not an actual threat, and her sudden loss of power probably made her a very tempting target. Even if it had not been following her from the start, it had almost certainly taken up the chase by now. And considering the display of speed that she had seen earlier, that was a disquieting thought indeed.

Valthyrra wished that she still had power enough to bring up her shields at stealth intensity—all she had left was battery power for environmental systems and herself—then the Dreadnought would have been forced to give itself away by targeting her with an impulse sweep. She was surprised and very gratified when that sweep came anyway. Perhaps the Dreadnought, fearful of yet another trap, was wondering what had become of the Maeridan, the first carrier that had attacked it. That sweep gave Valthyrra the very information she needed most. The alien weapon was indeed behind her, and coming up fast.

Fearful of being fired upon while she lacked the protection of shields, Valthyrra responded in the only way she could. Under her direction, the drone unit that had been standing idle just beside her raised its own shields to stealth intensity, a function very important to a reconnaissance probe. Then it turned and began to accelerate rapidly toward the Dreadnought, rapidly even by Starwolf standards. Being a fairly simple machine, it lacked the capacity to question any order it was given, as long as that order came from a valid source. It made its run directly toward the Dreadnought, which responded very predictably with another scanner sweep. It might have tried to open fire, but its discharge beams were barrage weapons and not designed for tracking such a small, swift target. Riding those impulse beams to their source, the drone rammed the Dreadnought at a combined speed over half that of light.

In a way, this was more than just a delaying tactic, but an experiment in itself. Normal shields were of three types. Defensive shields were designed to deflect or absorb energy weapons but could be penetrated fairly readily by solid objects, while navigational shields caught up any solid objects in a series of projected waves, clearing a safe path ahead of the ship, but were completely transparent even to delicate nuances of information in returning scanner beams. The Dreadnought's powerful shell was, of course, a defensive shield, but one of such great intensity that it should have seemed solid to any physical object striking it. Valthyrra wanted to know that for certain, rather than simply continue to assume that it worked that way.

If the drone went through, the combined energy of impact at that speed would have to be measured in megatons of force. Indeed, it would have simply vaporized a very large portion of the Dreadnought and probably shattered the rest, and that would have been the end of their problems all the way around. Unfortunately, Valthyrra knew immediately that the intensity of the actual explosion indicated the destruction only of the drone, although the shield continued to flash with great sheets and flares of discharge for several seconds afterward. That had probably been the result not just of the explosion itself but the distortion of the shield under that impact. A ton of spacecraft hitting at over a hundred and fifty thousand kilometers a second has a lot of force behind it.

"The main line is in place," Gheldyn reported.

"I am still getting no water into the pre-chamber," Valthyrra said. "Have you checked every valve?"

"We checked the valves a final time before I called you."

"Try it again." She paused to make a quick check of her operational plans and information on the matter. "Oh hell, each intake chamber has a valve that closes automatically if it detects anything except water coming in. You have to bleed the air from the line at the intake to each generator. There will be a simple manual cock-valve in the end of each line.''

"I am already on my way," Gheldyn assured her.

"Be sure to start with the big ones. I need all the power I can get."

"What about the Dreadnought?" Gelrayen asked.

"At least it stopped for a moment to take an accounting of itself," the ship replied. "I did buy us a little time there. It would have been on top of us already otherwise."

"Just what did you do to it, anyway?"

"I had the drone ram it," Valthyrra explained, then turned her camera pod toward the aft image on the main viewscreen. "Another sweep. One last look around for hidden dangers, and here it comes."

"Valthyrra, you should be getting power now," Gheldyn told her.

"Yes, the first conversion generator is coming up. And here comes the second."

Before Valthyrra could do anything with that power, the first discharge beam hit her from behind, connecting squarely on the back of her twin star drives. Unfortunately, she did not have either defensive shields or even her hull integrity shields in place to make some attempt to deal with that wash of tremendous energy; her only protection was the fact that the armored drive doors had been closed. Actual physical damage was limited to simple scoring and burning of the metal. The danger to the Methryn was that the discharge itself was running through her frame and power systems in the form of searing bolts of electrical energy. She brought up her integrity shields first, getting that discharge under control, then engaged her defensive shields at stealth intensity as she accelerated quickly into an evasive path.

"How are we doing?" Gelrayen asked, glancing quickly in Captain Tarrel's direction. A twenty-two G acceleration had put her out again.

"I, at least, am not doing well," Valthyrra reported. "Both of my star drives are down. The damage is entirely limited to the power conduits and the main phasing control, but it is nothing that can be repaired quickly and I cannot compensate with redundant systems. My rear battery is down and I have lost almost all ability to scan behind."

"Can we stay ahead of the Dreadnought long enough for it to lose interest in chasing us?" he asked.

She brought her camera pod closer. "I cannot out-run the Dreadnought in sublight speeds. Indeed, I can only assume that it will lose interest if I can achieve starflight. Commander, I want to try one last stupid idea. It will probably put me down entirely, but it might save this ship and my crew."

Gelrayen frowned. "I already do not like it."

"How do you suppose I feel about it?" Valthyrra asked. "I have already overridden the safety lock-outs and I am going to take myself into starflight with my main drives. We do not need to go far. But if I can just get myself past threshold, the Dreadnought will probably break off."

"We have no choice, do we?"

The lock-out devices that Valthyrra had removed were those intended to prevent feeding too much power to the main drives and burning them out. She knew that she would be damaging herself by this. The drives themselves would probably survive the punishment as long as she did not hold them at this level more than a few minutes; the worst damage would occur after, while they were cooling down. As long as she still had at least one functional drive on each side of the ship, she would still have enough thrust balance to maneuver. But she would never pass threshold if she lost a drive now. The ship began to shake and buck from uneven phasing.

"Coming up on threshold," Valthyrra reported. "That will be the hardest. Once in starflight, things will smooth out."

"How are your drives?" Gelrayen asked.

"Doing well. It seems that the Dreadnought cannot target those discharge beams effectively at higher speeds. I have not taken a serious hit since that first time." She paused. "Ready for transition into starflight. Hold on to something solid, Commander, and kiss Captain Tarrel good-bye. This might be very rough."

After all of that, her actual transition was not nearly as violent as she had anticipated. The carrier lunged sharply forward for several seconds as it was being pulled, then settled out into fairly smooth starflight.

"We have made it," Valthyrra reported. "The ship is maintaining extremely low starflight speeds. I will try to hold this for another five minutes and then bring us down. Unfortunately, we might not be underway again any time soon, at least not under our own power.''

"Well, we did survive and even came away knowing more than we did when we started," Gelrayen said. "I hope that it is worth it."

"I suppose that it was," the ship agreed dubiously. "I still wonder about just one thing. Whose stupid idea was all this anyway?"

—9—

When Captain Janus Tarrel first became aware of the fact that she was still alive, she was forced to approach that discovery with a certain ambivalence. One of the objects of the previous exercise had been to survive, so it had been successful in that regard. At the same time, she wondered how anyone who hurt as much as she did could have lived through it. High G accelerations were an enormously successful form of torture.

She tried to open her eyes and made two important discoveries. The first was the fact that her eyes were curiously unwilling to open. And even when she was able to open them, she was unable to see anything and was given to wonder if they had survived the ordeal. The eyes were very vulnerable to hard accelerations, second only to bad hearts and full bladders, and her own eyes certainly hurt enough. Then she discovered by touch that there were some type of medicated pads over them. She was relieved to discover that she really was not blind, although it did mean that she would have to earn her pension the hard way. No early retirement with benefits for her.

"The medic gave you something for the pain," a female Starwolf told her.

"It didn't work," she insisted. "Who is there?"

"Kayendel. The medicated pads are to keep you from getting black eyes. You have only been out for about half an hour, and the medic said that you can take off the pads when you come around."

"I don't want to look." Tarrel removed the pads, then discovered that she was doomed to spend the next few moments contemplating a very blurry view of the ceiling. "It was a stupid idea, anyway."

"What?"

"Coming aboard this ship," she explained. "Starwolves were specifically made to function under conditions that are deadly to creatures like myself. That should have been a strong warning to me about the advisability of trying to exist in your environment. Who took off my clothes, by the way?"

"Oh, we drew lots for that."

Ask a stupid question, get no satisfaction. "What are you doing nursing the invalid anyway? Don't you have duties to attend to?"

Kayendel shrugged both sets of arms. "What good is a helm officer in a ship that has no functional drives? We lost both of the star drives to the Dreadnought there near the end, and Valthyrra was able to get us away into starflight with the main drives. Were you still with us up to that point?"

"That was when I decided to take a nap."

"There is not much else to tell. Valthyrra knew that she might ruin her main drives by running them past their tolerances, and she was correct. We lost three drives to burn-out. The fourth is damaged, and that drive is on the outside. If we try to engage that one, the ship would be pushed so hard on that one side that the field drive steering would not be able to correct the uneven balance. So you see, Valthyrra actually came through this worse off than you did."

"Serves her right. So, what happens now? Is there any hope of getting the ship repaired enough to take her home again under her own power, or are we waiting for a tow?"

"Well, we do have some hope of getting the star drives running again," Kayendel explained. "The Maeridan is standing alongside and we have her repair crews on board. They expect to know something very quickly. Unfortunately, pulling off and replacing those damaged main drives will take a couple of days."

Tarrel glanced over at the Kelvessan. "You have replacements?"

"Of course. There are four perfectly good main drives facing forward to provide braking thrust, the exact same size and power as the drives we lost. We can take the two inner drives from the front and mount them in place of the outer drives aft. Any two drives can move this carrier perfectly well, even if it takes a little longer to build to speed.''

"I really don't want to go fast for a while," Tarrel commented. "What about Wally?"

"He came around a few minutes ago, in an enormously bad mood. He refuses to talk to anyone. At least we had already given him a room of his own."

Kayendel shortly had to return to her duties, since she was the second in command of this ship. Captain Tarrel got herself up and dressed very soon after that. The normal environment of the ship was just a little too cold for her, after the Starwolves had taken her out of her armor. And she felt responsible for Lt. Commander Pesca, although that responsibility was mostly directed toward keeping him from being a bother to the Starwolves. But she wanted to check his condition for herself, since she did not trust the Kelvessan to completely understand just how serious his problems might become. Unfortunately, he was already gone by the time she was dressed, and she did not find him in his cabin when she looked there.

After that, she got distracted by the efforts to get the Methryn back in flight condition. She knew from one of her previous tours of the carrier that she could see all of the holding and transport bays and much of the forward main drives from the observation decks above either of the fighter bays, which extended below the lower hull of the ship. As it happened, she was treated to a far more spectacular sight than she had anticipated. The Maeridan drifted belly-up only two hundred meters directly below the Methryn; considering the relative size of the carriers, they appeared to be very close indeed. The armor had already been pulled off the Methryn's two forward drives that were to be removed, although the actual process of physically removing the first drive appeared to be some time off yet.

Since nothing was actually happening on the outside, even a really great view became rather boring after a while, and Captain Tarrel understood that the view would probably be there for a couple of days. The whole trouble, she realized, was that she wanted to return to duty and had none. She was an advisor with no advice to give under the present circumstances, and the only thing she could do to help was to stay out of the way. She decided to go back to the bridge, where she could be in the middle of things and still remain out of the way.

Since their cabins were in the corridors behind the bridge, she decided to stop by on her way and see if Lt. Commander Pesca was about. She was almost surprised that he was there. He was locked inside his cabin and refused to come out at first, although the various thumps and bumps to be heard through the door indicated that he was busy at something. He could hardly be moving the furniture, unless he had unbolted it from the floor. Either his mood improved after the first few moments, or his curiosity got the better of him. He came out of his cabin dressed in armor, looking worn and beaten as if he had not recovered from the ordeal of the Methryn's battle.

"The ship seems nearly deserted," he observed, watching her closely.

"You just have to look in the right places," Tarrel told him. "The ones who are not trying to rebuild the star drives are probably outside the ship dismantling the main drives. They seem determined to take this carrier apart right here, in the middle of space."

"How long do they expect to take?"

"The first officer told me to expect a couple of days, but I suspect that she's being optimistic," she said. "There's no guarantee yet that the star drives will ever work, although I don't know what happened to them. We might get to see how you tow three kilometers of Starwolf carrier into starflight. I have been curious about that."

Pesca gave her another of his disquieting, calculating stares. "You like these Starwolves, don't you, Captain."

Tarrel shrugged. "They are interesting, I have to admit."

"Monsters," Pesca muttered under his breath as he turned back to his room.

Tarrel looked up at him sharply, realizing that things had gone far enough already. "Wally, I'm going to put you off the ship as soon as possible, back at Alkayja station if we don't meet one of our own sooner. There's no point putting you through all of this. The Starwolves aren't going to let you have what you want anyway."

"No, they probably won't," he agreed, looking embarrassed. "I guess I never was meant for this."

"If it's any consolation, I feel worse than I look," she assured him. "You might as well come out of that armor. Unless you plan to go outside with the Starwolves, you hardly need it in a ship that can't move."

In spite of the advice that she had just given, Captain Tarrel put herself back inside her own armor. When the Starwolves got around to moving one of those massive drives, she did indeed intend to go outside for a look. For as long as she had been in space aboard ships, she had actually been outside only very seldom, and that was true of just about everyone. Ship to station transfers were done through docking tubes, and most repairs were done inside pressurized repair bays not unlike the one where the Methryn had been built. Except for salvage and some emergency repairs, there was simply never any need to go outside a ship.

As she had expected, the bridge was nearly deserted. There was hardly any need for even a token watch, since Valthyrra herself would always be there anyway. Kayendel was on the bridge and apparently acting as the officer in charge, although the Kelvessan hurried over to join Tarrel as she shuffled her armored self onto the bridge. To her surprise, the first officer stopped before her and performed a reasonable facsimile of a salute.

"Captain, can you be on the bridge for the next few hours?" she asked.

Tarrel was almost too surprised to know what to think. "Yes, I suppose that I could be."

"Well, I was wondering if you would mind taking the watch on the bridge," Kayendel explained. "You do have command experience. And since you are a captain, you have the same technical rank as myself or any of the pack leaders and that makes you qualified to take the watch."

"What, me? Command a Starwolf carrier?" Tarrel asked, and smiled. "I can hardly make a mess of things, under the circumstances. I don't suppose that a Union Captain ever commanded a Starwolf carrier before. What does her worship think about this?"

"It was her idea," Kayendel said very softly. "There is no trick to this, since Valthyrra is in charge of the ship anyway. In theory, your only concern is to advise the ship and watch over the crew. Valthyrra knows what she needs to be doing and most of the crew is outside with Commander Gelrayen, and still under his command.''

"Well, if I'm going to sit in the chair, I might as well earn it," Tarrel commented. "My word, I wish circumstances could have been different. When I think of how much fun it would have been to go sliding into the Vinthra space complex in this ship—and a new ship at that, with less than a hundred light years on her—I feel better already."

"You do not get to keep her," Kayendel said on her way to the lift.

As far as it went, Captain Tarrel knew that she was only just sitting in the Commander's seat, but she could still appreciate the irony of the situation. The perfect complement to an inexperienced carrier unable to move herself was, of course, a captain from the enemy fleet. She certainly could not imagine her people's protocol allowing someone like Gelrayen or Kayendel to command a Union military ship, no matter what the circumstances; Starwolves were so refreshingly practical. But it made for a remarkable situation, just the same.

She carried herself up the steps to the Commander's station, aware that Valthyrra's camera pod was turning slowly to watch her, every heavy step of the way. Ignoring her for the moment, Tarrel secured her helmet in the rack behind the seat, before lifting herself in. She adjusted the angle of the seat until she was fairly comfortable, then settled back to enjoy her brief tour of duty as the Commander of a Starwolf carrier. After serving in hell, she now had a chance to rule in heaven.

Valthyrra moved her camera pod well into the upper bridge, holding it just above the main console of the station. "What course, Captain?"

"Right up the middle of the Rane Sector," Tarrel told her boldly. "I want to make life miserable for some incompetent Union Captains and their backward little ships."

"You know, I might be the only carrier who will never have fired upon a Union ship," Valthyrra observed, almost wistfully.

"You worry me," Tarrel remarked. "That's not the first time you've said something to that effect. But cheer up! The truce will never last. You'll be hunting Union ships within two months, after you destroy the Dreadnought. Just do me one favor. If you ever run across the battleship Carthaginian, you might think merciful thoughts.''

"Then you honestly believe that the war will return?''

"Of course. The Union is fundamentally greedy and ruthless. Many of the colonies are going to take advantage of our sudden misfortune to declare their independence. People like me will be sent out to punish them by dropping a few bombs on their heads, and people like you feel required to punish us in return and protect their independence. Unless, of course, our interplanetary network falls completely apart because the Dreadnought has destroyed so much.''

"And then we end up having to take care of you on a long-term basis,'' the ship observed.

"Are there enough of you?'' Tarrel asked. "You know, if you people are smart about this, you would move through as soon as you destroyed the Dreadnought and disable every Union military ship you can find. Then you could tell us how you expect us to behave, and we would have to listen. But I don't believe that you could make yourselves do that.''

"The circumstances are different than they have ever been,'' Valthyrra insisted. "Perhaps they would agree that it would be best to end the war as soon as it starts again, if you told them.''

"Wait just a moment. You seem to forget just whose side I'm on. As soon as you destroy the Dreadnought, my mission here is complete and I'll go back to my own ship.''

Valthyrra actually seemed surprised. "I had thought that you did not approve of many of the Union's policies.''

"No, I don't,'' Tarrel told her. "A lot of it is fairly nasty and ruthless, and all for the sake of greed. But it does work fairly well. I'm not sure that anything else would work any better, and there are a lot of systems that would be much worse.''

"The Republic works, and no one has to get hurt to make certain that it does.''

Tarrel nodded. "That is true, and it has given me something to think about. In Union space, we're taught that the Republic ceased to exist a long time ago, and I'm beginning to suspect that I now know why. But the situation there is just a little different. The Republic has the strong influence of the Kelvessan and your ships. You're a lot more perfect than we are, but you were built that way. We're only mortal. I've always believed in the Union, in spite of its problems, and I've been willing to enforce its policies. Did you think that the Starwolves had liberated me, that I was the Captain of a Union battleship because I was forced to be, or didn't know any better?''

"Frankly, I have had trouble remembering that you are not just another Starwolf," Valthyrra admitted. "You seem so much like them, far more so than I had ever expected that a human could be."

"Perhaps you're just not used to humans."

"No, I have seen humans often enough in my life. They are different from either you or the Starwolves. Perhaps it is because you are both warriors."

Captain Tarrel realized at that moment that she was discussing points of personal philosophy with a machine, and that they both seemed to be having some problem keeping in mind just who they were talking to. Whether naturally or by design, Valthyrra kept her camera pod always moving, changing angle, rotating lenses to focus on some small gesture of expression, all helping to create a strong sense of speaking with a real person who was actually there. In fact, Valthyrra was physically very large and distributed throughout the secure core of the ship. But, for the moment, Tarrel was more impressed with the complexities of Valthyrra's mind. She had expected the ship to think responsively in the same way as even the most sophisticated computers, all her thought processes generated only in reaction to external events and input. In truth, the ship seemed to engage in quite a lot of independent thought and speculation, and many of her responses seemed more emotional than logical.

"I hesitate to say this, knowing that you could easily find offense in it," Valthyrra continued. "In my experience, which I have been accumlating now for nearly six decades, I have generally found humans to be dull and very predicable in their lack of sophistication. Kelvessan, and the other ships, are always thinking beyond their own present concerns. They are more likely to tell you things that you would not expect, and they speak more plainly and honestly about what they really think and feel than humans, who seem mostly to feel some need to guard the privacy of their thoughts carefully. Perhaps that is also why you remind me more of the Starwolves."

Captain Tarrel chuckled to herself. "I could take offense at that, except that I've been thinking much the same thing myself lately. It might have something to do with being locked inside a ship with several thousand Starwolves, who are very interesting, contrasted with one human, Wally Pesca, who is definitely not a higher form of life.''

''I was wondering, perhaps, what your opinion might be of my own performance,'' the ship began hesitantly. Even the set of her camera pod suggested shyness. ''I was aware from the first that you were uncertain about my ability to handle myself, whether because of my lack of experience or just because I am a machine.''

''I don't trust anything that hasn't proven itself,'' Tarrel told her. ''But you did just fine. In fact, you surprised me. Your inventiveness and lack of hesitation was very impressive. You knew what you had to do to save yourself and you did it.''

Valthyrra turned her camera pod away. ''I admit that I am very embarrassed about my loss of power. That was a careless and stupid mistake that should not have happened.''

''I agree, although it wasn't your fault. Still, your professional pride forces you to blame yourself. I know I would.''

''I hardly know whether to feel good or bad about that battle,'' the ship remarked. ''To tell you the truth, except for that whole affair with the fuel element line, I thought that I did very well. I am now willing to take part in a serious attack on the Dreadnought.''

''Yes, I believe that you are ready for that.''

''I just hope that Commander Gelrayen agrees,'' Valthyrra complained. ''He seems to think that he has to tell me everything, as if I hardly know the first thing about taking care of myself.''

Captain Tarrel had to work at hiding her smile. There was still something of a child left in Valthyrra Methryn. Which was really just as well; Starwolf carriers had to grow up so fast.

Valthyrra lifted her camera pod sharply, then rotated only the pod itself to face toward the front of the bridge. Her reaction suggested that she had just become aware of something that had happened somewhere off the bridge, her gesture with camera pod being entirely a reflex. She turned the pod back again after a moment.

''Captain, I have experienced an unexpected problem,'' she said. ''There has been an unpredicted decompression of an area within my hull. Automatic doors have contained the pressure loss to that one area, but suit telemetry indicates that there is someone trapped within.''

''Suit telemetry?'' Tarrel repeated. ''Does that mean that this person is in no danger?''

''None for the moment, Captain. I should add that the decompression seems to have been a deliberate act. If I had been aware sooner, I could have used my overrides to prevent it.''

Tarrel nodded. ''Where is this? Does it have anything to do with normal repairs?''

''Not, it does not. It happened in a section well forward in the ship.''

''Can you show me where?''

Valthyrra cleared the main monitor on the Commander's forward console and brought up a schematic of that area of ship. It was like identifying a single block from a large city; relatively speaking, the problem was contained in a very small region. In fact, it was limited to a single chamber of unusual shape and size, perhaps five meters deep but at least thirty meters wide. Even more unusual, a dozen narrow passages or tubes led forward some distance until they emerged through the lower hull of the ship.

''Val, what is that cabin?''

''That is one of four chambers giving access to my forward missile tubes,'' she reported. ''The missiles are loaded from the storage bay by an automated conveyor rack. When fired, the missiles are kicked down the tube and away from the ship with a high-pressure blast of compressed carbon dioxide, and they do not engage their drives until they are clear.''

''Did you have missiles loaded?''

''Under the circumstances, yes. I loaded a full spread of missiles capable of both high sublight and short-range starflight speeds, directed through an achronic link by my own tracking systems, and armed with conversion warheads of variable intensity up to twenty megatons. One missile has been removed from its tube.''

''What, inside the ship?''

''No, it was pushed along the tube outside the ship. Both the inner and outer tube hatches have been blown manually, so I cannot close them.''

''I don't have to ask who,'' Tarrel commented to herself as she released the straps from her seat and began climbing out. ''I need a lift standing by to take me to the point as close to that launch tube as possible, where I can leave the ship. You need to warn Commander Gelrayen, and suggest having the repair crews get themselves back inside. And launch a pack of fighters to stand by.''

"I have no pilots on board," Valthyrra told her.

"Well, I suppose that you can fly at least one remotely," Tarrel said as she collected her helmet and hurried down the steps. "Can you control that missile remotely?"

"Yes, but it can still be fired and detonated manually," Valthyrra said, swinging her camera pod around to follow while she still could. "What are you going to do?"

"This is my problem," Captain Tarrel insisted just before she moved out of range, then waited until she was inside the lift. "Val?"

"I can still hear you," she said through the lift com.

"Wally Pesca is my responsibility," Tarrel continued. "I brought him on board this ship. I knew that he was having problems, but I was too busy playing with the Starwolves to pay him enough attention. Don't you try to talk to him through his suit. I'm the only one he might listen to now, and I doubt even that."

"I will leave him to you, Captain," Valthyrra promised. "I might remind you that you do not have a weapon."

"Is he likely to have one?"

"Aside from a conversion missile? No. All of the ship's small weapons are accounted for, and he did not come aboard with anything."

Tarrel said nothing, but she wished very much that she did have a weapon of some type. She really did not anticipate that she would be able to save Lt. Commander Pesca unless he surrendered to her voluntarily, and she did not believe that he would. The fact that he was using a conversion device against the Starwolves indicated that he did not expect or intend to survive his own attack; he probably meant to move it into a position where it would do the most damage and detonate it manually. Although she did not know for certain, she suspected that anyone willing to make a suicide attack was probably too devoted to his cause to be talked out of it very easily, or could even be forced to surrender. If threatened, he would simply set off the device immediately.

The fate of entire worlds could well depend upon the survival of these two carriers, two of only sixteen fighting ships left in the Starwolf fleet. In that balance, Walter Pesca's life was a small concern. If she had had a gun and could have taken him by surprise, Captain Tarrel would have shot him without the slightest hesitation to get him away from that missile. But aside from the rather obvious problem that she did not have a weapon in the first place, Pesca was wearing the best armor there was. Dispatching him quickly and easily was more a problem than it seemed. That was why she wanted heavy firepower in the form of a fighter to back her up, if she could direct the fighter into position before he saw it.

"Captain, this is Valthyrra," the ship said after a long moment. "I have considered the matter carefully and I have decided not to warn the crews that are working outside, or make any attempt to secure the ship. That would warn your companion that we know what he is doing, and he might be frightened into detonating the device. I have discussed this with Commander Gelrayen and he agrees. We will leave this for you to handle."

"I appreciate you confidence," Tarrel said, uncertain whether she intended that sarcastically. "I need some firepower at hand immediately."

"A fighter is too large and obvious," Valthyrra explained. "I am sending you a probe, the smallest of my surveillance remote units. It operates entirely by field drive, and it has a mobile camera pod with an attached small cannon."

"Enough to pierce Starwolf armor on the first shot?"

"It should."

The lift, which had made four changes of direction already, pulled to a smooth stop and the doors snapped open. Captain Tarrel found herself facing a narrow, dimly-lit corridor in what looked to be a very remote portion of the ship.

"Listen to me quickly," Valthyrra told her. "The corridor you see gives access to the minor airlocks along the ventral groove, and you are only about three hundred meters back from the nose of the ship. Walter Pesca is moving the missile along the ventral groove a short distance back from your present position, no doubt using the groove as the only effective cover. He probably expects to fire the missile before he begins moving outward along the wing, and I suspect that he intends to target the open bays along the Maeridan's lower hull."

"Can he fire that missile with any accuracy?" Tarrel asked, surprised.

"He can try pointing it in the general direction. Considering the range, he has a very good chance of hitting something. Go down the corridor to your left and take the first passage to your right. That will put you at a small airlock leading out into the ventral groove."

Tarrel found the passage quickly enough, a narrow tube sealed at the inner end by a heavy hatch in the event that the passage between the inner and outer hull was damaged. The airlock itself was hardly more than a service port, small enough that she had to bend slightly to get her helmet under the top. The ventral groove was familiar territory from her visits while the Methryn had still been in her construction bay, larger than the slender line that it looked to be from a distance, with the massive heat-exchange bars of the solid-state cooling system at top and bottom. There was hardly any more detail to be seen, since they were in the smothering darkness and bitter cold of intersteller space. The brilliant floodlights illuminating the area of work about the main drives was still nearly a kilometer away.

"Where is he?" Tarrel asked.

"About fifty meters back from where you stand, moving away from you," Valthyrra reported. "Since he is carrying the missile, he is moving much slower than you will."

"Carrying? How large is that missile?"

"Perhaps I should have said that he is pulling it in freefall, since that missile is five meters long and weighs two tons under one standard G. If you stay well back in the darkness of the groove, he might not see you until you are fairly close. Unfortunately, your armor is Command white. His armor will be white with black trim, but the missile itself is dull black."

"What about that firepower you promised?" Tarrel asked.

"Right behind you."

Captain Tarrel turned and was startled to see the dark shape of the probe drifting immediately behind her. This machine was much smaller than she had anticipated, an armored, wedge-shaped remote with its folding wings fully extended so that it looked now like some curious flying or aquatic creature. Its camera pod, lifted to regard her, was in a protective flare at the end of a flexible snake-like neck. The focusing lens of a comparatively small gun was located beneath the camera; with power coming up from within the main hull of the machine, it could be a great deal more dangerous than it looked.

"How can I talk with him?" she asked.

"You are aware of the switch for the external speaker on your collar?" Valthyrra reminded her. "When you press that, I will shunt the signal to a second audio channel. It will only work while you are holding the switch, so you will control what you want him to hear."

She had to weigh her options very quickly, trying to decide whether to give Pesca a chance to surrender, or if she should take the safest course by simply allowing Valthyrra to ambush him with the remote. But if Valthyrra shot and missed, he would still have time to detonate the missile.

"Val, can you control his suit remotely?" she asked as she hurried along the deep ledge of the ventral groove.

"Yes, it was designed to allow me to care for an injured pilot as best I could, by adjusting temperature and oxygen content."

"Can you vent the suit and suffocate him?"

"No, there was no foreseen value in that function."

"But you can cut his oxygen completely?"

Valthyrra considered that briefly. "I can certainly cut down the oxygen content to a level at which a human could not remain conscious. Believe it or not, that really is a useful function with Kelvessan. It will be as much as a couple of minutes before he goes under."

"Do it, then. Leave all other levels where they are. He might not even notice for some time."

Tarrel hurried the best that she could; there was no artificial gravity outside the ship, and her boots held to the hull only by an electromagnetic device that was pressure-sensitive to each step. The hold seemed to stick for just a fraction of a second with each step, until the sensors registered the lifting of her leg and released the lock, but it was just enough to slow her down. The probe drifted silently behind her, its lenses glittering in the reflection of the distant lights between the two carriers.

"The missile just began a one-minute delayed count," Valthyrra reported. "The overload level is full power, twenty megatons or more. Lieutenant Commander Pesca seems to have panicked. His respiratory and cardiac rates are climbing rapidly, and he is pressing buttons on the missile's manual control apparently at random."

"He scared himself," Tarrel observed. "Can I have a channel to him now?"

"The second audio channel is ready."

"Wally, can you hear me?" she asked, trying to sound both authoritative and strongly reassuring. "Wally, you have to turn the damned thing off. You have it set to overload in less that a minute."

"I can't, Captain," he answered, almost hysterical. "The controls aren't in Terran. I was trying to fire it, and I don't know what I did."

After weeks of trying to find any clue to the secret language of the Starwolves, he had to do it the hard way.

"I can direct him to key in the manual override to lock out the controls and return the missile's systems to inert status," Valthyrra said softly over Tarrel's com.

"Wally, Valthyrra Methryn is going to tell you how to turn the thing off. Will you listen to her?"

"Where is she?"

"Walter, this is Valthyrra," the ship said. "We use the standard Terran character set, so you will recognize that much. To deactivate the missile, type in the characters and numbers in reverse order of the access code that you will see inside the lid of the control panel. Can you do that?"

"I can't see the numbers!" Pesca insisted, deeply frightened. "I don't have a light. I can only see the keyboard because the keys are illuminated from the inside."

"Walter, I will read you the sequence from my inventory. But you have to hurry, because you have only twenty seconds." Valthyrra paused. "Damn. I suspect that he just fainted."

"Give him back his oxygen," Tarrel suggested.

"I did when I realized that he was willing to deactivate the missile. You will have to do it. The missile is only twenty meters ahead of you now."

She looked up, but she could barely make out the black form of the missile drifting above the outer edge of the ventral groove. Pesca must have pushed against it as he passed out, for the tapered nose of the missile was swinging slowly out away from the ship. "Val, I'll never get there in time. Do you have enough control of that missile to fire it away?"

"Yes, I do."

"That's the only way you can save yourself now. The nose

of the missile is pointing away into open space, so get it the hell away from here now.''

''Walter Pesca might be caught in the drive wash,'' the ship protested.

''Perhaps his suit will protect him,'' Tarrel insisted. ''Val, you gave me temporary command of this ship, and now you listen to me. I'm ordering you to fire that missile. The decision and the responsibility are entirely my own.''

The missile suddenly disappeared in a blinding flash of light that streaked away to disappear into the distance. Tarrel was still blinking from the flare of that drive when a second flash of brilliant light filled the blackness of space several kilometers out from the ship. She wondered at first if it had gotten away in time, when it seemed that the explosion was reaching out to take them, but the shock wave that moved across the ship seconds later was hardly enough to rock it gently, a light pressure that did not even threaten her hold on the hull. She turned and hurried to find Walter Pesca, fearful as Valthyrra had been that he had been caught in the tremendous energy of its drive wash.

''Captain, your companion did not make it,'' Valthyrra said softly.

She stopped short. ''He's dead?''

''His suit telemetry stayed with the missile. I must suppose that he had fastened himself to it with a short tether.''

''Then he died in the explosion?''

''He did not survive the acceleration of the missile,'' the ship answered. ''I tracked his telemetry until the explosion. He was dead already.''

With nothing left to do, Captain Tarrel returned to the airlock and took the lift back to the bridge. She hardly knew what to think, the situation had arisen and was gone again so quickly. Her thoughts at the time had been only practical ones, above all her awareness that the survival of the Union, if not human civilization itself, could depend upon the welfare of these two ships. With the danger past, she now had time to realize that she had given an order that had caused the death of a junior officer under her command. Oddly, she felt vaguely disappointed with herself, with Walter Pesca, and with her own kind in general; having to face aliens after a demonstration of the violent failings of her own race. She did not know if the Starwolves would ever be able to understand the fear and suspicion that had driven Pesca mad, or if they agreed with her decision to sacrifice him to save the two carriers. They possessed the strength and speed to have gotten to that missile in time.

Commander Gelrayen had returned to the bridge by the time she arrived. He met her at the lift and led her into the corridor leading behind the bridge. "Are you well?"

"Yes, fine," she insisted. "Is something else wrong?"

"Valthyrra is taking it very hard," he explained. "She has never had to kill anyone before. Fighting the Dreadnought was one thing, since its actual sentience is in doubt. But she had not anticipated that she would have to take a life deliberately anytime soon, no matter how necessary it was."

"The choice was mine," Tarrel answered. "I had been given the bridge, and it was my order as temporary commander of this ship. I told her that."

"Even I cannot order Valthyrra against her will," Gelrayen said. "She made the decision to do what you told her, and she was the one who actually fired that missile. She just needs a little time to adjust."

"Is there anything that I can do?"

"Valthyrra will feel better when we get her repaired and under way on her own power. We have begun moving the main drives, and I need to get back to the repair crews. Will you watch the bridge for a while yet?"

Tarrel was surprised by that request. "Yes, I suppose. If you still trust me with your ship."

Gelrayen smiled. "You have taken good care of her so far."

—10—

After nearly three days of hard work, the Methryn was ready to get underway again under her own power, if only barely. She had half as many main drives working as she should have, and her star drives were expected to operate at only one-third of normal capacity, if that. A part of her sensor array remained out, along with her rear battery and some of her perimeter cannons, as well as several external cameras and a section of her heat exchange. All the same, she had been very lucky in many important respects. Her armor was completely intact, and her main battery and her shields were both fully operational, even at stealth intensity. Her star drives could be restored with only a modest amount of work, and the phasing crystals and major components could be salvaged from her four damaged main drives. Four or five days of work in a construction bay would have her in fighting condition once again.

The most serious problem she faced was being able to beg those repairs when she did return to Alkayja station. Opinions varied greatly aboard ship about whether she would be returning in favor or disgrace. She did not have detailed interior scans of the Dreadnought, but she had proven that it could be fought successfully. Valthyrra herself was very pessimistic. She remained very embarrassed over the incident with the incomplete water line that fueled her conversion generators, even if that had been the responsibility of the station construction crew. And that was directly responsible for the damage that she had suffered.

She also felt that she was very much to blame for the sabotage attempt and Walter Pesca's subsequent death. She had known that he had been wandering the remote areas of the ship, spying, but she had assumed that it had been a part of his linguistic research and she had not anticipated that he would do her any harm. He certainly should not have been able to steal an entire conversion-warhead missile from out of her own launch tube. She saw that as giving her very bad marks for carelessness.

Captain Tarrel was delighted to point out that there was one advantage to the Methryn's lame condition: The carrier was no longer capable of crushing accelerations. Valthyrra was herself polite enough not to respond that she could still make at least one person's life very miserable, even on only two main drives. They eventually made something of a running joke about it, which helped to restore a better mood aboard the ship. Although Tarrel was somewhat annoyed when the Kelvessan were so endlessly fascinated to find that she did indeed have a sense of humor.

She had accompanied Commander Gelrayen on a final inspection of the major components of the ship. The star drives had been ready for some time and the functional main drives had not needed repair in the first place; they had only been moved. The two damaged main drives had been mounted into the two empty forward slots, being too valuable as salvage under the circumstances. Although the Starwolves never said a word on the subject, Tarrel suspected that they were also reluctant to leave large pieces of their machinery drifting about in Union space. With the inspection complete, they took a lift directly to the bridge to prepare for immediate departure.

"Well, everything worked well enough when we powered up for a static test earlier," Gelrayen remarked as the lift hurtled along the length of the ship. "Of course, we will know nothing for certain until we are actually underway, especially where those star drives are concerned."

"We have to take the chance," Tarrel commented. "Just as long as there were not too many parts left over, we should be all right."

Gelrayen looked uncertain. "Actually, there were about a hundred thousand parts left over. I wonder if that is relevant, considering the size of the task."

"Is that supposed to be funny, Starwolf?" Tarrel asked. She was still very worried about those star drives, knowing that the carrier would be going nowhere without those.

"I am very sure of my drives," Valthyrra assured them over the lift com. "Captain Tarrel, the entire bridge crew wishes to express its delight that you do not need the protection of your armor due to my incapacitated state."

Tarrel was not allowed time to wonder why the Starwolves would have been concerned about that, since the lift drew to a stop in the next moment and the doors snapped open. When she stepped out onto the bridge with Gelrayen, they could both see what the bridge crew had in mind. They were all seated at their stations, ready for duty, except that each and every one was completely naked.

"Kelvessan do appreciate a good joke," Gelrayen said very softly as they went directly to the upper bridge, ignoring the dozen and more naked Starwolves who were studiously pretending that nothing had happened.

"I suppose that they must, considering the great lengths they will go to for the sake of a bad one," Tarrel observed. She lifted herself into the seat at the Commander's station. No matter how lame the Methryn might be, she would not try to ride out any acceleration standing up.

"Valthyrra, are you ready to get underway?" Gelrayen asked.

She brought her camera pod around. "I am as ready as I can be."

"Secure all bays and locks for flight and begin warming up your main line of generators."

Kayendel glanced over her shoulder. "Commander, the members of the bridge crew would like very much to step outside for a moment to collect our proper uniforms."

"No, I need for you people to stand by your manual controls until we see how those main drives are going to handle," Gelrayen replied, as if refusing them with great reluctance. "We have a long haul ahead of us, and every minute counts. You can certainly understand that."

They understood that he was taking advantage of the situation.

"Commander, the Maeridan is moving clear," Valthyrra reported. "Khallenda Maeridan reports that she will stand by until she knows that we are away, before she returns to her patrol. I have sent her and her crew my regards, in the innocent hope that I am going somewhere."

"Well then, feed some power to those drives and we will see what happens," Gelrayen told her.

There was really no reason to worry that the main drives would not work properly unless the Starwolves had not put them together right, and the static tests would have detected that. As it happened, everything functioned exactly as expected. The two rear drives engaged and built thrust to cruising power smoothly, phasing flawlessly all the way across that range. Although the Methryn did not leap forward with her usual vigor, she was still moving out smartly by Captain Tarrel's standards.

"No worries or surprises," Valthyrra reported. "I am increasing power slightly to move us on up toward threshold."

"If you feel that you can handle it," Gelrayen agreed. "The real test, of course, will be those star drives."

"Commander, if the ship is performing well . . . " Kayendel began, turning in her seat to look up into the upper bridge.

Gelrayen motioned for her to turn around. "I understand your desire to maintain proper appearances, but I believe that we really should not leave the manual controls unsupervised until the Methyrn is safely in starflight. You do agree, Valthyrra?"

"Oh, most certainly," the ship insisted, swinging her camera pod around to the upper bridge. "I would feel better about it. Besides, Kelvessan hardly need to wear clothes in the first place. I doubt very much that you could be cold."

"Well, I was thinking about Captain Tarrel," Kayendel remarked.

"Are you bothered, Captain Tarrel?" Valthyrra asked.

"Not in the slightest," she replied. As a matter of fact, about the only thing she could see of the Starwolves at the moment was the backs of their seats. But as far as it went, she did not think that the curious frames of the Kelvessan looked all that human in the first place. Since they were without exception powerfully muscled, and were by design incapable of carrying any real fat, the natural state was actually quite becoming to them.

"The ride home is going to be a long one," Valthyrra observed in a softer, less contrived tone of voice. "We will need fourteen days at our present speed to reach Alkayja. I do hope to adjust phasing on the star drives to run them slightly hot, which will give us an extra ten to fifteen percent. That might cut things to nine or ten days."

"No danger to the drives?" Gelrayen asked.

"None. If we actually do get into starflight, that is. After that, my only concern is for what happens next. I believe that I have some feel for the way the Dreadnought behaves, and I wish to continue my mission. That will depend upon whether the Great Powers are pleased with my performance so far, or if they see only my mistakes. And if they have four new main drives to give me any time soon.''

"Finding parts for you will be the only problem," the Commander assured her. "There is no question about whether or not you deserve them."

Captain Tarrel said nothing, but she knew how unpredictable the Great Powers could be. She remembered how reluctant they had been to allow the Methryn to go out the first time, when actual battle had not been the purpose of her mission. No matter what they thought of her performance, she still might find herself passed over in favor of more experienced ships. Although Tarrel would not mention it aloud, she even wondered if the Methryn, rather than receive the repairs she needed, might find herself stripped of useful parts to keep some of the older carriers flying. Valthyrra might very well be going back into the construction bay for months, or even years.

For her own part, she suspected that she would be watching the next stage of this battle from the bridge of yet another ship. She even had to admit that it probably would be best for the Methryn if she did have to wait out the rest of the battle with the Dreadnought. She knew that it was largely a sentimental response on her own part, that she wanted to see this young carrier get her chance to fight. If she was asked, Tarrel certainly intended to testify that Valthyrra had proven herself quite clever and resourceful enough to have earned special consideration.

The trouble was that the Methryn had learned more than anyone had really expected, but still less than they needed to know. She had proven that the Dreadnought could be fought and even hurt, but even her brief scan during the moment that the alien weapon's shield had been down had not revealed any great secrets. The ship continued to defy any interior scans, and little enough could be inferred from the limited exterior view. If Valthyrra had been going home with a clear idea of how to destroy the Dreadnought, those same Great Powers would find it harder to deny her.

"I am sitting at threshold," Valthyrra announced soon enough. "Shall I attempt the transition into starflight?"

"When you feel ready," Gelrayen told her.

"Ready to engage star drives," she warned the bridge crew. "Stand by all manual controls."

As it happened, the only failure that was likely to require any member of the bridge crew to intercede with manual controls was the failure of Valthyrra herself, and that was extremely unlikely to happen for any reason except for complete power loss. The star drives began to phase very smoothly, especially so because they were slow to develop even the limited power available to them; so gentle, in fact, that it seemed for a moment that the carrier might even fail to pass threshold. Once she was in starflight, she continued to build speed at a leisurely but steady pace.

"I am settled into starflight to stay," Valthyrra announced. "My drives might be weak, but they remain responsive. I will continue to build to my best cruising speed as things are before I try tampering with the star drives to boost their efficiency."

"Commander?" Kayendel asked; she was one of several crewmembers looking over their shoulders.

Gelrayen looked up at the camera pod. "Val?"

She knew what the game was, and she was eager enough to play along. "I really do not want any of those monitors or manual controls unsupervised for even a moment until I am settled into my best possible speed and we all feel certain that nothing will go wrong. Say, another ten hours? I hope that no one minds taking such a long watch without interruption."

"We should be comfortable," Kayendel remarked sourly as she turned back to her monitors.

Gelrayen was looking so amused, Captain Tarrel decided that it was time to take a part in their little game for herself. "Valthyrra, I have been thinking."

The camera pod turned toward her. "You do it well."

"You know, I have been very uncomfortable with the temperature aboard this ship since I first came aboard." As a matter of fact, she really did not mind it much at all. "It occurred to me that part of the reason you have to keep it so cold is so that Kelvessan can wear clothes that, as you pointed out earlier, they hardly need. If none of the Starwolves aboard this ship wore their clothes, you could move up the temperatures to a level that I would find more comfortable."

"Yes, that sounds very reasonable." Valthyrra turned her

camera pod to Gelrayen, who was looking very surprised by that time. "Commander, it would be very hospitable of us if we made that suggestion a standing order."

Watching Gelrayen try to explain his way out of that one proved to be very entertaining.

Valthyrra had to fuss over her ailing star drives every step of the way, but she managed to bring herself home on her earliest projected schedule of nine days and was still able to avoid damaging herself in the process. When she finally dropped out of starflight well inside the Alkayja system, she was not the only one to feel extremely relieved to have actually made it. She transferred full power to her two remaining forward drives, struggling to cut her tremendous speed with only half the thrust that should have been available to her.

She had, of course, sent her full report on ahead to Alkayja by a tight-beam achronic message as soon as she had escaped from the Dreadnought, a week and a half earlier. Nothing that she had to say would come as a surprise, but Fleet Commander Asandi and his associates were still awaiting direct reports and observations, not only from her but Commander Gelrayen and Captain Tarrel as well. In fact, Asandi was in communication with the Methryn as soon as he was told that she was in system.

"Commander Gelrayen, your ship seems to have done quite well for herself," Asandi began enthusiastically. "We will try to have a construction bay ready for you as soon as you can get here. I'm afraid that we are still working on getting all the replacement parts she needs, however."

"Thank you, Commander," Gelrayen responded, standing over Captain Tarrel's seat as he used the com on the upper bridge. If Valthyrra Methryn was very much in favor with Commander Asandi himself, that served as a good indicator about her future.

"It seems a shame to have had our newest carrier damaged on her first flight, but we expected that," Asandi continued, then paused. "Commander, why are all the members of your crew naked? Not that it really matters to me, of course. That is entirely your own business."

"Val, this was supposed to be audio only," Gelrayen complained softly as he realizing that the ship must be supplying a visual image through her own camera pod. "Well, yes Commander. That was Valthyrra's suggestion actually. We are keeping portions of the ship warmer than usual, for Captain Tarrel's comfort.''

"Very considerate, especially considering that we supplied her with self-warming clothing before the Methyrn departed,'' Asandi observed, seeming to realize that someone had been having a little joke at the expense of the Starwolves, known for their unfortunate tendency to be a little too gullible. "We will be having a quick meeting to discuss your observations as soon as you can secure the Methryn in her bay. I might add that most of us do plan to dress for the occasion. I will see you soon.''

"Thank you, Commander,'' Gelrayen replied, then glared at the camera pod. "Valthyrra Methryn, I was worried enough about our credibility as it was.''

"Commander, I never honestly expected you to go along with that silly idea in the first place,'' Valthyrra told him. "You could have simply said no.''

Actually, Valthyrra knew perfectly well that it was entirely her own fault. She had never taken advantage of anyone in her life, even as a jest, and she had found it impossible to resist. Digging into her vast archives of information, she had been able to tell Gelrayen that the Kelvessan had not been allowed to wear clothing, except for their armor, for the first five thousand years of their existence, a time when nudity had been a sign of their status as the property of the Republic as an artificial race. They had gotten into the habit of wearing clothes, and then only when it pleased them, simply because they were now allowed to. No member of the Methryn's crew had thought to ask what relevance that had to the present situation. Being motivated by an instinct to be helpful, they had gone along with the scheme.

For her own part, Captain Tarrel had done nothing to interfere. She was not entirely certain, but she believed that it had been good for them. Of the few known intelligent races, only humans and Kelvessan were in the habit of wearing clothes. The Kelvessan had no racial identity beyond the rather uncomfortable association of being an artificial race—property and genetic weapons of war but not real people—and they were very good at avoiding the question of what their true identity should be. As long as they could hide their alien and yet vaguely human forms in clothes, then they were able to wrap themselves in the illusion that they were in some obscure manner mostly human. Forcing them to look at themselves, in the collective sense and meaning no vulgar innuendoes that did not apply, also seemed to force them to think about just what it meant to be Kelvessan.

Captain Tarrel had various reasons to be interested in this experiment, enough so that she had actually spoken privately with Valthyrra Methryn on the matter. Whether they knew it or not, the Kelvessan wanted a racial identity of their own. And if they came to feel secure and satisfied as a race in their own right, they probably would lose interest in maintaining the endless war that they had been bred to fight. Either they would go their own way and leave human space to deal with itself, or they would contrive a quick end to the war on terms they would be prepared to enforce. Whichever way things turned out, Tarrel believed that it would be best for everyone involved.

Valthyrra had agreed that it did the Kelvessan good to face such questions, but she doubted that they would come to any sudden answers, although she did agree that beginning the process now would help them to work their way slowly toward a solution over the next few generations. As she pointed out, the real problem that the Kelvessan faced was only of physical appearance; the fact that they still looked vaguely human kept them trapped in the illusion that they needed to act human. The Aldessan of Valtrys, who had executed their actual genetic design, had done them no favor in failing to make their appearance alien and unique enough to differentiate them. Valthyrra was even prepared to suggest that they would be well served by some additional genetic modifications that would be passed through their entire race over the next few generations and slowly alter their appearance, perhaps changing the complete shape of their faces and giving them a full coat of fur.

The Methryn was assigned a construction bay, the very same where she had spent the first six decades of her existence. Once she had dropped her great speed coming down from starflight and had installed herself in orbit, getting herself back inside the bay was simple enough. Such maneuvers were accomplished entirely on field drive, and that was her one function that was not impaired. Valthyrra settled herself into the docking brackets quickly and deftly.

"Secure the ship, and stand by to switch over to external power as soon as the connections are complete," Gelrayen ordered, then glanced up at the camera pod with a sour expression.

"You might also decrease the ship's temperature to the normal levels and ask the crew to dress for company."

"Perhaps they should," Valthyrra agreed grudgingly.

Captain Tarrel accompanied Commander Gelrayen and Valthyrra Methryn into the station only a few minutes later, giving them all just enough time to dress for the occasion. For the sake of convenience, Valthyrra had transferred one aspect of her awareness into a probe, one of the small remotes just like the one that had gone outside the ship with Captain Tarrel in the hopeless attempt to stop Walter Pesca from detonating the missile he had stolen. Valthyrra kept the small machine's wings fully swept back, making it less cumbersome in the corridors of the station.

Fleet Commander Asandi was waiting for them outside the meeting room, where the Commanders of the other carriers in system and many other Kelvessan had begun to gather as soon as the Methryn had arrived. "Captain Tarrel, I cannot tell you how sorry I am about your young companion."

"It was entirely my own fault," she insisted. "I should have been more aware of his condition, but my thoughts were on other problems. I knew that he was having trouble, but I never realized how much."

"Well, we do appreciate what you have done for us," Asandi assured her. "Valthyrra, I still feel very bad about asking you to go out and risk such damage on your first flight."

"It is my job," the ship replied simply.

"I will get you replacement components as soon as they become available," he promised her. "Commander Gelrayen, I hardly recognized you."

Kelvessan did not blush, but Gelrayen still managed to look embarrassed. "That was actually Valthyrra's idea."

"And a long story, no doubt. Perhaps it can wait until after this meeting is concluded."

They were hurried into the meeting room and took their seats; Valthyrra settled her probe on the arms of her own chair, having observed that the remotes sent by several of the other ships had done the same. Captain Tarrel was led to wonder about this apparent change of policy, since none of the ships had themselves been present at any meetings during her previous visit to Alkayja station. Valthyrra began the discussion with a detailed account of her own experiences with the Dreadnought, concluding with a display of the single image of the machine that she had captured when it had lost its shield.

"I was given the opportunity to acquire additional information concerning many of those questions about the Dreadnought that we have been trying to answer," she said. "I still do not believe that it is fully self-aware, or many of its actions would have been more subtle. But just how clever is it? None of its actions during this incident indicated that it is very clever at all. It responds most often in a very simple, automatic manner. But we have in the past seen it function in a more clever, even unpredictable manner. My own conclusion is that it is a machine, but one that we must be careful not to underestimate.

"How fast is it, and just what type of drive can it be using inside that shield? My captured images show the back end of the Dreadnought, assuming that it even has a back or front in any conventional sense, and we can clearly see that it does not employ main drives or star drives as we know them. But I did observe evidence of unexpected speed. My own guess is that the Dreadnought uses a very refined version of a jump drive, technology that we do possess but never bothered to refine."

"But not a very powerful version of a field drive?" one of the Kelvessan engineers asked.

"Even a field drive has a very strong static power emission, but I did not detect anything. Any final speculation about that drive must wait for one piece of information that my files do not possess. Can Kelvessan sense a jump drive in operation? My crew was able to sense the Dreadnought's generators while its shield was down, but not a drive."

Not even any of the ships knew the answer to that question, but somewhere in that station were the records dating back to the time when the first jump drive had been tested aboard the carrier Valcyr, which had disappeared on her first flight.

"There is one observation that I certainly would not have expected to have found," Valthyrra continued. "I believe that the Dreadnought is nearly blind. Now it is only logical to realize that it is receiving no visual information through that light-consuming shield, but I now suspect that its ability to receive common scanner information is very limited. Once it had restored its shield, the Dreadnought pursued me at a following distance of less that a thousand kilometers. I was open to passive scan as well as being very visible against that planet, and yet it seemed unable to see me."

"Do you have any theories on that subject?" Asandi asked.

"For that matter, I believe that I have proof. Meaning no criticism, I suspect that our scientists here at Alkayja invented an explanation for why it could use its scanners through its own shields, when in fact it cannot," She began feeding images to the main viewscreen. "Because I did have the Dreadnought targeted clearly against the planet, I was able to get some detailed images of its shield. In these images, you can in fact see several relatively tiny objects protruding through the Dreadnought's shield. Several are knob-like projections about a meter across coming only just through the shield, which I believe are scanner beam projectors. There are also dozens of whip antennas, coming through the shield to a length of four or five meters, which are probably active and passive scan detectors. When the Dreadnought is under attack or trying to evade detection, it draws these units back until they are obscured from scan by that shield, but this severely limits the effectiveness of these devices."

"In that event, if the Dreadnought was attempting to avoid detection by one carrier, a second carrier might be able to slip in close enough to fire cannons through those shields?" Trendaessa Kerridayen observed.

"Yes, I believe so," Valthyrra agreed. "And that brings me to one very encouraging observation about the Dreadnought. I suspect that it might not be as tough to crack as we feared. Once a cannon bolt finds a way through that shield, it seems to take damage very easily, if only temporarily. It also seems to get shaken, as if it cannot decide whether to take an offensive or defensive stance. These are things that we can exploit to our advantage."

Asandi nodded slowly. "Since you have fought the Dreadnought with reasonable success, what do you recommend?"

"Is the Kerridayen fitted with an impulse scanner?" Valthyrra asked.

"Yes, but the ship is not yet fully repaired."

"Then my suggestion is that the Kerridayen and myself coordinate an attack, luring or driving the Dreadnought within range of an ambush. Once it has come within moderately close range, two or three carriers could match frequencies with their main batteries until they pierce that shield, standing by with either missiles or conversion cannons when it fails. Once we know where it is, we should be able to find a place to arrange an ambush easily enough. I will admit that this plan is not perfect, but it is the best that we have at this time."

"And you believe that you should be allowed to fight the Dreadnought?" Asandi asked.

"I believe that I should be allowed to coordinate the attack," Valthyrra declared frankly. "I have a feel for how the Dreadnought operates and reacts. I think that I have proven that."

"One might also argue that you were lucky," Asandi remarked. "It was my thought that we should have you repaired but held in reserve, in case our first major attack against the Dreadnought should fail. Captain Tarrel, what has been your impression of Valthyrra's performance?"

"Actually, I believe that she has done very well," Tarrel insisted. "I hesitate to speak plainly in her presence, however."

"I prefer that you should," Valthyrra told her.

"Then the bad news first," she continued. "Valthyrra still seems to be getting used to stressful situations and dealing with events beyond her own control, experiences she could not get sitting inside a construction bay. At the same time, she allows nothing to interfere with duty. When the time comes to act, she never fails to act cleverly and decisively. Although I must admit that my experience with the Starwolf carriers is limited, it did seem to me that she is more inventive and quicker to react than I found the Kerridayen to be. I believe that her desire to lead the fight against the Dreadnought has to be considered for the very reason she gave, although we must still consider all the alternatives."

"Some achieve greatness, some have greatness thrust upon them, and some are just built that way?" Asandi asked, amused. "Frankly, I do see reason to be impressed with our young ship. But regardless of her qualifications, the Methryn is still wrecked. Half of her main drives are out, her star drive is operating at half of normal efficiency, and a portion of her sensor array and her weapons have been destroyed. Will she be in any condition to fight any time soon? I cannot in all conscience send her into battle crippled."

"The star drives can be repaired easily enough," Gelrayer said. "Those can be fully operational in a few days. She does have four heat-damaged main drives that will need weeks to rebuild, but we could replace those here in station in a matter of hours.''

Asandi looked uncomfortable about that. ''As it happens, we have a full set of eight main drives in surplus here at the station, and the Methryn will get the four she needs. Fortunately, she is the first carrier to come home needing replacement drives.''

''All other repairs will be simple enough,'' Gelrayen continued. ''We can go out again in perhaps as little as four or five days.''

''What do you think about your ship's ability to fight?''

''I learned very quickly that I can trust her completely. She was making all the decisions and giving the orders during that battle.''

Asandi nodded slowly. ''What about her ability to lead others, and to deal with people? Does she have the experience to deal with others?''

Captain Tarrel smiled. ''You saw the state her crew was in. Valthyrra talked them into that quite cleverly. That was, by the way, a little joke that turned into a philosophical experiment.''

''A what?'' Gelrayen asked, perplexed. ''What does tricking several hundred Kelvessan into running around naked have to do with philosophy?''

''Well, Valthyrra and I discovered that the most amazing thing happens when you take the clothes off a Starwolf,'' Tarrel commented. ''He begins to contemplate the meaning of his existence and his place in the universe.''

''Oh, is that what causes it,'' he said, looking greatly surprised. ''Well, a Starwolf just has to be careful about the strange thoughts that seize the mind when he is naked.''

''If you don't mind . . .'' Commander Asandi suggested, rubbing his face. ''Captain, you need to be careful when you play games with my Starwolves.''

''It was Valthyrra's idea,'' Tarrel insisted.

''Was not!''

''If you don't mind,'' Asandi interrupted, then shook his head slowly. ''I would like to give Valthyrra what she wants, but I just do not feel that this is the time to stick out our necks and take a risk. I really believe that we should arrange a more conventional attack on the Dreadnought, at least this first time. Commander Daerran, the Kerridayen is in her bay, ready for battle. What do you think?''

"It seems to me that the question really comes down to deciding between two options," he answered. "No matter who leads the attack, the first question we have to ask is whether we plan to throw a majority of our resources into this first battle with the Dreadnought in the hope that it will be the last, or do we take only the ships here in station and leave the rest of the carriers running their patrols."

"Exactly," Gelrayen agreed. "Just how many carriers do we have here?"

"The Kerridayen, the Destaen, and the Mardayn are fully functional and ready for battle," Commander Asandi explained. "We have nearly completed work on the Vardon's hull, and the Methryn seems to think that she can be out again in four or five days. That gives us five fighting ships here at Alkayja, as well as the freighter Taerregyn to carry replacement components."

"I should probably add at this point that we only have operational sets of auxiliary shield generators for four ships," Dalvaen, the leader of the Kelvessan research team, told them. "At the same time, the Kerridayen is now fitted with a fully functional impulse scanner."

"That settles matters for me," Daerran said. "My own suggestion is that this group of five fighting ships should go out as soon as possible, locate the Dreadnought and try to arrange an ambush. The Kerridayen and the Methryn can direct the attacks of the other ships. If we feel like we need more help, we can call in two or three of the carriers on patrol near that area."

"Do you need the Methryn?" Commander Asandi asked.

"I honestly believe that we should pool our experiences before we go, and the Methryn's experience fighting the Dreadnought will certainly be valuable. But I doubt that we are going to have any idea of just what is best to do until we find the Dreadnought. As for having the Methryn come along, I would certainly like to have her at hand."

The other Starwolf ships and Commanders were quick enough to agree with his judgement, and that seemed to settle the matter. Commander Asandi looked thoughtful, but not necessarily upset or annoyed as he capitulated to their wishes. Still, Captain Tarrel was certain that he had his own ideas about the Methryn's immediate future, and not necessarily just to have her in reserve, as he had said. But, whatever his real reasons might be, they were nothing that she could guess.

The final decision was to send out the main battle fleet consisting of the Mardayn, the Destaen, and the Vardon, supported by the Kerridayen and the Methryn. They would be able to direct the other carriers with their impulse scanners, since those three ships would actually be fighting blind. This arrangement was actually to their advantage, since the attacking ships would be able to correct the impulse images transferred to them by the surveillance carriers that would be standing off, but without betraying their own presence with beams. These three ships were to receive a pair of auxiliary shield generators each, with the Kerridayen receiving the last available pair in the event they were needed. The fact that the Methryn was passed over for receiving a pair seemed to indicate that she was held to be inferior in status to the older carriers. The Starwolf freighter Taerregyn would accompany this fleet, carrying a wide variety of replacement parts, extra drives and construction crews from Alkayja station, and she would be standing by to tow any carrier that could not be repaired in space.

Commander Asandi intercepted Tarrel in the hallway once the meeting had been concluded. "Captain, I was wondering if I might speak with you privately for a moment."

"Certainly," she answered, falling into step beside him.

"First, I should tell you that I appreciate the difficulty of the decision you made when you ordered Valthyrra to fire that missile, and I commend your ability to act quickly and decisively," he began, then hesitated. "If it is your intention, however, to go out with the Starwolves yet again, then I feel that I should warn you about the danger of tampering with their social self-image."

"Danger?" Tarrel asked. "That was actually Valthyrra's doing, and it began only as a joke. They were trying to call each other's bluffs, and that young machine out-bluffed them all. I just happened to observe the results."

Commander Asandi looked uncomfortable. "Those Starwolves are insidious. They can be so candid and good-natured that you find yourself compelled to love them. Even you, an honored Union Captain; you are beginning to love them yourself. You want to help them. I want to help them, and that makes it only that much harder to deny them. But the fact remains that we have been working to keep their self-image in balance for tens of thousands of years, and this is certainly not the time to upset things."

"Pardon?"

"That happens to be my real job, you understand," he told her. "What real good am I to the Starwolves otherwise, the human senior commander of a Kelvessan fleet? I supervise what they think and do, as far as I am able. I limit their numbers as best I can, and they do not seem inclined to reproduce when you send them down to a planet. I take their best scientific minds from the carriers and assemble them here, then I give them busywork. We do not want them making technical advances, and their carriers are essentially the same machines they were thirty thousand years ago. They could have perfected the jump drive long ago, and any number of new weapons. We are satisfied that they have everything they need as it is."

He indicated for her to precede him into the tram, then waited until they were away. "The Kelvessan were designed to be naked. The Aldessan of Valtrys meant things that way. That is all part of the balance, keeping them between two cultures and never really a part of any. They use the Aldessan language and names, but with the Terran alphabet. They do not look very human, but we encourage them to dress themselves as if they were human. Everything they have amounts to bits and pieces of other cultures, and very little is entirely their own."

"But what possible danger could they be?" Tarrel asked, frankly shocked by what she was hearing. "The Kelvessan are the most amiable people I've ever met, at least to have as friends and allies. Would they ever have reason to turn on us?"

"Oh no, they would never be a danger to us in that sense, unless we do something to deserve it," he agreed. "Captain, the Republic and the Union might be opposing camps, but consider this. Together our worlds define a very specific region of space, and we are not interested in looking beyond those boundaries. Although we are not the only civilized race within those limits, we are certainly the preeminent race in numbers, power and prestige. Neither side really wants to see that change."

"No, I suppose not," Tarrel admitted. "Still, I don't see how they can be a threat to us even in that sense. They aren't prolific and I don't see them as being interested in establishing commercial empires."

Asandi nodded. "Yes, but consider this. Our interplanetary systems of commerce are dependant upon trade and travel through space, and space is the element the Kelvessan were designed to conquer. If they were free to pursue their own future, they would control a large portion of interstellar space because their ships are larger and faster than anything we have. They would take the responsibility of seeing that the space lanes and the frontier are safe. In addition to that, all new technology would be coming from Kelvessan researchers. We would come to be dependant upon the Kelvessan. Although we would prosper under their leadership, our prosperity would be dependant upon their leadership.''

''Is that so bad?'' Tarrel asked, watching the corridors of the station pass by the tram's windows.

''Perhaps not, but would we be able to accept that?'' he asked. ''One of our greatest strengths, and also one of our greatest needs, is to command our own destinies. We are human. However much you might like them, the Kelvessan are still only highly advanced biological machines. Perhaps some day they might evolve into a real sentient, free-willed race. But right now they are still guided by the instincts of compassion and duty that they were given. Their eagerness to defend even their old enemies from the Dreadnought is proof of that. I certainly was not in favor of that. I knew that they would need new weapons to fight that thing, and I knew that it would be difficult to maintain the old balances through all of this. The Starwolves are happy with what they are.''

''Slaves,'' Tarrel commented sourly.

''Slaves are people held in bondage against their will,'' he told her. ''The Kelvessan are satisfied to be exactly what they are, fulfilling the needs and goals that they were given. Do not teach them expectations of themselves that they are not yet ready to confront.''

''No, I don't feel qualified to teach them anything; it just seemed to me that the process was beginning naturally,'' she said, and smiled wryly. ''That was certainly the last thing I expected to find.''

''What is that?''

She glanced at him. ''I was just thinking how alike your side and mine really are. We both seem willing to nominate someone else to make sacrifices for our benefit.''

—11—

Once the Starwolf fleet had found the Dreadnought, preparing an ambush for it proved to be simple enough. After determining which system it was most likely to strike next—and they had certainly proven their ability to predict its movements—they had hurried to arrive first. The Methryn and the Kerridayen positioned themselves well out at opposite sides of the system where they could sweep it with their impulse scanners very efficiently, and the Methryn had already shown that low-intensity pulses were effective at showing up the Dreadnought's location without alerting it that it was being scanned. The other three carriers had hidden themselves behind planets deeper within the system, where one of them might easily be able to slip in close behind the Dreadnought on its sub-light approach. Captain Tarrel had used her authority to order the local station abandoned, but not removed or powered down, with the Union's System Fleet of twenty-three large ships still moored at their docks. With bait like that to hold its attention, the Dreadnought would run straight in to attack.

Once the carriers were in position, they had no way of knowing if they would be waiting hours or days for the Dreadnought to arrive. At this point, there was little else for them to do. Once the alien weapon was identified, and assuming that it was not alerted to their presence in the process, then one of the three carriers deeper in the system would try to move in close behind it and match the frequency of its shield with her impulse cannons, repeating the Methryn's successful attack earlier. This time, however, that trick would be attempted from a greater distance, at least a thousand kilometers, so that the attacking carrier would have time and room enough to hit the Dreadnought again with either missiles or a low-intensity discharge from her conversion cannon. That would surely disable the Dreadnought long enough for the other carriers to move in for the kill. If everything went according to plan, the Methryn and the Kerridayen would never even enter the fight.

Neither of those two ships were pleased with that arrangement, and not because it failed to include them as anything except surveillance platforms. Trendaessa Kerridayen was convinced that they were again underestimating the Dreadnought's strategic abilities. She believed that it had already proven itself too clever to make the same mistake twice. Valthyrra Methryn agreed with her completely. She strongly believed that she knew just how to attack the Dreadnought; she believed that they had been making the same mistake from the first, trying to fight it as one large ship against another. Captain Tarrel believed that Valthyrra was taking the right approach, but she did not have a vote in the matter and the other three carriers had overruled Valthyrra Methryn and Trendaessa Kerridayen. The Starwolves themselves seemed reluctant to interfere with the authority of their ships, allowing the carriers to decide the matter among themselves.

In the two weeks since these battle plans had been made at that meeting at Alkayja station, Janus Tarrel had kept her counsels very much to herself. She found herself having to do something that she had never expected: she was having to reconsider her personal beliefs. What she could not figure out was why Fleet Commander Asandi's little speech about the Republic's secret attitude toward its Starwolves should be so upsetting to her, since it supported everything that she had always believed. The Starwolves were property, genetically engineered weapons of war to be used and discarded; her own kind came first. Justice had to be weighed against the greater good, and even towering injustices were sometimes necessary for the benefit of the greatest number. Those whose rights and welfare needed most to be sacrificed for the benefit of a larger society most often needed that judgement forced upon them, since they were not likely to accept such sacrifices willingly. As a Union Captain, she had enforced that very philosophy often enough in the past, always reluctantly, but always comfortable in the belief that it was proper and necessary.

Now she was beginning to wonder if there was ever any hidden justice in injustice, and if any society that demanded the innocent to pay the price for someone else's benefit was inherently corrupt. She understood now why the Starwolves believed in that philosophy, blissfully unaware that they were enforcing a moral belief that was secretly denied to them. She could also understand why that was such a driving force in luring the Terran colonies, raped of the little wealth they generated, into making ill-advised attempts at independence.

Absolute justice was always preferable, but she still had to remind herself that it was not always possible. Although she was tempted to warn the Kelvessan about how they were being used, she could not yet convince herself that it would be best even for them if she did. Commander Asandi had warned her against teaching them to expect something that they were not equipped to have, and in this case there was indeed some justice in denying them the right of freedom and self-determination because such things were meaningless to their present existence. For good or bad, they were exactly what they were designed to be.

Of course, the matter could well be out of her hands. Valthyrra Methryn had become deeply fascinated with the Kelvessan and the development of their racial consciousness. She had turned up her thermostats and ordered her crew out of their clothes again as soon as they had left Alkayja, and she was now trying to convince them to make that a permanent condition. Tarrel suspected that her goal was to undress the entire Starwolf fleet, encourage them to think about their racial identity, and eventually suggest that they should attempt some additional, purely cosmetic tampering with their genetics. Valthyrra obviously believed that external appearances were the key to encouraging the Kelvessan to develop greater self-awareness and social independence, and she was most likely correct.

But, with battle threatening at any time, the ship's temperatures went down more than usual to cool the electronics and the Starwolves kept themselves inside their armor at all times. Captain Tarrel stayed inside her own armor as well, having developed an instinctive fear of being caught without it. When the time came, it happened suddenly and sooner than they had expected. The Dreadnought entered the system along the predicted approach and passed almost directly over the Methryn, at least in relative distances. In fact, the two ships missed each other by half a million kilometers. Valthyrra identified it even before it dropped sub-light.

"Contact," she warned, sending the members of the bridge crew hurrying to their stations. Then she spun her camera pod around in a circle. "Perdition! I never thought about that."

"Thought about what?" Gelrayen asked as he helped Tarrel with the straps of her seat. "This is no time for anyone to be making a mistake."

"I cannot warn the ships deeper in the system even with a tight beam, not without the Dreadnought intercepting it." She paused a moment. "I am relaying my information to the freighter Taerregyn. Since she is sitting well outside the system, she can relay the report to the other ships by tight beam from a different angle."

"Is everything going according to plan?" Gelrayen asked as he descended the steps to the main bridge level.

"It does seem to be. The Dreadnought is going straight in toward the one inhabited planet. Because I am closer than the Kerridayen, she has signaled that I should provide the only surveillance contact for now. I am using a very low-level sweep every twenty seconds, and I am now feeding the scanner images to the main carrier fleet through my link with the Taerregyn. The Mardayn is beginning her maneuvers that will eventually bring her slowly in behind the Dreadnought."

"No impulse beams from the Dreadnought?" Gelrayen asked.

"None that have been detected so far. The other carriers are now much closer, and might be able to detect an impulse sweep on their own passive impulse scanners. However, the Mardayn reports that she cannot detect my sweeps even knowing that they are there, but she does not have sensors."

"Then you need to watch very carefully," he reminded her. "Those ships are depending upon you to tell them when to run."

Over the next few minutes, the Mardayn fell in directly behind the Dreadnought and began to close the distance quickly as the alien weapon continued to brake on its approach toward the colony. Valthyrra was beginning to feel increasingly uncomfortable with the situation. The Dreadnought was not using its impulse scanner on routine sweeps, as it had in the past. She knew that it would never simply forget and she could not believe that she had damaged its impulse scanners beyond repair during their last encounter. That led her to the uncomfortable conclusion that it was up to something. Could it have refined its own sensors so greatly that it was reading the achronic echoes of her own sweeps? Even as the Mardayn moved in to attack, with every outward indication that she remained undetected, Valthyrra felt certain that the ambush was about to turn back on them.

"Commander, we have to decide something immediately," she said at last. "I want to terminate this attack right now, before we get into trouble. This is not right. The Dreadnought is not making regular precautionary impulse sweeps, as it has been seen to do in the past. It knows."

"How could it know anything specifically?" he asked. "Even if it is aware of us, how can it know the present location of our ships?"

"I suspect that it might be reading the echoes from my own sweeps. I also suggest that a Starwolf carrier puts a fifteen million ton dent in the fabric of space, a very small gravity well, but made very conspicuous by the fact that it is moving."

Gelrayen made his decision quickly, and nodded. "Relay your suspicions to the Mardayn."

"I am, Commander," Valthyrra reported. "She agrees with my judgement of the situation, but she refuses to break off yet. She still wants a shot at the Dreadnought, in the hope that it is not entirely certain of how matters stand."

With the Mardayn unwilling to withdraw, the other carriers had to hold their own positions for fear that any movement might alert the Dreadnought to their presence, if it did not know already. Distances within a system were deceptive; a system looked like a relatively small and crowded space, with no part of it more than a few minutes away to a fast ship like a Starwolf carrier. But those distances were still great enough that none of the five carriers could have moved quickly to assist another. Tracking with cannons would have been impossible at that range, and a missile would need minutes of flight time.

"Commander, I can see the flaw in this plan," Valthyrra warned. "As the Mardayn comes closer to the Dreadnought, we will have to terminate our tight beam transmission of scanner images or the other ship is going to detect that signal for certain. And that is going to leave the Mardayn blind. I am now ordering the Mardayn to break off."

"She can simply ignore you," Gelrayen remarked. "Keep feeding her all the data you have, no matter what."

"The Kaeridayen is supporting my decision to terminate the attack, and the Mardayn seems likely to agree. This is the very reason why I should have been the one to go in after the Dreadnought."

Unfortunately, by the time the Mardayn agreed that it was time to retreat, it was already too late for her. The Dreadnought made no change in either course or speed; it simply attacked. The Starwolf carrier suddenly found herself caught in a broad, pale beam that was stripping away power from her shields faster than she could pour more energy into them, leaving her nothing left over for her weapons or drives. She called for help, loudly and directly, and the other carriers hurried to her rescue. The Methryn hurtled herself in through the system so quickly that Captain Tarrel lost consciousness during the first few moments.

If any of the other ships could have drawn a part of that fire or made a distraction of themselves, it would have helped. Unfortunately, they were simply too far away to be a threat. Even as the Mardayn struggled under that first assault, a single beam of intense power struck her in the nose and began to eat steadily along her length through the core of her main hull. After only seconds, that narrow beam had cut into her engineering regions and the powerful conversion generators already struggling to meet the demands placed upon them to maintain the shields. The Mardayn was lost in a blinding flash, like that of the explosion of a small star; an explosion so great that it knocked even the Dreadnought from its course a thousand kilometers away.

The other carriers reacted furiously to the sudden, violent death of their sister, turning to strike without hesitation. As soon as the Methryn was able to resume her transmission of impulse images, the two closer carriers hurtled in to attack while the Dreadnought was still disoriented from the force of that explosion. Captain Tarrel admired their determination. The absolute destruction of a Starwolf carrier was such a rare event that she found herself shaken almost beyond the ability to think clearly. Granted, the Starwolves and their ships were probably designed to always keep going, no matter what.

"I am advising the other carriers to keep themselves moving constantly and quickly," Valthyrra reported with deceptive calm. "These new weapons are obviously effective only if they can be locked on target for several seconds. We can counter that by darting in and making rapid strikes with our main batteries."

"Do the other carriers understand?" Gelrayen asked.

"They have acknowledged," Valthyrra said, bringing her camera pod around to face where he stood behind the Commander's station. "No doubt in response to its failure in its battle with me, the Dreadnought determined the need to increase its effectiveness. Either it had these more powerful weapons in reserve, it adapted weapons it already had, or it created new ones."

"Trendaessa Vardon was right," the Starwolf commented sourly, watching the impulse scan on the main monitor. "That machine does have more tricks than we gave it credit for."

"You people seem to be missing the whole point," Captain Tarrel declared, sounding rather desperate even to herself. "That machine just took out one of your carriers. What can you do now but throw bolts at a shield that you know you can't penetrate this way?"

"Yes, you have a perfectly valid point," Valthyrra agreed, lifting her camera pod slightly. "Commander, I am ordering the packs to the fighter bays. This is what we should have done from the start."

Gelrayen nodded slowly. "I can see no other way that we might salvage this situation."

Valthyrra Methryn was taking herself into the system as quickly as she could, building her speed steadily to take herself just barely into starflight for the few moments she needed. The Vardon and the Destaen were trying to engage the Dreadnought by themselves, since neither the Kerridayen nor the Methryn would come into range for another couple of minutes. They were trying to fight a ship that they could not track directly, through the impulse images being relayed to them by Valthyrra. Their attack so far had proven to be completely ineffective, but at least the Dreadnought seemed unable to lock its new, more powerful weapons on the carriers as long as they kept moving.

After a quick conversation with Trendaessa Kerridayen, Valthyrra began braking somewhat early. Since she was the only carrier that lacked auxiliary shield generators, she would stand off a short distance and provide accurate impulse scans of the Dreadnought to help the other ships to coordinate their own attack. That also gave her the opportunity to get her fighters moved down to the bays and launch her packs, something the other carriers could not manage while they were engaged in quick evasive maneuvers.

"Commander, the first packs are moving into the bays now," Valthyrra said. "The Kerridayen has joined the Vardon and the Destaen in battle."

"Are they having any success?" Gelrayen asked.

"That is extremely hard to measure. The objective now is to blind the Dreadnought completely by depriving it of all external sensors, and we can only judge whether that plan is effective by the deterioration of the Dreadnought's tracking control. I am not yet certain that we have had any success, but it will take time."

As Captain Tarrel interpreted that, the Starwolves would know that their attack was effective if the Dreadnought failed to destroy them. They knew, or assumed with very good reason, that the Dreadnought was able to see by means of sensors extended through the shield, and that it could be blinded by burning off those sensors with cannon fire. She agreed with Valthyrra that the fighters, quicker and far more maneuverable than the carriers, and much smaller targets, were better suited to this task. The carriers had been doing the fighting so far on the assumption that they were more durable than the fighters, but that assumption was possibly in error. The Dreadnought had the weapons to destroy a carrier, but the fighters might have a superior defense in their ability to evade.

But even if the Starwolves did succeed in blinding the Dreadnought, and silencing its weapons, that still did not mean that they had won the battle. As Captain Tarrel saw it, the Dreadnought could either run blind or simply sit tight where it was like some creature safe in its shell. When their first trick had failed, she felt that it was time to clear out before things got worse and send the Starwolves back to their drawing boards to work on some new weapons for cracking that shield.

"Commander, the Kerridayen is down," Valthyrra warned.

"What happened to her?" Gelrayen asked, hurrying to consult the scanner image.

"The Dreadnought was able to lock on her with a discharge beam," the ship explained. "Her main generators seem to be down; no doubt the discharge was powerful enough to disrupt her main power grid. She is trying to retreat on secondary power, but the Dreadnought is chewing her to pieces."

"Move in to intercept," Gelrayen told her. "We have to give her time to get away."

"I am moving in now, and the Freighter Taerregyn is coming into system to assist in towing. I am launching my first packs now."

The first group of four packs hurtled out of their bays on the Methryn's belly, drives flaring as they emerged beneath the carrier's nose. Guided by Valthyrra's scanner images, they moved off quickly to intercept their prey, assuming their standard Vee formation before each ship at the end of the wings moved to take positions one above and the other below the pack. As soon as the bays were clear, Valthyrra moved away the empty racks and began bringing forward the next groups of fighters.

At the same time she was holding herself on a course to intercept the Kerridayen, ready to do whatever she could to distract the Dreadnought. The Destaen was there ahead of her, sitting off to one side of the Kerridayen and turning the full power of her main battery against the Dreadnought, heedless of the discharge beams ripping apart her enhanced shields. The alien weapon continued to focus the greatest part of its attention on the stricken carrier, blasting away sections of her unprotected hull. A large portion of her nose and wings were gone already, torn apart by internal explosions and burning furiously.

"Valthyrra, be careful!" Gelrayen warned her sharply. "If you lose your impulse scanners, then we will be the ones who will be blind and helpless. The Kerridayen has to have lost her own already."

"Trendaessa Kerridayen is dead," Valthyrra said softly.

Gelrayen looked up at her camera pod. "What do you mean?"

"Her main computer grid is destroyed. What remains of her crew is trying to abandon ship, and we have to buy them time." Valthyrra turned her camera pod to the main viewscreen. "I am ordering the packs to stand clear of the Dreadnought, and I am charging my conversion cannon. Transports from the Vardon and the Destaen as well as my own are standing by to collect escape pods from the Kerridayen."

"Conversion cannons have no effect on the Dreadnought," Captain Tarrel reminded her. "The Kerridayen tried that one before."

Valthyrra turned her camera pod. "I do not anticipate damaging it."

Before she had a chance to act, the Destaen also took a very bad hit in her main engineering regions and was shaken by a series of explosions that disabled her drives and most of her main conversion generators. The damage was very serious, but not a threat to the survival of the carrier as long as she was protected from further harm. That left only the Methryn and the Vardon in any condition to fight; the Taerregyn was a freighter and possessed only minimal weapons. Valthyrra rotated about, locked her conversion cannon on target and discharged the stellar reserve of energy that she had assembled in her conversion holding chamber. She released that flood of searing power slowly, pouring it over the Dreadnought's shield for as long as she could.

Valthyrra cleared her impulse scanner as quickly as she could, as soon as she had exhausted her reserve of energy, fearful of how the Dreadnought would respond. Perhaps she had done in one stroke what the other carriers had been unable to manage, blinding the Dreadnought by burning away the sensor array and other detection devices extended just outside its shield. The immense machine remained drifting on its previous course, deflected slightly by the Methryn's conversion discharge, its weapons still. Valthyrra doubted that this condition would last for long; she instructed the other ships to hurry in their rescue efforts, and ordered the packs to keep clear of the Dreadnought for fear of provoking a response.

Now that the Destaen was crippled, the Taerregyn had no choice but to tow it to safety, leaving the burning hulk of the Kerridayen's remains behind. If the Dreadnought left the wreckage alone, perhaps they could return later to discover if any of Trendaessa's memory units remained intact and could be salvaged. The Taerregyn moved in directly above the Destaen and settled until the two ships were nearly touching, and the freighter locked onto the carrier's hull magnetically with retractable grappling units. Once the two ships were secured, the Taerregyn engaged her main drives and began moving them both to safety. The Methryn and the Vardon remained behind, waiting for their transports and capture ships to gather in the Kerridayen's escape pods.

"Judging by the number of escape pods I have counted, I believe that we can hope to recover one third to one half of the Kerridayen's crew," Valthyrra reported. "I have ordered the packs to return to their bays, since there is no hope in continuing this fight. The Dreadnought is still distracted with her own condition."

"Are we giving up?" Gelrayen asked.

"No, but we are going to do this the way I knew it should be done from the first. As soon as we have all survivors aboard, then we are going through that shield to destroy that monster."

"According to the plans we have discussed?" Gelrayen asked, although he knew what her answer would be. "How many fighters do we have modified so far?"

"Only two, but I have every reason to expect that to be enough. The question of pilots for those two ships remains. Granted that I expect you to claim one of those ships for yourself, and I do not intend to protest that. This mission will require your experience and judgement. Will you take Pack Leader Teraln with you?"

Gelrayen looked unhappy. "The problem in deciding is that we have never had a chance to see our packs in operation, so all I have to judge them on is their records. Teraln looks like the best choice."

"I am moving the fighters to the lower left bay and having them fitted with auxiliary weapons," Valthyrra told him. "We should be ready to launch in a quarter of an hour."

"I want to go down to the bay now and have a look at that ship," Gelrayen said, then turned to Captain Tarrel. "Would you like to come with me?"

"Yes, I'm very much interested in this great plan of yours," Tarrel said as he helped her from the seat. "My Starwolves seem to be keeping secrets these days."

"Well, you *are* the enemy," he told her as they descended the steps from the upper bridge. Gelrayen paused to collect his helmet. "When Valthyrra observed that the Dreadnought is able to see by extending probes and sensors through that shield, she began to wonder how that was done. A shield that dense should seem completely solid to any physical object, and its tremendous power should have fried any electronics being poked through. And yet we know that the Dreadnought does extend some of its most sensitive sensory devices through its shield. How?"

"Good question," Tarrel agreed as they stepped aboard the lift.

"The answer is so simple that Valthyrra only had to think about it for half a minute," Gelrayen explained. "Any shield is simply a projection of a great deal of energy, and there would always be static discharge between the ship and the shield except that the shield is grounded to the ship. Under those circumstances, anything that is also grounded to the ship is grounded to the shield as well. That tells you how to put something through a shield."

"Yes, I see," Tarrel agreed. "Then modifying a fighter to penetrate that shield is very simple. The tricky part is actually doing it."

The concept sounded reasonable enough and she believed that the Starwolves might actually make it work. It involved some piloting that she would not have attempted, but the flying skills of the Starwolves were legendary. There was something about this business that bothered her a great deal, but she was not going to mention anything to Commander Gelrayen at this time. By the time that the lift had carried them all the way back through the ship to the bay, the packs that had been launched earlier had already come back aboard. Two packs had returned to that bay, and the overhead handling arms were lifting the large black fighters into their racks for safe storage.

Gelrayen went immediately to the pair of fighters sitting in their racks at the front of the bay. The only difference in these two large ships, at least that Tarrel could see, was that they had been fitted with some curious harpoon and cable device under their long, tapered noses. Each ship also carried four featureless black pods farther back along their extended forward hulls, things that looked suspiciously like explosive devices. Pack Leader Teraln was already waiting for them, standing beside the nearest of the two fighters while one of Valthyrra's probes hovered at his side.

"Has Valthyrra explained the theory to you?" Gelrayen asked.

"Theory, yes," Teraln agreed. "What she has not explained is why I get to volunteer for this."

"Your name started with a T," Gelrayen offered. "If you have no interest in going along, I can find another volunteer easily enough."

Teraln looked surprised and annoyed at the idea that he could be replaced. "Oh, yes? Who?"

"Captain Tarrel, for one."

"Oh. Then I certainly volunteer."

"I wonder if I should be offended?" Tarrel asked Valthyrra, but the remote gestured "no" with its camera pod.

"Valthyrra, what is the Dreadnought doing?" Gelrayen asked as he climbed the boarding platform beside the cockpit.

"Absolutely nothing, last time I looked," she responded. "I have decreased my impulse scans to one each minute, to avoid calling an excess of attention to myself."

"Then I believe that we should go immediately," he decided. "If we wait until that thing starts to move, we might never get a chance to attempt this maneuver. We will be dependant upon your scans to lead us to it."

"As long as she can place us to within twenty kilometers," Teraln amended as he hurried to his own fighter. "From that range, you can actually see the beast. That shield is actually a shade darker than background space."

"Then do not alter your scan interval, unless it begins to move again," Gelrayen added as he settled himself into the cockpit, while a bay crewmember helped him with his straps. "If it stays in one place, we already know all we need about where to find it."

"I understand," Valthyrra said.

"Complete your rescue efforts quickly, and then you and the Vardon should begin to withdrew slowly. I will need you back immediately once that shield goes down, so put Captain Tarrel back in her seat. Teraln and I will get ourselves well clear before you come into range. If, by chance, this does not work and I do not come back, then you are to have sole command of the ship, but listen to Kayendel and Captain Tarrel. Your first duty is save yourself and the other ships. Anything else?"

"Take good care of yourself," Valthyrra called to him. "I love you."

Gelrayen paused and stared. "What?"

"Hey, bear with me. This emotional stuff is all very new to me."

The two fighters sealed their cockpits, and began to power up their major systems. Valthyrra and Captain Tarrel joined the bay crew in retreating a short distance, as blast barriers came up from the lower deck to protect the ships farther back in the bay from the drive wash. The two pilots signaled that they were ready and Valthyrra gave them a count with the lights above the forward bay door. The two fighters engaged their main drives at the final green light, but left their racks and moved out of the bay relatively slowly, dropping down to avoid the transports and capture ships bringing escape pods to the transport bays near the front of the carrier.

"Well, what are their chances?" Tarrel asked.

"Very good, I should think."

Tarrel glanced down at the probe. "Valthyrra, did you ever have a chance to discuss this plan with Fleet Commander Asandi?"

"Yes, I discussed it with him by com during my approach to Alkayja station after my last battle with Dreadnought. He said then that the plan was too dangerous, that the packs would not survive in close range to the Dreadnought. We have already seen that they can. Commander Asandi told me that I should not discuss this plan with the other carriers."

"I see." Tarrel turned toward the lift, expecting the probe to follow her. "Did it ever occur to you that Commander Asandi deliberately sent this fleet into a battle that he knew would be too dangerous? To phrase things a little more plainly, do you suspect that it might have been in his interests to commit a portion of his fleet to their own destruction?"

"Is there any reason to suspect why he should?"

"Commander Asadi indicated to me that the Republic fears the Kelvessan and has reason to make certain that they do not prosper. I am betraying his trust in me, but I believe that he has failed in his trust with the Kelvessan and their ships."

"I had suspected that the Republic, or at least the Fleet Commanders, had a history of failing to encourage Kelvessan scientific and cultural development. I am not convinced that Commander Asandi contrived the destruction of this fleet, only that he displayed poor judgement in refusing to consider my plan more seriously. I must discuss this privately with the other ships."

Tarrel stepped inside the lift that opened at her approach, then moved aside as the probe drifted in behind her. "You carriers can make up for the lack of support from the Republic."

Valthyrra looked up. "How?"

"You seem to have made a good start. Don't let them wear their clothes. Do whatever it takes to keep them thinking about their own racial identity. Talk them into altering their appearance. Just do what you think best."

The two fighters moved cautiously into position, engaging their main drives no more than absolutely necessary. They really did not believe that they were fooling anyone with such subtlety; least of all the Dreadnought, with its proven instinct for seeking out and destroying any machine it found in space, including many smaller and less obstructive than a Starwolf fighter. Their only hope was that the Dreadnought would remain drifting on its present course and continue to stubbornly ignore anything going on about it, and they simply wanted to encourage that condition to continue for as long as possible by being reasonably discreet.

Considering the fact that the Dreadnought had just devastated a fleet of Starwolf carriers, destroying two and severely damaging a third, the ability of two lone fighters to face and destroy that beast seemed very unlikely.

The Methryn's scan gave them the Dreadnought's position easily enough, bringing them slowly in with perfect accuracy, behind the target that they could not see. Eventually as Pack Leader Teraln had said, the Dreadnought could be seen. At very close range, it was darker than background space, and no stars could be seen through that blackness. It had been very considerate so far, staying on course and ignoring their presence if it knew they were there at all. Even Valthyrra had been unable to offer any explanation on what the Dreadnought could be doing while it drifted, seeming to have closed itself tightly inside its shield. It might have been contemplating strategies, believing that it had failed in its mission because it had been unable to destroy all the Starwolf carriers. It might have simply been repairing a wrecked sensor array. Whatever it was doing, it certainly went about it with single-minded determination and an absolute belief in its own invulnerability.

Commander Gelrayen brought his fighter in close behind the Dreadnought, so close that the fighter's forward lights diffused into the shield only three meters away. The plan now depended completely upon their finding a sensor or scanning device protruding through the shield. Valthyrra had insisted that the Dreadnought would never leave itself completely blind unless it was trying to protect its array from direct attack. After several moments of frantic search, fearful that the Dreadnought would move away at any time, he finally saw the slender whip of a receiver extended barely half a meter outside the shield. It was black and difficult to see, even in the flood of the fighter's auxiliary lights.

Gelrayen moved quickly, activating the remote device that Valthyrra had designed and built, now attached below the nose of his ship. A long probe extended forward of the ship, far enough that he could see the simple clawed end, and he moved his fighter forward until that claw touched the sensor probe just above the point where it disappeared within the shield. The claw rotated, sharp edges cutting away the insulation until it sensed contact with bare metal, then detached itself from its arm so that the fighter was tethered by a short cable. Gelrayen waited until Teraln's fighter attached itself in the same manner, and the two ships pivoted carefully until they were facing the shield.

The next step had to be done quickly and nearly in unison, for fear that the Dreadnought might react to the intrusion. The harpoon device under each fighter's nose opened into a spread of four long, slender legs, each one ending in an electromagnetic pad. The harpoons were launched, driven through the heavy resistance of the shield by their own small solid-fuel engines, but they did pass through and signaled back through the heavy cable trailed behind them that they had locked onto the ship within. The pilots hastily shut down the drives, main generators and major electronic systems of their fighters, then activated the powerful winches that pulled the small ships through the darkness of the shield. There was some static discharge—pale lights that raced along the sharp edges of their hulls—but nothing of consequence. And then they were through.

The device that Valthyrra had designed had included a powerful array of auxiliary lights, enough to flood vast areas of the interior of the Dreadnought's shield. She had never anticipated that the ship itself would have been illuminated, and yet large areas of the Dreadnought were brilliantly lit. Even the darker regions of the immense ship, especially near the end, were partially lit by icy white sheets of light from small, powerful lamps.

And there was certainly enough to see. After the Methryn's previous encounter with the Dreadnought, their one brief glimpse inside the shield had been enough to show them a complex array of shapes, rather than the smooth, armored hull they would have expected. Now they could see for the first time that the Dreadnought had no outer hull, and that it was in fact only a sweeping spaceframe containing the ship's various generators, reactionless drives and other components. The outside of the frame bristled with countless slender towers or projections, no doubt the supports for sensors and probes that could be extended through the shield, and a scattering of machines as large as a Starwolf fighter that were built onto pivoting stands, probably the discharge cannons. The shield itself fit up close against the shell of the Dreadnought, averaging no more than twenty meters of clearance, although somewhat more at the end where the two fighters had penetrated. They were standing almost nose-down against the frame as it was.

"Well, that explains a lot," Gelrayen commented aloud.

"That explains what?" Teraln asked.

"This ship has no physical hull. The shield must be intended to stay up at all times; the power assembly must be designed to feed it constantly without taking power from any other systems. Under the circumstances, an armored hull would be ten or fifteen million tons of superfluous weight. Of course, it does have one serious defensive flaw that we just exploited. I wonder if their original enemies ever figured that out."

"Perhaps the Dreadnought has a software problem," Teraln suggested. "They could have prevented this kind of little problem by having it shoot anything of any size that came within a certain range. But, if they did, that feature is malfunctioning. There is one thing I do wonder about, Commander."

"Yes?"

"All of these lights. Could this machine be an inhabited ship, or might it have been one originally? We knew already that it is nothing more than a giant, automated hazard to navigation. Perhaps it was meant to have supervision in handling more complex problems."

"I suspect that these auxiliary lights are meant for visual inspection of the ship by its own maintenance remotes," Gelrayen answered. "Nothing about the Dreadnought is a flaw or deficiency if you consider that this machine was probably built to destroy an enemy whose almost infinite numbers made up for an inferior technology, less complex than our own. If they had been on about the same level as the Union, they never would have been able to track it, much less fight it."

He disconnected his fighter from the harpoon, jettisoning the entire winch assembly now that the device had served its function, keeping only the rack of auxiliary lights, anticipating a future need for those. Then he rotated his fighter around and began to move slowly forward along the length of the Dreadnought, using only field drive. The fact that the Dreadnought did not have a physical hull made their task a great deal easier, and the effectiveness of their attack potentially considerably greater. The machinery was built on a scale that was vast even by the standards of the Starwolf carriers, with enough room to navigate the fighters slowly through the interior of the ship. The conversion devices could be planted deep inside, where they would do the greatest damage.

As they moved along the length of the Dreadnought, they came soon to the first of four areas that were the most brilliantly lit. This was the result of long rows or grids of crystalline lights set into long, rectangular recessed areas in the side of the ship, obviously designed to serve some function other than simply providing illumination for the maintenance of the ship.

"Radiant intercoolers," Gelrayen observed.

"You expected to find something like this?" Teraln asked.

"Valthyrra checked her archives and found that radiant intercoolers were associated with experimental jump drives. You might notice that these grids are surrounded by reflective pans designed to direct the light outward into the shield, where it is likely absorbed as energy and directed back into the power grid. Very efficient. Considering the fact that these drives are idle at the moment, I would not want to be here when they are engaged. We would be fried."

Since he had seen enough of the exterior of the ship, Gelrayen directed his fighter inward, finding an opening around the radiant intercoolers. The passage was often tight or dimly lit, but they were always able to find a way through. The maze of machinery meant little in itself, but Gelrayen was able to begin piecing together a general design of the Dreadnought. He found that it was built in segments; four short segments that appeared to contain the jump drives with their intercooler grids facing outward. To either side of each drive segment was a power segment, containing nothing except stacked arrays of scores of vast conversion generators. The Dreadnought was perhaps ten times the size and weight of a single Starwolf carrier, but its generating capacity was at least a hundred times greater. The armored double tube of the power core ran along the center length of the ship, distributing and directing that tremendous power to where it was needed. The power core was itself surrounded by the bundled tubes of the flux coils that generated the powerful shield.

Gelrayen was able to plot his pattern of destruction easily. He was fearful of trying to destroy any of the conversion generators themselves, knowing that an overload could cascade through that entire array of generators with the power to destroy a large part of that entire system. Instead the two fighters moved along either side of the power core, placing their conversion devices between the shield flux coils and the jump drives. The detonation of those relatively weak devices would wreck the drives and destroy that section of both the flux coils and probably the power core itself, leaving the Dreadnought disabled and fairly harmless. At five second intervals, each of four pair of conversion devices was set to detonate. The shield would almost certainly come down with the first blast, and that would give the two fighters time to get away.

Once the conversion devices were in place, the two Starwolves retreated as far as they could to the back of the Dreadnought, using the ship's bulk to protect their fighters from the explosion. They had no way back through the shield on their own. Even if they could have reattached the grounding cables, there was no way to pull the fighters back through. And taking an active drive through that shield would have been disastrous.

"Be ready to run the very moment the shield comes down," Gelrayen warned. "There is still a chance that the generators will overload."

"It seems a shame to destroy this machine," Teraln commented.

"The shame is that we did not try this plan sooner. I should have been more supportive of Valthyrra, but too many elements of this plan sounded impractical. I would have never expected the Dreadnought to simply sit still and allow us to destroy it. Coming up on the first round of detonations."

They engaged the primary generators of their fighters and brought forward engines to hold the ships stationary. As long as the drives were at least idling and warm, they would respond much more quickly to a sudden demand for full power. If the Dreadnought did happen to explode in a massive overload, a blast that would likely be measured in billions of megatons, then the Starwolves would have to race a double shock wave. The first would be a mass of radiation across a wide spectrum, the greatest and most deadly amount being a seemingly solid wall of intense light and heat, and an electromagnetic flare that would wreck a ship's electronics. This shock wave would be moving at or very near the speed of light, meaning that the fighters would have to get into starflight to outrun it. Pushed to its limits, under an acceleration that even Kelvessan would find hard to endure, a fighter could kick itself over threshold prematurely after a thirty second run. The second wave, superheated plasma—the vaporized remains of the Dreadnought itself—would be much slower and would dissipate fairly rapidly, and so was of no consequence.

"On the mark . . . now!" Gelrayen warned.

There followed a distant flare of light and a deep shudder passed along the frame of the Dreadnought, imperceptible to the fighters isolated in the vacuum of space within the shield. Because that first set of detonations was some ten kilometers up the length of the ship and contained deep within its machinery, the effects were outwardly deceptively restrained. The only drastic result was the abrupt failure of the shield, which collapsed without even an instant of hesitation. As soon as the two pilots could see the stars, they engaged their main drives and accelerated away. They were already well beyond visual range before the next set of explosions wrecked the second jump drive assembly.

"Commander, were you successful?" Valthyrra asked as soon as she was able to identify the two fighters and establish contact.

"Valthyrra, are you anywhere near?" Gelrayen asked in turn. "That machine has an array of generators that could feed an entire Union sector with power, and I cannot say whether or not they will explode."

"I will maintain a safe distance," she agreed. "I am detecting a series of major explosions within the Dreadnought."

"There will be four in all," he told her. "We set our conversion charges to explode in pairs every five seconds, with the objective of destroying the Dreadnought's four major reactionless drive units as well as the power core and shield coils. That should be the end of it."

"I am happy to hear that," Valthyrra commented. "The Dreadnought is beginning to move, using the drives it still has in operation."

"Where is it going?" he asked.

"Toward this system's sun. This might be a self-destruct gesture."

Perhaps anticipating the loss of self-control, the Dreadnought had set itself on a course that would carry it to certain destruction. Even if it now shut down entirely, leaving it a half-wrecked and drifting hulk, Gelrayen wondered if they would be able to deflect its path in time to avoid that act of self-immolation. Perhaps it would be best to simply let it go. Aside from the mystery of its origin and purpose, there was nothing of the Dreadnought's technology they wanted except the secret of its reactionless drives. And he had already wrecked those.

"Commander, I have detected your final explosion," Valthyrra announced. "The Dreadnought is completely disabled unless it still possesses field drive, and it has accelerated itself to nearly the speed of light. At this speed, it will destroy itself in less than three minutes."

"I forgot how fast we expected it might be," Gelrayen said. "It might have been able to match your best speed using only one of those four drive assemblies. It appeared to have been designed to have a reserve capacity for power and speed several times what it could actually use. Do we have time to attempt to capture that ship and turn it away?"

"It might not be able to move, but it can still fight," Valthyrra reminded him.

"There seem to be very few actual cannons. The fighters will be able to go in and destroy those in reasonable safety, and then we could shut down that weapon while it is still reasonably intact."

"I cannot believe that we have the time," Valthyrra answered. "You know how hard it would be to target those weapons on a ship moving that fast, and then I would still have to come in and attempt to turn it aside. That is not something I care to try at that speed."

"No, there is not enough time," Gelrayen agreed. "I was able to collect detailed interior scans. Perhaps that will tell us all that we need to know."

"Just what are you interested in?" the ship asked. "Are you lusting after reactionless drives?"

"Why not? You are not too new to refuse a refitting."

"Commander, the Dreadnought has begun building power,"

she interrupted him. "Entirely too much power for a ship that has no drives."

"I should have gone after the generators after all," Gelrayen commented to himself. "Does it seem to be doing anything with that power?"

"No, just holding it." She paused, and when she spoke again she seemed honestly frightened. "Commander, can you anticipate the power involved if every generator in that machine was forced to overload?"

"Yes, I warned you about that already."

"Then can you imagine what would happen if the Dreadnought brought every generator it has to a level just below overload and then hurtled itself into that star at nearly the speed of light? It would be bad enough just to throw a hundred million tons of machinery into a star at that speed, but I had calculated that the star would have survived that. The power of those generators alone would explode that star, but the combined energy will create a shock wave that will destroy the closer planets in this system. I am moving to intercept."

"Val, what can you do?" he demanded. "Can you get yourself in range in time?"

"I doubt that very much," she admitted. "But I still have to try. There are two hundred million colonists in this system who are not out of range of that blast."

"If you cannot stop it, then you will never get yourself out of range in time," Gelrayen told her as he brought his fighter around. "Take yourself and your crew to safety. I will ram that monster."

"Commander?"

"The sacrifice of one is preferable to that of an entire carrier, and I have a better chance of getting there in time. Teraln?"

The other fighter had already pulled ahead of his own, moving quickly to overtake the Dreadnought from behind.

"You save yourself, Commander," Teraln answered. "Valthyrra Methryn needs you. This is work for peons."

Valthyrra interrupted the discussion. "If you gentlemen are finished being noble and self-sacrificing, you might be interested in knowing that the Dreadnought is changing course."

Now that the Dreadnought no longer had its concealing shield, it was open to even common scanners. Before any of them could respond, or even begin to wonder why the Dreadnought was turning away, the massive machine had used its own limited resources and the pull of the star's gravity to take itself close enough to speed of light to kick itself through threshold and into actual starflight, if at extremely low speed. Once it was into starflight, however, the greatly reduced drag of acceleration permitted it to build its speed more rapidly. After everything that had happened, the Dreadnought was still about to escape. And it almost certainly had the ability to repair itself, even after so much damage. Although it had lost several vital systems, it had only suffered destruction of well under a quarter of its total machinery.

Valthyrra responded out of desperation, locking her scanners on the fleeing ship and forcing herself over threshold prematurely. She knew that she could keep pace with the Dreadnought if she could only catch it before it was able to disappear from her own scanner range. She could hardly imagine how that machine could have gotten itself into starflight without the use of any of its primary drives, until she locked in her scanners for a detailed analysis. The Dreadnought, as Commander Gelrayen had observed, had been built with multiple redundancies and capacities that far exceeded the needs of normal use. Its secondary drive system, a very refined and powerful version of her own field drive that would have normally been reserved for close maneuvering, was in fact powerful enough to carry it past threshold. After it had used its primary drives to take it nearly to light speed before they had been destroyed, it had used the gravity of the star as an added boost to get it clear of the Starwolves as soon as possible.

Under the circumstances, the Dreadnought certainly no longer possessed the power to outrun a Starwolf carrier; its only hope had been to get itself into starflight before it could be tracked. Valthyrra had not forgotten that it still had its complete array of weapons and could probably defend itself as well as ever. She launched a spread of six missiles, each carrying conversion devices and given a very precise set of instructions. The missiles did not attempt to strike the Dreadnought itself but paced it, moving in close beside its massive hull before detonating. Shaken by that rapid series of concussions, the Dreadnought lost power and dropped down out of starflight.

When it again began building its remaining generators to an

overload, Valthyrra accepted that gesture as an honest one and remained in starflight to take herself to safety as quickly as possible. That was just as well for her. The Dreadnought's generators reached their capacity in a matter of seconds, and the explosion of the first caused a cascade of detonation through the complete power array. The Dreadnought was consumed in a sudden blast that was quite literally equal to that of an exploding star, its cumulative capacity for self-destruction far greater than anyone had anticipated. At least its brief run into starflight had carried it well outside the system, and its passing did no harm to anything except itself.

Valthyrra Methryn circled around to collect her fighters, and to make a final check for survivors.

—12—

Captain Janus Tarrel did not accompany the Starwolves back to
their base at Alkayja station. While the freighter Taerregyn carried the damaged carrier Destaen home for extensive repairs, the
Methryn and the Vardon had remained in system for a time to
attempt to salvage the wreck of the Kerridayen and search for
additional survivors, including the ship itself. Commander Daerran and his bridge crew were still missing and none of the ship's
memory units that had been located so far had survived intact,
but the Starwolves still had some hope that the Kerridayen herself
could still be rebuilt; as much as sixty percent of the carrier's
hull, including her forward-thrust main drives, her star drives
and her generators, were still reasonably intact or could be repaired. The ship itself would probably fly again, after years of
refitting, and possibly with a new guiding sentience.

As much as she wanted to stay with the Starwolves a while yet,
Captain Tarrel left the Methryn within hours of the destruction
of the Dreadnought. Because the Starwolves had been able to
intercept the alien weapon before it could attack, the local system, including the System Fleet, had survived undamaged. After
the System Commander had made contact with the Starwolves,
he offered a heavy cruiser for her use. Hardly two hours later,
she found herself on her way to Vinthra with only the special
armor that had been made for her and a great many new aches
to remind her of her time among the Starwolves. When Valthyrra
Methryn had moved to intercept the Dreadnought during its
attempt to escape, she had used some very sharp accelerations.

Tarrel did not believe that the Starwolves simply wanted to be rid of her now that her usefulness was at an end. The circumstances of her sudden departure had not been of their contrivance, nor did they operate in that manner in the first place. In fact, they were very anxious to know if the Union intended to extend the truce now that the Dreadnought was destroyed, and they looked upon her as an important source of information. But she had been given the means to leave, and no one could think of any good reason for her to stay.

Since she was once again only a passenger on someone else's ship, she had time to wonder whether or not she had unfinished business with the Starwolves. She wanted very much to be able to encourage them to re-evaluate their standing with the Republic and to seek their own destiny. That seemed certainly to be in the best interests of the Kelvessan themselves and she believed that it would also be in the best interests of her own kind, if not necessarily best for the Union. At the same time, she knew only too well that the actions she contemplated would be viewed as improper if not actually treasonous by the Union, and she remained a Union Captain with all the duties and moral responsibilities that involved. So perhaps it was just as well that the matter had been decided for her, even though she could not escape the feeling that this was not yet over.

The massive military and commercial complexes above Vinthra had survived intact only by virtue of the fact that the Dreadnought had not come here. And that had been entirely a matter of chance. That sprawling array of docking components, warehouses and repair facilities would have been one of the most tempting targets in Union space, if the Dreadnought had known of its existence, and it certainly could not have been moved to safety. Captain Tarrel watched the final approach to station through the wide bank of windows in the cruiser's lounge, wondering if she would see her own Carthaginian nosed in to a docking slip, although she was not surprised when she did not. She was able to see only a small proportion of the ships moored at the station, and there was even the chance that Carthaginian was out running errands at the moment.

After all that she had been through, she almost expected some recognition of her efforts. Still, she was practical enough not to be surprised when no one was there to meet her as she came off the ship. She arranged to have her bags sent to visiting officer's quarters on the station, then presented herself at Sector Commander Victor Lake's office. At least he was on station at that time, but he was away for the moment. His personal secretary was away also, and the computer indicated that she was welcome to wait. Since only the computer was there to look at her, she elected to stay rather than leave a message. The fact that Lake was due back at any moment decided the matter, since she did not feel like waiting long for anyone.

Victor Lake arrived in a hurry, glancing at her briefly and without much concern on his way through the outer office to his own. Then he stopped short and stared. "Janus Tarrel? What the hell are you doing here?"

"What am I doing here?" she asked, then paused and made a face. Since she had not asked the Starwolves to send a message, the news had not arrived any faster than herself. "Of course, you don't know. The Dreadnought is dead, blasted to little tiny pieces these last nine days."

"So the Starwolves finally came through," Lake commented. "We were beginning to think that they were waiting to see us whipped first."

"The Starwolves took a real beating for our sakes," Tarrel said sharply. "They did the best they could. You had my reports."

"We took quite a beating ourselves," Lake insisted. "I'm not asking for sympathy after all you've been through, but I've had the Combined Council and the heads of every trade company demanding to know what I was doing. I must have invented half a million ways to avoid telling them that the matter was out of my hands. Do you tell people like that to sit tight and trust in the Starwolves? Why don't we go into my office."

She followed him through the inner doors into his office, where he went immediately to the bar and began preparing drinks for them both as if that was his most pressing duty of the moment. Tarrel wondered if she looked like she needed it; her weeks among the Starwolves had left her fairly beat up, but she had had time since then to recover. If he was to be serving drinks, then she decided to help herself to the stuffed leather sofa, reclining sideways across its length to encourage him to take the chair opposite.

"Why did you send me that Walter Pesky person?" she asked sourly; her opinion of the departed had not improved in the weeks since his death. "Was nobody aware of the severity of his xenophobia?"

"Apparently not," Lake insisted. "The only thing in his record was praise for his precise, diplomatic politeness in dealing with aliens, due no doubt to the fact that he secretly hated and feared them. It seems that he only lost it once in his career, but then he lost it all the way."

"Well, it was partly my own fault for not sending him home when I should have," Tarrel admitted. "I was just afraid of leaving him alone and completely unsupervised until they had a ship free to bring him back. Of course, my only concern was that he might do something to embarass us politically."

"I can hardly imagine anyone putting anything over on Starwolves. They deal with their enemies fairly harshly."

"Their enemies, yes. We were theoretically friends and allies by that time, and Starwolves can be so damned trusting with anyone they consider their friend. You probably have to know them better to believe that."

"No, I've heard something to that effect before." He handed her a glass, then settled with his own drink in the chair opposite her. "Drump nut liqueur in iced mint tea. I still recall your odd drinking habits."

"I was never a serious drinker in the first place," she reminded him, taking a quick swallow. "When did you start keeping mint tea at hand?"

"Since I knew that you would be coming back here when your mission was done."

She nodded absently. "What about my ship?"

"Actually, I seem to recall that the Carthaginian is out running errands somewhere in the Sector. She should be back within the next few days, which means that you get a short vacation."

Tarrel shrugged. "I'm in no state of mind to run a ship right now anyway, even if we're not at war with anyone for the moment."

Lake spent a moment watching the ice in his glass. "Can we talk business for just a moment? I have to go out there very soon and announce that the Dreadnought has been destroyed, and I need to be prepared for some very hard questions."

"Go ahead."

"Did the Starwolves ever find out what it was?"

"In general terms, it was a big machine designed for the single purpose of wrecking the space-faring capabilities of a civilization less technically advanced than itself," she explained. "We would have never found a way to destroy it ourselves; you can tell that to anyone who says that we should have never made a truce with the Starwolves. The only reason we survived is that we had someone willing to protect us who possessed the ability to understand that thing and fight it on its own terms. Except for Starwolves, we would be sitting here waiting to die."

"No question?"

"No question."

Lake nodded. "Was it sent to attack us specifically, or did it just happen to wander into our space and begin executing its primary function?"

She shook her head hopelessly. "There never was any way to know that for certain. There was no evidence one way or the other, and no way to talk to that thing. It was willing to listen, but it shot anything that did not give the proper recognition code immediately."

"The fact that there was only the one suggests that the Dreadnought had simply wandered in," he suggested.

"I don't consider that conclusive," Tarrel insisted. "If it hadn't been for the Starwolves, the one would have been enough to destroy us. Some unknown enemy would likely have never considered that we would receive help from the Starwolves after we'd been at war with them for thirty thousand years. I guess that we'll know the answer to that question if a certain amount of time passes and they don't send out a modified Dreadnought, one better protected against Starwolves."

"Is that possible?" Lake asked.

"Even the Starwolves can't fight it. They just happened to find a way to sneak in through its shield and destroy it from the inside. A design flaw that will probably not be repeated."

"In that case, will the Starwolves be able to destroy a second Dreadnought if one is sent?"

"If that flaw is corrected, then no. But I believe that they have the ability to come up with some new weapons in a hurry."

Victor Lake spent a brief moment regarding his glass, then finished his drink in a quick swallow. "There are certain questions of a very sensitive nature that I would like to discuss with you off the record. I never asked these things, and you never spoke to me about them. But these questions will be asked. If some powerful elements of the Union wish to break the truce, then I do not have the power to stop them. I can even be ordered to break the truce, and I can't refuse short of resigning. And I should warn you that there are strong incentives to break the truce as a quicker way to recover our losses.''

She had anticipated that much already, although it still saddened her to realize that it was indeed inevitable. The truce was doomed, and they both knew it. "I understand.''

"You've said that the Starwolves took a beating. How bad?''

Tarrel frowned; this was the part that she hated the most. It was the balance between doing her professional duty, without regard to the consequences, and doing what she had come to believe was right. She could not escape the feeling that she was betraying a friend, but she was compelled to answer. "Is this off the record?''

"This entire conversation is completely off the record," he assured her. "If I don't believe that it's in the Union's best interest, then I can pretend that I never heard any of this. You don't seem to think that we should break the truce.''

"Let's just say that I have a much better idea of just what the Starwolves can do, and I can see the futility of fighting them. I've also seen that they can be reasoned with. If we weren't so greedy and impatient, we could have everything we want without fighting.''

Lake looked more amused than impatient. "I know that already, and I don't doubt that clever people have been figuring that out since the war first began. Unfortunately, the Union is designed to insure that greedy people are always in control. So what about the Starwolves?''

Tarrel sighed heavily. "I saw the carrier Mardayn destroyed outright, and the Kerridayen was almost certainly destroyed as well. The last I saw, the Starwolves were trying to salvage the pieces. The Destaen was towed away with serious damage, and she probably faces months if not years of repair. Even before that last battle, the Kerridayen, the Karvand and the Methryn had all taken damage in separate attacks, and I can recall it being said that their resources have been stretched to the limit. I doubt very much that they have the ability to repair their damages any time soon.''

"Then if we are going to violate the truce, we might as well do it soon and consolidate our own gains before the Starwolves can get their fleet back up to strength.''

"I'm not so sure about that," Tarrel mused. "What are our own losses?"

"We don't have any good figures about commercial losses on ships, but more than seventy Systems were hit with the loss of at least that many stations. Our military losses are somewhere above twenty-five percent, enough that we will feel it for decades to come. Still, the loss of even a single carrier hurts them more than losing a thousand ships hurts us.''

"Perhaps." Tarrel sounded uncertain. "A single carrier might be worth a thousand of our own ships, but I'm not sure that the loss of one or even two hurts them all that much. They apparently keep a second fleet of carriers in their own space. Some of those ships might be moved up to cover their regular patrols, especially if we provoked them.''

"Why didn't they use those ships against the Dreadnought?" Lake asked.

"They were extremely reluctant to. Those carriers were in reserve to fight the Dreadnought if it came into their own space.''

"Then you are not convinced that we can expect to have an easier time of it because of their recent losses?''

"I'm saying that we cannot count upon the Starwolf fleet being too far below strength to respond to a breaking of the truce," she insisted. "They have more ships than we knew, although I cannot predict whether those ships will be transferred to Union space. They might still be concerned that another Dreadnought might turn up, at least in the next few years. That possibility also worries me. If we break the truce immediately and annoy the Starwolves now, are they going to be very sympathetic if we go begging for their help again soon?''

"But you know how to destroy a Dreadnought now," he reminded her.

Tarrel shook her head firmly. "I know the general theory, but the main ingredient in that recipe is Starwolves. You first have to be able to see the damned thing, which requires technology we do not have and cannot anticipate developing any time soon. Then you have to beat it senseless and blind it by shooting off its external sensor array, which you can't do if you can't see it. I can write you a fairly detailed report on how they did it, but that still doesn't mean that we can do it ourselves.''

Lake glanced at his glass, then got up to pour himself another drink. "I agree with everything you say, and I'll do my best to present that side of the matter. But, like I say, I don't get to vote on the matter. That privilege belongs to a small group of greedy old men who have already convinced themselves that the colonies and independent worlds have taken advantage of this situation and deserve to be punished. Were you aware that few independent worlds and fringe colonies were attacked?"

"Of course not," she declared. "The damned monster was programmed to go after major holdings. It went first through the most developed parts of each Sector."

"Yes, *we* can see that," he told her. "But minds that already hunger to rebuild our losses by raping the outer worlds can easily convince themselves of a conspiracy. They won't listen to you or me if we tell them something they don't want to hear. They decide policy, and they delegate us to deal with the consequences."

Tarrel shook her head. "Nothing surprises me any more. Would you believe that the Starwolves have their own old men to screw their lives around?"

Lake paused in pouring his drink to look at her. "They do? Why?"

"They're afraid of the Starwolves," she explained. "They don't want to end the war because they're afraid of what that many unemployed Starwolves would do."

"Starwolves are not actively hostile," Lake mused. "They only react to provocation. If I didn't have Starwolves as enemies, I would trust them completely. So what do they believe so many unemployed Starwolves would do?"

"Go into business for themselves and be so good at it that mere mortals like ourselves could never compete."

"I never would have thought of Starwolves as particularly mercantile."

"I don't believe that they would leave us begging, but I have recently come to think that Starwolves can do just about anything they want," Tarrel said. "You might recall that they've largely financed their side of the war by stealing our ships and goods and selling it all back. That seems clever enough."

"Damn, you're right," Lake agreed, and decided to pour himself an even larger drink. "You know, I wonder if I should tell the High Council all of this. The best way to convince them to extend the truce indefinitely is for them to believe that the Republic is using the war for its own purposes."

The Carthaginian dropped out of starflight and began an immediate scan of the system, clearing the way for the supply convoy that followed her two minutes behind. The military escort was largely a matter of tradition or old habit, a fearful response to the presence of old enemies seen and unseen, and an even deadlier enemy that might or might not return. Captain Tarrel settled back into her seat, enjoying the satisfaction that very little was likely to go wrong. Escort duty in peace time was almost like a vacation. And like all vacations, it would not last forever.

"Captain, I have detected a Starwolf carrier settled into orbit at our destination," the surveillance officer reported.

The first excited response to that was entirely the result of old habits. In previous times, they would have warned away the convoy before it could leave starflight and then sit tight and hope that the carrier did not notice. But, under the terms of a treaty that had not yet been broken, the Starwolves were friends and allies, even a source of protection against other dangers. The members of the bridge crew calmed themselves after that first response, although the old, instinctive sense of threat and excitement remained just under the surface.

Tarrel nodded in acknowledgement. "Send the Starwolves our regards, and politely ask what ship."

"The ship responds that she is the carrier Methryn," the communications officer responded after a moment, sounding slightly confused. "She asks to speak directly to you."

"Old friends indeed," Tarrel remarked. "Bring the convoy down and direct them into orbit. And give me that channel at my own station."

"Yes, Captain. You have your open channel."

She settled her headset. "Valthyrra Methryn, have you plugged your first Union warship yet?"

"No, but I do keep hoping," the carrier responded. "I see that they put you back to useful employment."

"Then they gave you a patrol in the Rane Sector?"

"This used to be the Kerridayen's patrol," Valthyrra commented sadly. "Ah yes, I see that they put you to escort duty."

"What else is there to do these days? So, how is everyone?"

"Doing well enough, in the sense that things are slow to

change in the daily existence of Starwolves. Commander Gelrayen asks if you would like to come over for dinner. I can turn up the heat. The Starwolves are more indifferent to clothes than they used to be, and not just my own. We seem to have started an anti-fashion trend.''

''Is that a fact?''

''Of course, they always were rather indifferent to clothes. Will you be in-system very long?''

''A few days, at least.''

''Give us a call when you get everything settled into orbit.''

Tarrel removed her headset and settled back into her seat, waiting out the final deceleration into orbit. Matching the convoy, they would be dropping down from threshold for the next five hours. That would give her plenty of time for reflection. She had always felt that she had unfinished business with the Kelvessan, but she had never expected that she might ever have the chance to run across the Methryn, and she did not know any of the other ships well enough for this matter. In a civilized universe that was generally not cleverly run, perhaps some things were fated after all.

Janus Tarrel felt obligated to stay on the bridge until every ship in her convoy was secured in orbit and the first freighter was taken away for unloading. Her own turn of duty ended by that time, and she put in a private call to the Methryn to arrange a time for dinner. As it happened, Starwolves were always hungry, and in this occasion the attire was semi-formal; both she and her first officer were expected. Under the circumstances, she thought that it was just as well. She could hardly imagine how young Chagin would react to dining with naked Starwolves. She was surprised enough that the offer to come abroad had been extended to anyone beyond herself. The crew of the Methryn seemed to like her well enough, but they had never been given any reason to trust her associates.

Entirely as a sentimental impulse, she retired to her cabin, removed a large trunk from storage, and dressed herself in the white Starwolf armor that she had been given during her stay aboard the Methryn. Chagin was surprised to see her when she joined him at the Carthaginian's small docking bay, as was every other member of the crew she passed. Because she could not tell if Valthyrra had been serious about turning up her thermostats, Tarrel had warned Chagin to dress warmly.

"Captain, that's certainly one hell of a souvenir," he commented with droll humor. "How does a person get one of those?"

"The hard way."

"I almost feel under-dressed. What will the Starwolves be wearing?"

"I hesitate to guess," she admitted.

Whether as a considerate gesture, or one of precaution, Valthyrra had sent one of her own transports to take them to the Methryn. The trip over to the carrier was short enough, since she had moved herself in to within five kilometers of the station. Commander Gelrayen and his first officer Kayendel were there to meet them, both of them dressed in their simple command uniforms of white, the first officer's tunic trimmed with black. Chagin was obviously surprised and fascinated; like most people, he had only seen Starwolves in their armor before, and they looked so much smaller and less threatening without it. Kayendel offered him a tour of the ship, and the two first officers went their own way. They were to join Captain Tarrel and Commander Gelrayen later on the bridge.

"How is everyone?" Tarrel asked as they took the lift from the transport bay to the bridge, a relatively short ride. "I admit that I've worried about the Kerridayen the entire six months since the Dreadnought was destroyed."

Gelrayen looked unhappy. "We never did find any part of Trendaessa that was still intact, and the area of the bridge was completely gone. If fact, they finally had to abandon any plan of rebuilding the carrier. Every machine and major system in that ship was wrecked by power discharge, and her frame was damaged. She was the last of the old ships, and her memory units lacked the protection built into a newer ship like the Methryn."

"Have your losses left you short in your patrols?"

"No, the Karvand is back out again, and that leaves only the Destaen still under repair. We have moved three of our reserve carriers into the regular patrols. We know that the Union will begin intimidating the colonies any time now, and the truce will be broken."

"Yes, they started rearming from the first," Tarrel agreed. "I suppose it's no secret to you that my convoy is moving supplies into the fringe to be ready to move against the colonies any time now. The trade companies will be appropriating ownership and control of agriculture and mining. I tried to convince them to keep the truce. We can't be certain yet that we won't be fighting a new war with the builders of the Dreadnought any time.''

"Perhaps, but it seems very unlikely," Gelrayen told her. "My interior scans of the Dreadnought, and the analysis of debris we collected, indicated that it was at least a quarter of a million years old. We were able to make sense of the few transmissions it made. It seems that it would have never attacked anyone except your people. It confused you with the enemy that it was designed to destroy, for the simple chance that the level of Union technology and ship design almost exactly matched, and your physical appearance was very much the same. When it tried to talk to the Starwolf carriers early on, it was simply telling us to mind our own business.''

"Oh, fine. I'm glad to know that it was all stupid and pointless in the first place," Tarrel complained.

"Your superiors will be pleased to hear that."

"I believe that everyone would be much better off if they never knew," she said, then hesitated. "There was something that I should tell you. I don't know if it's in the best interests of the Union to do this, but you deserve to know. The last time I was at Alkayja station, I had a little talk with Fleet Commander Asandi. He told me that the Republic fears the Starwolves and that it conspires to keep you from developing your technology or your own social identity, and that it has kept you fighting the war to give you something to do."

Gelrayen seemed to be hiding a smile. "Valthyrra said that you seemed to be concerned about us. That was why you conspired to keep us naked. The Republic used to keep us naked as a sign of our slavery."

"And they put you in clothes to encourage you to stop thinking about how your were different."

"Captain, we know exactly what has been going on," he insisted. "The fact is, we are satisfied with the way things are for now."

"You are?"

"Captain, with the exception of certain individuals such as yourself, no one has ever been honestly concerned about our future and what might be best for us. Unfortunately, we do not yet have a future. When we were designed, the Aldessan of Valtrys gave us free will. We are not compelled to follow any order that we are given, and that insures that we can never be used for evil intent.''

"Are you certain of that?"

"Yes, very certain. At the same time, the Aldessan made a great mistake in our design. They gave us an instinct, even to the point of an actual compulsion, to help anyone that we might find in danger or distress. The Union has been our enemy for centuries. But when you were in danger, we did not hesitate to help you. That compulsion to help completely negates our free will and it leaves us slaves to our own instinct to protect."

"Then you don't see any hope for yourselves?" she asked.

"Yes, we have one hope," he said, then paused as the doors of the lift opened. They stepped outside the lift, then waited a moment in the corridor outside. "The Kelvessan have been evolving rapidly from the first. We evolve in stages every few thousand years, very suddenly and quickly. It might take thousands of years yet, but one day we will have evolved to the point that we have complete control over our own actions and we will simply assume our right to govern of our own destiny. Until then, all we can do is wait."

"And you are satisfied with that?" Tarrel demanded.

Gelrayen considered that briefly. "Actually, yes."

Unfortunately, his answer proved that he was probably right. Perhaps because they were capable of so much already, Captain Tarrel had wanted the Starwolves to enjoy even more. She realized now that they were simply very good at being what they were designed to be. For all that she believed that they deserved the same rights and freedoms that all other races enjoyed, she could not give it to them, and they did not seem ready to demand it for themselves. But she felt more sorry for them than ever. To some degree, they really were machines, compelled to fulfil the function that they had been designed for until they finally did acquire the ability to desire more.

If she felt sad and dissatisfied, perhaps it was entirely her own fault for thinking that anything should have been different because of all that they had been through together. The truce would end soon enough, and everything would be exactly the way it had always been. The Union was still the Union, with all its faults and injustices. The Starwolves were still the Starwolves, endlessly solving everyone else's problems over and over. Only she herself had changed, and somehow she did not feel the better for it.